JORDAN'S ACCIDENTAL ADOPTION

Hounds of the Hunt 4

TONI GRIFFIN

Edited by SANDRA C STIXRUDE

Edited by JAYMI E

Cover by LOU HARPER

CONTENTS

COPYRIGHT

Cover Artist: Lou Harper © 2019
Editor: Jaymi E

First Edition

PUBLISHER
Mischief Corner Books, LLC

DEDICATION

To Freddy MacKay, without your constant (and I mean constant!) nudging, this book would have never been finished.

And to my readers for being so patient with me.

Enjoy!

TRADEMARKS ACKNOWLEDGEMENT

The author acknowledges the trademarked status and trademark owners of the following wordmarks mentioned in this work of fiction:

Atari: Atari Interactive
BioShock: Blizzard Entertainment, Inc.
Bluetooth: Bluetooth Special Interest Group
Call of Duty: Activision Blizzard, Inc.
Coke: The Coca-Cola Company
Cuphead: Studio MDHR
FaceTime: Apple Inc.
Game Boy: Nintendo Company, Ltd.
Great Northern: Great Northern Brewing Co.
Half-life 2: Sierra Entertainment, Inc.
Messenger: Facebook, Inc.
Nintendo: Nintendo Company, Ltd.
Overwatch: Blizzard Entertainment, Inc.
PlayStation: Sony Interactive Entertainment

CHAPTER ONE

Darwin sucked. Nicor always hated it when they had to travel to the far north. While the rest of the country froze during winter the great far north had to be contrary. Nicor had to admit that June through August was the more pleasant time to visit. Unlike December, when you couldn't take two steps outside without being covered in sweat from head to toe, no matter the time of day or bloody night it was.

Right now, it wasn't too bad. It wasn't mind-meltingly hot, and thankfully, the humidity that made people want to kill themselves in the later months had disappeared. It might actually make a nice change from the freeze-your-balls off temperatures in Melbourne.

Nicor stared once again at the BOM website and the temperatures listed there. Every other capital city was in single digits, or low teens. Darwin, however, settled in the high twenties.

Sighing, he glanced up at Adze. He had called everyone into the living room for a meeting.

It looked like the never-ending search for the mermaid responsible for the missing dozen women would be put on hold again, for now. It had been nearly a year since the ringleader had managed to give Pyro the slip that night. They had yet to find a single, miniscule trace of the mermaid. She'd obviously gone to ground somewhere. It wasn't like she could disappear into thin air. Water, yeah, but the women she took couldn't survive. Nicor was confident they would find her in the end, though. It was just taking a little longer than they'd all thought.

The right here and now, however, meant they had a new situation to deal with.

"Matti's been keeping an eye on a situation in Darwin over the last couple of weeks," Adze had told them, leading Nicor on a search of the BOM site for the current temps as the meeting begun.

"What kind of situation?" Daevas asked.

"The kind where nearly half a dozen pregnant women have died suddenly—their bodies disappearing not long after."

Nicor racked his brain trying to think of what the hell could be the cause of something like that. He came up blank.

"What does Matti think is doing it?" Pyro asked.

Adze glanced around the room at the five of them. Both Callum and Archie were at work right then, Archie having gone back to the accounting firm part-time a little while ago. It was only two days a week to see how he coped, but so far so good.

"Matti believes we have an aswang on our hands."

"Seriously?" Cacus asked.

"I thought they were only prevalent in the Philippines," Oriax remarked.

"So did we, but apparently one decided to travel and seems to have taken up residence in the far north."

"When do we leave?" Nicor asked, resigning himself to the trip to Darwin.

Adze grinned. "We leave tonight. As soon as Archie and Callum get home."

Nicor nodded. He didn't envy Pyro and Adze having to leave their mates behind, but it wasn't like they could actually come with them.

As Nicor sat on the private plane later that night, he thanked whoever would listen that they didn't have to fly commercial. The long flight to Darwin was already bad enough, he couldn't imagine what it was like to be stuck in the middle of all those people, unable to get up easily and walk around.

He wasn't an easy flyer at the best of times, though he'd gotten used to it over the years from all the travel they had to do. Still, Nicor found himself feeling like the walls were closing in on him and he'd have to get up and do laps of the small plane.

The others left him alone to pace and play his games, knowing how he felt about flying. After a half hour of pacing he finally settled enough to sit again. He pulled out his Switch to distract himself with one of his many games. Nicor plugged his headphones in, so he didn't disturb the rest of his pack and concentrated on the small console in front of him.

A couple of hours into the flight, Nicor paused his game and pulled his headphones off. "So, what's the plan?" he asked as he looked up at the others in the cabin.

"It's not going to be easy that's for sure," Adze replied. The others all ceased their chatter and tuned into their conversation. "As you know, during the day the aswang looks just like any other human. At night it can shapeshift. Matti's come across a couple of reports of people thinking they'd spotted a Tasmanian Devil in Darwin, which is what pointed her towards the aswang being responsible for the women's deaths."

"A Tassie Devil? In Darwin?" Oriax asked incredulously.

"Yep."

"Great. Well, at least we know what to look for."

"Only during the night. During the day the only way to tell is either with garlic, which they're vulnerable to, or by looking them in the eyes and having your reflection turned upside down. We'll be looking for someone of Pilipino decent, which in Darwin, doesn't really help as they have such a large population of people with Asian backgrounds."

Nicor nodded. With Darwin being nicknamed the gateway to Asia, it was understandable they would reside there. Plus, the weather was remarkably similar to their own countries.

"How many women have died?" Daevas asked.

"At last count, five. The problem is, once an aswang

kills their victim and devours the unborn child it can create a doppelganger of the deceased from any plant life around them and send it home in place of the real person. The doppelganger then falls ill and dies within a couple of days, making it look like all the women have died from various ailments and at different times than they actually did. The real bodies have either been consumed over time by the aswang or are being hidden."

"Well, that certainly makes things *interesting*," Oriax commented.

"We'll split into two teams," Adze continued. "A day team in human form and carrying garlic at all times—the aswang is most vulnerable during the day. And the night team to be in hound form and on the lookout for a Tassie Devil. Remember the best way to kill an aswang is by beheading it."

"Where do you suggest we start? Even though Darwin is the smallest of the capital cities, it's still a decent enough size that this could take weeks," Nicor said.

"Funeral homes and hospitals would be the best place to start. I currently have Matti looking into if any dead people have gone missing. Aswang not only eat unborn babies, they also enjoy snacking on corpses. So, we check out the hospitals and funeral homes for anyone that's been hanging around that maybe shouldn't have been and go from there."

"Sounds like a good place to start," Pyro agreed.

They settled back in their chairs and lapsed into silence as they all took in the updated information.

The team had never had to deal with an aswang before. With the creature being from the Philippines, they tended to stay close to home. This one though, seemed to have caught the travel bug. Nicor was actually surprised Matti and the others had been able to figure out what the creature was. But he supposed that was their job, to know what to look for and what creatures fit the profile, no matter how obscure.

Lost in his ruminations, the rest of the flight went by in a jiff, and not too much later they finally landed.

As Nicor stepped out of the plane he wanted to curse a blue streak. Even though back home was bloody cold right now, Nicor honestly thought he'd prefer to be there than here. It was supposed to be the dry season in Darwin. The temperature would actually be quite pleasant if it wasn't for the humidity that was hanging around when it shouldn't have been.

The sun beat down brightly on them, nary a cloud in the sky to offer them any kind of protection. Nicor placed his sunnies on, giving himself a little reprieve from the harsh light of day.

They crossed the tarmac as a group, duffle bags in hand, and headed to the car rental to pick up their transport.

Half an hour later they stepped foot through the penthouse door of the Evolution building on Gardiner Street just on the edge of the city.

The cool air was refreshing after the humidity outside. This place was one of the few things that Nicor enjoyed about coming to Darwin. They'd purchased the two-story, six-bedroom, eight-bathroom penthouse with its own private pool off the plan. When they weren't here on business the place was rented out for several grand a night. It was actually surprising the number of people who were willing to part with that much cash.

Nicor headed up the stairs to his room and threw his bag on the bed. The two-story windows gave a spectacular view of the city, even if it wasn't much compared to Melbourne. The pool looked all kinds of inviting, but that would have to wait.

There was still several hours of daylight left so plenty of time for them to get out there and see what they could find.

Nicor, Adze, Pyro and Daevas all headed back downstairs to meet up with Oriax and Cacus, who had the rooms on the first floor of the penthouse.

They all took a seat in the living room and started going over plans.

"Who's our local police contact?" Nicor asked.

"Captain John David. I'll contact him as soon as we're done here to let him know there's definitely a Sup in his area and we're here to track it down," Adze replied.

They were broken into two teams—Adze, Nicor, and Cacus would take the first run of day shifts, with Pyro, Oriax and Daevas starting at night. They'd then swap after three days if they hadn't located the suspect before then.

"So, where to first, hospital or funeral home?" Nicor asked as they were in the lift, heading back to the basement and their car.

"Shops first to pick up a few bulbs of garlic, then to the hospital," Adze said with a shrug. "Easier to blend in as there's more people."

"Sounds logical," Cacus said.

The lift dinged to alert them to their arrival, and they stepped out into the stifling car park.

A quick stop at the supermarket to pick up the garlic, and they were on their way to the hospital. Unfortunately, that was a good twenty to twenty-five-minute drive away, all depending on traffic. The AC in the car blasted and the afternoon radio jock was giving away tickets for listeners to go to the movies. Nicor tuned it all out as he sat in the back of the car and watched the scenery go by.

"Why is finding a car park always such a pain in the ass?" Adze bitched as he drove around for the second time. Thankfully he spotted someone pulling out not far ahead and he indicated to say he was taking the spot.

Women in hospital gowns were sitting in wheelchairs with baby cribs next to them, congregated far enough away from the entrance that they were allowed to smoke. Nicor had never understood what humans found so fascinating about ingesting poisons into their bodies.

To each their own he supposed.

Maternity was on the sixth floor, but as they were looking for pregnant women and not brand-new babies, they stayed away from the ward. Plus, the doors there were locked and you had to buzz through. None of them wanted to bring that much attention to them being there. Instead they lingered for as long as possible on the other side of the floor, in the waiting room. One by one they headed in and took a seat, picking up a magazine and started to pretend to read it, like they were waiting for their partner. They were looking for any pregnant woman who looked like she could be of Pilipino descent.

Women of all stages of their pregnancy came and went, as the time slowly ticked by. Nicor signalled to the others, placed his second, or maybe his third magazine back on the little coffee table and headed out.

He waited by the lifts for the others, thankfully not having to wait too long.

"Well, that was a bust." Nicor pressed the button to call the lift.

"Yeah, didn't really think we'd be that lucky on day one," Cacus said.

"I know, but one can live in hope. Let's quickly check the rest of this place, well, as much as we can, then move on to the private hospital."

Thankfully, the private hospital was literally just next door. Problem was the security was even tighter than it was at the public hospital and their search was over in no time flat. They left the hospital no closer to finding the aswang.

The sun was slowly setting as the three of them all piled back into the car.

"We gonna go check out a funeral home before the sun goes down?" Nicor asked.

"I think the one on Amy Johnson could be our best bet at this time of day," Adze told them.

"Sounds good to me," Cacus agreed.

THE SUN HAD long since set as they rode the lift back up to the penthouse. The funeral home had been a bust. No one there who looked suspicious in the least, only one poor woman in her late seventies, who'd obviously been crying as she talked to the funeral director about the plans for her husband's service.

Nicor didn't feel right about eavesdropping on their conversation, but he'd prefer that than not and possibly letting the aswang get away from them.

They stepped through the doors and immediately the scent of cooking meat struck Nicor. God, he didn't know if there was any scent better than that of a barbeque. The three of them headed up the stairs, the twinkling lights of the city around them shone through the windows.

Pyro was at the barby, beer in hand, while Oriax and Daevas were floating in the pool.

"Beer?" Pyro asked as he poked at something on the hot grill plate with his tongs.

"Hell, yes," the three of them replied all at once.

Nicor didn't wait around for his beer, though. He'd been dying to jump in the pool since they'd arrived that afternoon. He wasn't going to wait any longer. It didn't take him long to strip down to his underwear.

The glass-panelled gateway was thankfully open and Nicor took off running. When he reached the edge of the pool, he launched himself into the air, tucked his legs to his body and held his breath as he started to fall, right in between his two packmates who were peacefully floating in the pool.

Water rushed over him as Nicor sank to the bottom of the pool, air bubbles swirled around him. Laughter wanted to burst free, but he held it back—opening one's mouth underwater was not a smart thing to do.

Pushing off from the bottom of the pool Nicor broke the surface. Curses and laughter greeted him along with water being splashed in his face.

Nicor gave back as good as he got. He dived down, then grabbed Daevas's leg and pulled his brother under before quickly swimming away. When he surfaced he got a face full of water from Oriax. Nicor laughed and splashed back, soon the water had changed from calm and peaceful to jagged and wild.

"You're fucking dead," Daevas bitched as he came up coughing water.

Nicor could see the grin on his brother's face though, so wasn't worried the man was really pissed at him.

"Like you could ever catch me," Nicor taunted.

Daevas growled and lunged. but Nicor managed to stop him at every turn. He couldn't remember the last time he'd laughed this much, playing and relaxing with his brothers.

"Oi, dickheads! Dinner's ready," Pyro called from the edge.

"Truce?" Nicor asked the others as they all headed for the edge of the pool.

"Fine, but after dinner is another matter," Daevas agreed.

Nicor laughed. "You've got a deal."

Nicor flew to the edge of the pool then and hoisted himself out of the water. Adze handed him a towel and he gave himself a cursory dry before he wrapped the towel around his waist and took a seat at the table. A cold bottle of beer waited for him at his spot. Nicor took a long drink.

Pre-made salads from the shops along with grilled onion and potatoes and a platter of meat sat in the middle of the table.

"Thanks, guys. This looks great," Nicor said as he grabbed a bread roll and started buttering it.

It didn't take long before all the food had been devoured and they were all sitting back in their chairs with full stomachs. Nicor was silently thankful that he'd been given the day shift. The last thing he wanted to do right now was go hunting.

Too bad the others had to.

Pyro, Oriax and Daevas headed out an hour later, ready to start their shift.

After watching a little television with the other two, but Nicor called it a night not long afterwards and climbed into bed. He played a few games on his iPad for a little while before turning out the light and letting sleep take him.

Travelling always took it out of him.

Four days later they were no closer to catching the damn aswang and Nicor was starting to get annoyed. He wanted to go home. Unfortunately, trying to track down a being that could blend in with the rest of the population was proving much harder to do. It was like looking for a needle in a haystack.

Night had once again fallen. This time it was Nicor, Adze and Cacus's turn to hunt, the two teams having swapped shifts that afternoon.

Being a Friday night, the city would be teeming with life and Nicor silently hoped that tonight would be their night. Not many people roamed the streets of the suburbs alone after dark, the city though, was an entirely different matter.

Unlike Melbourne, which was bloody big and odd shaped, Darwin city was only small and bordered by four roads, making for a nice large rectangle for them to patrol. The waterfront district, which attached to the south-east side of the city was a little different, but once again not so overly large that the three of them couldn't handle it easily.

There would be plenty of dark, covered places on the esplanade for an aswang to take its victim and devour it.

Nicor loved being in his hound form. He always felt like he was coming home whenever he shifted.

We'll head to Daily Street, then split up and patrol Cavanagh, Smith and Mitchell Streets until we get to Bennet, Adze said. *Then head down to the waterfront, check that out then come back along the esplanade before repeating.*

Let's do this, Nicor said.

The three of them took off, bounding down the road and keeping to the shadows as much as they could.

Some streets were easier to do that than others. Once they reached Daily Street they split up and all headed for their assigned streets. Adze took Mitchell as it would be the hardest one to stay hidden on, known as Darwin's party strip. The majority of pubs and clubs were all located on that one stretch of road. Music drifted down from street, along with the heady scent of drunken humans.

Thankfully it wasn't his assignment.

Nicor got Smith Street while Cacus had Cavanagh. It wasn't until he got closer to the city centre that Nicor started to see more people. There were a few hotels and restaurants on Smith Street. Not to mention the one and only gay club Darwin had to offer. It was still a little early for that by the looks of it. Down the next side street was a titty bar. Nicor shuddered. That was the last place he wanted to go, he'd much prefer to stake out the front of the *Throb* and watch all the men and women entering there.

Glancing down the side street, there were women standing on the sidewalk in stiletto heels and barely anything else. The bra and G-string they were each wearing left absolutely nothing to the imagination.

No, no pregnant woman would be hanging out around here, so Nicor continued on his way.

Macca's on the corner had its fair share of customers. He could only imagine as the night went on the place would get even busier. Since the last time Nicor and the pack had been here, someone had painted a massive pride flag in the middle of the intersection right in front of the entrance to the outdoor mall. The thing took up practically the entire intersections. All the colours of the pride flag were on show, including brown and black.

Nicor would love to know if it was just an artist or if the council that had done that. He'd have to look it up when he got home. The painting did look rather permanent, so he hoped it was.

Crossing the road, Nicor made his way down the outdoor mall. At least here he didn't have to contend with vehicles. Just people walking or on push bike.

He kept his ears peeled and his eyes sharp, looking for anything that might be considered out of the ordinary, especially any Tassie devil-looking creatures.

The three of them met up on Bennet Street at the end of the mall.

Anything? Adze asked.

Nada, Cacus replied.

Nicor shook his head.

Let's keep moving.

The three of them took off past the bus depo and down through the darkened civic park. After the pool earlier, Nicor's hound was in a playful mood. He wanted to run 'round and roll in the grass, maybe chase some crickets. But one look at Adze halted Nicor from taking off. He had to remember the serious reason they were here.

They made their way through the trees and down the steep embankments to the waterfront district. Restaurants and pubs were in full swing with people everywhere. The place was lit up, with barely a shadow to be had. They had to move cautiously down here.

They'd covered as much ground as they could without seeing anything out of the ordinary at the waterfront, so they headed back to the city.

They'd been doing laps of the city for the last three hours. Evening had worn into the early hours of the night. Everyone louder. More reckless. Women had long ago removed their heels and were now walking barefoot along the footpaths while they carried their shoes.

Throb had opened its doors, the music blaring to beckon the partiers and the lonely alike. Nicor had to admit to enjoying walking past there and seeing all the people lined up out front.

Darwin was a small city compared to the rest of the country. As such they only had the one LGTBQ+ bar. But every time they came to town, the place was always hopping. One thing Darwin seemed to do well was Pride, as shown by the massive flag painted on the ground down the road. There definitely wasn't any hate anywhere around here. Everyone was out looking for a good time, no matter who they were with, and that made Nicor happy that in this place and time, people were free to be who they wanted to be.

As much as he would have loved to shift and join in with the partiers, Nicor continued on his way. He was halfway down the mall for what felt like the thousandth time, but really was only the fifth or six time that night when he heard something.

Nicor paused. Not sure what he heard. His ears perked up as he concentrated on his surroundings.

Might have something. South side of the mall. Standby.

Let us know. Will head to you now, Adze replied.

It took a moment before he heard it again. There, the smallest of whimpers. Nicor slowly made his way towards the sound. As he got closer it seemed to be coming from down the Star Village arcade off to the left off the mall.

The arcade was dark, all the shops having long since closed for the day. The through entrance to the alley behind had also been closed up, meaning there was only one way in and out of there. Being a hound, the dark didn't bother Nicor, but from experience bad things always seemed to happen anywhere there was a lack of light.

Nicor heard the whimper again. The noise sounded fainter the closer he got.

He didn't know if it was a victim slowly running out of life, or the aswang trying to confuse him, or something else entirely. He wasn't so stupid to think the aswang was the only paranormal creature in all of Darwin. Either way, Nicor had to get in there and put a stop to whatever it was.

Adze and Cacus joined him at the entrance to the arcade seconds later. That was one good thing about Darwin, it really didn't take long to get anywhere.

Senses on high alert, the three of them stalked over the bricked entrance through the dark. His hackles rose with every step into the arcade they took. A sense of excitement started to grow within him as they hunted their prey.

A large staircase sat in the centre of the arcade, leading up to the shops on the first floor.

A noise to the right as they entered the main section of the arcade caught Nicor's attention. He turned in time to see a black creature with a white strip across its chest and wickedly sharp teeth pounce on him. The creature growled and snarled as it snapped its teeth together, attempting to take a bite out of Nicor.

The aswang was the largest Tassie devil Nicor had ever seen. Nicor was knocked off his paws at the impact and the two of them went tumbling. His paws slipped out from underneath him as he scrambled to stand again. Nicor squared off against the aswang, who was currently hissing and spitting at him.

Cacus, race home and grab our clothes. Call an ambulance. I'm not sure how long this woman has left, Adze's voice sounded in his head.

Nicor ignored it, not allowing himself to be distracted as he and the aswang circled one another. The worry in Adze's voice had sunk in, though. There wasn't time. They needed to get the human help. Not wanting this creature to survive even a second longer, Nicor attacked.

As large as the aswang was in this form, Nicor was bigger, meaner when he had to be. They battled, teeth and claws ripping into each other. Nicor ignored every bite, every cut he received, determined to end this. The need to save the woman trumped any small injury he could get. He could heal, but the human, their lives were so fragile.

Out of the corner of his eye, he saw Adze leave the

woman he'd been checking over and make his way towards where the Nicor battled the aswang.

The demon must have seen him as well as she whirled around, now having attackers on two fronts. Adze and Nicor stalked forward, closing the distance between them and their prey. Nicor knew they had to behead the creature to kill it before they could set it alight. They just had to get the right opportunity.

Moments later their opportunity came when the aswang turned to attack Adze. Nicor didn't let her get very far. He leapt, barrelling into her. His claws dug into fur and flesh on the devil's back. The scream from the creature echoed in the small courtyard. Nicor tilted his head, opened his jaws and bit down hard on the sup's neck, teeth sinking deep on either side of the spinal column.

Jaws locked tight, Nicor tugged with all his might. The sound of flesh tearing wasn't pleasant, but the head jerk was necessary. The head must go. Nicor spat out the flesh and bone in his mouth, the aswang limp under him. Her eyes wide and sightless, her tongue lolled to the side.

Adze shifted to his human form and stalked over to the creature. He reached down, grabbed the sup's head and ripped it from the body. The strength of the man had never ceased to amaze Nicor.

Blood covered the bricks beneath their feet as it spilled from the broken body of the aswang.

"You good?" Adze asked him, his hands and arms blood soaked.

Nicor nodded. The taste in his mouth was foul, but nothing he couldn't live with until he got home.

A whimper from the corner of the arcade had Nicor whirling around. He'd momentarily forgotten about the woman. He trotted over to her. Her large pregnant belly had been sliced to ribbons by the creature, no doubt trying to get to her unborn child.

The arcade was shortly bathed in bright green light as Adze set the body of the sup on fire. The light only made the scene in front of him look even worse. Nicor shifted as quickly as he could. They had to try to stop the woman's bleeding as much as they could until the ambulance got there.

It looked like Adze had already licked at the wounds, hoping the healing properties in their saliva would help. Nicor could see that the bleeding had slowed, he didn't know if that was because it was healing or because she was running out of life.

Before he could do anything else Cacus had returned with the others trailing behind him.

"Here, let me look out for her, you get dressed," Pyro said as he pulled a shift from the backpack and knelt on the ground next to Nicor.

Nicor nodded. Cacus showing up meant the ambulance had been called. The last thing they needed was for it to arrive and have Nicor and Adze standing there buck naked. Not a good look for them at all.

Once he had jeans and sneakers on, Nicor knelt once again next to the woman. He lightly brushed the hair back from her head and whispered, "Everything's going to be okay."

Her eyes were closed, and Nicor assumed she'd passed out, but that didn't stop him from talking with her.

Adze was on the phone in the background. Nicor assumed he was chatting with the local "Matti", then their police contact, informing them what had happened and that clean-up of one aswang body was required. The next phone call would be to the local police contact in Darwin to bring him up to speed on the events of tonight.

It wasn't long before the small arcade was swarming with cops and paramedics. Thankfully their contact had driven off with the aswang's remains as the ambulance arrived. Nicor and Adze told the ambulance officers what they could, but seeing as how they didn't even know who the woman was, there wasn't much they could tell them. It wasn't like they could say a Pilipino demon called an aswang tried to rip the lady open so it could eat her unborn baby. Nicor could only imagine how well that would go down.

He had a feeling it was going to be a long night for everyone, whether they liked it or not.

CHAPTER TWO

Jordan stared at his sketchpad once again. For the last month all he'd been able to draw was a damn dog. A huge, hulking dog that was so real to him he felt a deep need in his bones to draw it. He didn't understand why he was so damn obsessed with this creature. He couldn't even remember seeing any dog like it recently.

He flipped the page and picked up his piece of charcoal. Jordan always preferred charcoal to pencils if he was sketching. Hopefully he could actually draw something other than a damn dog this time. He closed his eyes and took a deep breath, centring his breathing and hoping.

Something felt different, if he was being honest with himself. *Something* had felt different in the city for the last month. Some kind of shift had happened. Being an incubus, Jordan found himself tuned in to the feelings of those surrounding him, and recently *something* had changed. He hadn't been able to put his finger on what, though. Of course, some of his kind would say he didn't understand the feeling because he was a broken incubus so it affected his mind. Jordan knew better. Now anyway. He wasn't broken. Just unique, *different*, among most of the incubi and succubi in the world.

Eyes still closed, Jordan placed the charcoal stick to his sketch pad and started drawing. When he opened his eyes again and looked down there was another dog, its big eyes staring up at him like it needed something from him. Why would a damn dog need *him*? Or was it chastising him?

"God damn it," Jordan swore. He hoped whatever he felt would disappear soon. He had work to do. His agent would be pissed if all he had to hand over was pictures of black dogs. Oh no.

Jordan glanced at his watch. "Fuck."

His agent was going to kill him. Immediately if possible—*if* Amanda had the psychic ability to know when he'd forgotten about their meetings. Jordan dumped his sketch pad and charcoal down, racing for the bathroom. As he stripped, his phone started ringing.

Jordan hopped on one foot while he tried to pull off his pants and he tapped his watch to answer the phone. Hopefully it wasn't the impeccable, irrefutable Agent Amanda White. It *might* not be her.

"Hello?" he asked breathlessly.

"Where are you?" Mandy asked in a clipped tone. Of course it was her. Mandy *had* to be psychic. Some kind of latent ability passed down from partial demon heritage she wasn't even aware she had.

"Where would you like me to be?" Jordan asked. He raced into the bathroom and turned on the shower. Clothes. He needed them all off.

"You're supposed to be in front of me. We have things to go over in preparation for your exhibit."

"I'm coming. I swear."

Mandy sighed resignedly. Jordan could picture her pinching the bridge of her nose like she did when she was exasperated. It happened with him more often than she liked. Mandy really should have known him better by now. She had been his agent for the last five years for crying out loud. Jordan couldn't recall if he'd ever actually made it to one of his meetings on time. Nope. Not once. Hell, he usually ran late for his opening nights. It was one of those things that weren't imperative to him. Not like his art. His art consumed him, making Jordan forget time all together. Food and people and schedules ceased to exist.

"I'll be there shortly," he promised as he yanked his socks off.

"See that you are. You're not my only artist you know."

"I know, but I am your best," Jordan said cheekily.

"Jordan!"

He laughed and hung up the call. It would be at least a half hour before he was standing in front of Mandy.

The water in the shower took his breath away as he

stepped under the spray. Cold, *too* cold. Jordan washed quickly, then dried himself and dressed in short order. One last glance in the mirror—not too shabby, the electric turquoise blue of his shirt contrasted well against his dark russet skin—and he grabbed his keys. Presentation was important after all. He headed to the attached garage and climbed into his SUV. The car was far too big for him and he didn't love driving it, but the size was necessary as he often transported large paintings in the back. Plus, the little red convertible parked in the next bay was completely useless this time of year.

Jordan couldn't wait for the warmer months when he'd be able to take his baby out on the road again. Until then he had to drive this behemoth or deal with the Sydney public transport, and no one willingly wanted to do that.

Reversing cameras are a thing of miracles, Jordan thought as he slowly reversed out of the old brick building. Once clear, he clicked the button attached to his visor and waited for the roller door to close. One could never be too careful in this day and age. Home break-ins were once again on the rise in the city and the last thing Jordan wanted to deal with was someone invading his private space.

He joined the busy traffic and headed toward the gallery. It didn't seem to matter what time of day or night, the traffic in Sydney never seemed to ease.

Jordan glanced at his watch and groaned as he pulled into the small lot at the back of the gallery then climbed out of his car.

Mandy waited for him right inside as he stepped into the gallery.

"What time do you call this?" she asked him, trying to look stern.

"Jordan time?" he replied with a shrug.

"You're impossible." She sighed.

"You've been dealing with me for five years," he reminded her.

"I keep hoping you'll get better."

Jordan shook his head. "Not gonna happen." If it hadn't happened in the two centuries before now, it wasn't going to happen ever. "Lose all hope now."

"Right, let's get started then, shall we?"

"Let's."

Jordan followed Mandy as she took him to the back room. A large screen hung on the back wall with a laptop already connected sat in the middle of the small conference table. It showed Jordan an image of the gallery with his already finished art on the walls on the screen, and plenty of blank places for the work he hadn't yet completed. For now, it was all computer images. The visual made moving and rearranging the art to Jordan's exact specification so much easier. It wasn't until they got closer to the opening day that art would start going up on the walls. Nothing was final though until Jordan had his last walk though.

Mandy had to make a living and she couldn't do that if they shut down the gallery for months at a time in preparation for a next exhibit. She currently had a mix of other artists' work out front, that would all be removed and his work showcased when they got closer to opening day.

His theme for this exhibit excited him and kept images of the dog from crowding into the picture.

Mandy clicked into the walls, to give Jordan a closer look. His newest work lined along them with little white plaques placed next to each painting with an explanation about its meaning. A lot of his work was based in traditional aboriginal paintings, but over time, Jordan had evolved his own style. They now involved colours that wouldn't naturally be found in the bush when he'd first been born. Blues, pinks and purples stared back at him in thousands and thousands of little dots, as did greens and yellows. He loved the more vibrant colours he was able to use in this day and age.

The ochres, browns and blacks from centuries past had gotten their use over the years, but he wanted to explore new horizons. Only two pictures on the wall used those traditional colourings now.

Jordan held up his hand for Mandy to pause as she clicked through to the next wall. Here was one of the two pieces he'd done using traditional colours. It seemed appropriate to honour his mum in that way. It had been a long time since she had passed away. Nearly two hundred years, but he could still see her image in his mind, clear as day, as if he'd only looked upon her countenance the day before. He hoped wherever she was, she was happy and proud of the man he'd become.

"Love you, mum," he whispered, then cleared his throat, forgetting that he wasn't alone in the room.

His mum wasn't the only portrait on the walls, images of people he'd met over his long life stared back at him. All people who had influenced him during the years. The majority of them were from aboriginal descent, but there were a few Europeans thrown in there for something a little different.

This new style he'd been toying with gave the portraits the impact he'd been looking for. And he couldn't wait to see them hanging on the walls for real.

The one hard part was changing up his technique enough so that he wouldn't be compared with himself from previous lives, but making sure it still felt like him when he looked at his art. Living an exceptionally long life was a burden at times.

Not all his work was limited to regular canvas paintings this time around. He had thrown in some other fun "canvases" too.

"We've already had some major interest in the surfboards," Mandy informed him as she showed him how they would be displayed. "I've also taken a number of calls from manufacturers of the products, wanting to know if you would be interested in designing for them."

"Nope," Jordan replied without having to think about it too much.

He wasn't interested in his artwork being stamped on surfboards left, right and centre. That would take away from the uniqueness of what he created. A little bit of his soul went into the designs, the idea of it mass produced made him shudder. People paid good money to get a one-of-a-kind piece from him and Jordan wasn't about to screw his customers out of that.

"I didn't think so, but it's my job to at least ask the question."

"Thanks for not trying to talk me into it."

"I've known you long enough now to realise that would be a fruitless endeavour," Mandy replied as they continued their virtual walk through. "I did receive a call, however, about something you may be interested in."

"Oh yeah?" Jordan answered, not really paying attention, too busy making sure his art was in the right place and telling the story that he wanted.

"Yep, the city council called me," Mandy said.

It took Jordan a moment to realise Mandy had stopped talking. Not only had she stopped talking, but she had stopped clicking as well. He turned to see her sat, staring at him, frozen on the screen was a piece he'd done about the early settlement of Australia. Those weren't easy times.

"I'm sorry, what did you say?" he asked, giving her his full attention.

"I said, the city council called me."

"Why in the world is the council calling you about me?"

"Have you seen the artwork that's going up on the sides of buildings in the city recently?" Mandy asked.

"What are you going on about now? You know I've been holed up at home for months working on all of this." Jordan waved, motioning to his art on the screen.

Mandy sighed again. "I was afraid you were going to say that. Which is why, when we're finished here, we're going for a drive."

"I don't have time for that," Jordan replied as he stared back at the screen, waiting for Mandy to continue the virtual tour.

"You're going to want to make time," Mandy announced. "The council would like to commission you to paint the side of a building."

Jordan turned to take in Mandy. A commission? Of his art? For the masses to see? Talk about opportunity for showcasing what traditional art could do.

"What kind of building and where is it located?"

"I've no idea. That's information for you to work out with them. As for payment, we're already in discussions over that. " Mandy smiled, knowing she had his full attention. "There's a massive movement going on at the moment to beautify the city with artwork. They've commissioned several artists to paint the sides or backs of building which were previously eyesores as people drove down alleys. Now, though, they're stunning pieces of art on a massive scale. Some old buildings are a single story, some works are as big as five to six stories."

In all his years, Jordan hadn't ever painted a building before. The idea intrigued him. He would have to take a look to see what had already been done and talk with the council to see where they were thinking of giving him. It would take a lot of time he was sure, several weeks with planning and all at least.

Mandy held out a piece of paper, waiting for Jordan to take it. He did, excitement thrumming through him about the potential project. He tucked the paper in his pocket, he'd call as soon as he arrived home.

THE DRIVE through the city had been eye-opening. He couldn't believe he'd missed this happening in the last several months. Some of the artwork on the buildings was stunning—bigger and more eyepopping on such a grand scale. The excitement he felt at the gallery intensified over the thought of his work being on display like that for tens of thousands to see on a daily basis.

Jordan pulled the details from his back pocket and grabbed his phone as he collapsed on his couch. His stomach rumbled in hunger, but Jordan ignored it, he'd gotten good at doing that over the years. It wasn't a hunger that food could quench.

He dialled the number listed and waited for the call to connect.

"City of Sydney, this is Harry."

"Harry Donovan?" Jordan asked.

"That's me. How can I help you?"

"Harry, my name is Jordan Makan, I was asked to call you."

Jordan could practically hear the guy on the other end sit up and take notice as soon as Jordan told him his name.

"Mr. Makan, thank you for calling me back. I assume you were made aware of the reason for me reaching out to you?"

"I was, and I must admit to being intrigued with what you're trying to do."

"Thank you. It was hard to get started, but since the first one, more and more artists are willing to sign up. We'd love to have you on board as well."

"What would I have to do?" Jordan asked.

"Would it be possible for you to come up with a couple of design options and come in for a meeting on Friday? We can consider which design would work best, designate you a building, sign a contract and let you get started."

Jordan thought long and hard about that. It didn't give him much time. But he already had a couple of ideas in his head after his drive with Mandy.

"I think that's doable," Jordan answered. More of his art. More of how he saw the world was about to be on display for everyone. He settled on a time with Harry for their meeting on Friday then disconnected the call.

Three designs. Three proposals with his style of art that could be easily expanded and transferred on to the side of a building. All him. Jordan had his work cut out for him. He threw his phone on the couch beside him, picked up one of the many pads and pencils he had scattered over his home and settled back to see what came to him.

Hopefully.

The fine lines curved out from the pencil, but his fingers itched. Where was his charcoal?

CHAPTER THREE

A few weeks had passed since they arrived back from Darwin and Nicor couldn't believe he was thinking he actually missed the weather in Darwin. That hot, humid, smack in your face weather that wanted to melt everyone, human or Sup. Melbourne in the middle of winter was miserable. Being cold sucked.

Yes, the cold didn't affect them as much as it did humans, but it did still affect them. Hellhounds revelled in the heat, not the cold. And when he said heat, Nicor meant a dry heat. Not like Darwin. The weather in Darwin tried to maim people.

The rest of Australia seemed to be quiet at the moment. None of them were willing to say it, though, in case they jinxed themselves. Hell, even thinking it was bad luck.

As nice as it was to have a couple of days off where they weren't tracing down a sup gone bad, Nicor longed for someone to share that time with. Watching

Adze with Archie and Pyro with Callum had him thinking and wishing about his own mate. Their unconscious affections in front of the single packmates could drive a hound mad.

Before Adze mated, Nicor hadn't allowed himself to think about the possibility of a mate all that often. He hadn't wanted to get his hopes up only to find out they didn't exist. But with the appearance of Archie, then Callum, hope had seeded itself deep in Nicor's heart. To stop himself from wallowing in what he didn't have, Nicor found an outlet for his frustration.

The character on the screen exploded under a hail of bullets, blood splattering the lens. Nicor picked up the weapon and continued on. His headphones on, his favourite music blasted away as he lost himself in the game. When arcades first became the thing, it was like he had found himself. Then came the Atari, Nintendo, PlayStation, Xbox, Game Boy, Sega Genesis—it didn't matter the console, he loved to lose himself in the game—all of which he still owned and played. Games gave him an outlet. Something to do while he waited.

When FPSs came on the scene, Nicor found his jam. There were a lot of great games out there, but first-person shooters were by far his favourite. The hunt and kill aspect appealed to his hound but in a human form.

Half-Life 2 and Call of Duty had been religious experiences—as much as any hellhound could have.

He was so engrossed by the action on his television, he jumped a mile when a hand landed on his shoulder. Nicor's heart pounded as he dropped the controller and pulled the headphones off his head, thankful he hadn't screamed when he saw the amusement on Cacus's face. He'd totally meant to scare Nicor.

"Yeah, yeah. Fuck off," he bitched.

"You should have seen the look on your face man." Cacus started chuckling.

"Piss off. What did you want?" Nicor picked up the remote to his stereo and paused his music, glaring at Cacus.

Cacus continued chuckling as he turned for the door. "You're wanted in the living room. Apparently, Callum has something to talk to us about."

Nicor groaned. He had jinxed the lot of them and his quiet days of killing alien invaders were over. At least he'd have something to do rather than wait. Waiting sucked. Nicor saved his progress then shut everything down. Everyone had gathered in the living room by the time he got out there.

Nicor took a seat next to Oriax on the couch and waited for the other shoe to drop. He didn't have to wait too long.

"Thanks for coming guys, sorry to interrupt what you were doing," Callum said. The man looked tired. Like he'd had a bloody long day at work. He hadn't even changed out of his suit yet.

"No worries, how can we help?" Daevas asked.

"I took a call today from a Detective Lewis in Sydney. It seems he's got a series of missing women come across his desk."

Nicor sat up straight, as did a couple of the others. That bit of news wasn't going anywhere good.

"He called me to ask if we'd caught the person or

persons responsible for the kidnappings last June."

"What did the detective have to say?" Adze asked, his phone already out of his pocket and he was tapping away. Matti was about to get busy by the looks of things.

"They've had four women go missing in and around Hyde Park and the Royal Botanic Gardens in the last three weeks. The disappearances were similar enough to our cases he decided to give me a call."

"All right," Adze said with a nod. "Matti is looking into it and will let me know shortly. But it might be a good idea to pack a bag. Looks like downtime is over."

The team got up, grumbling, but all broke off to pack.

Nicor had always liked Sydney, but something about it felt different this time. He shook it off thinking it was because their prey had gotten away from them last time. He didn't like the idea that the mermaids had skipped town and seemed to have moved location. Not that it wasn't exactly unexpected. Nicor didn't know what it was, but he felt good about what they were about to do. He had a feeling they were finally going to get the bastards.

This time, Nicor wasn't walking away empty handed.

Sydney, much like Melbourne, had grown over the years, not only out but *up*. The number of skyscrapers in the city had increased yet again. None of the cities in Australia rivalled American cities, though. Their tall building numbers were plain ridiculous. Nicor shuddered thinking about having to police the numbers the American packs had to. Hell, if he remembered correctly, New York City and Los Angeles had two packs each. There wasn't anywhere else in the world that had that. Most countries had one or two packs—full stop.

The plane touched down with a slight bump and Nicor couldn't wait to disembark. Tin cans flying through the air didn't sit right with him no matter how many times he flew. Thankfully the flight was only an hour and a half, unlike the trip to Darwin. Nicor still felt the confinement of being in the locked cabin.

There hadn't been much talk during the flight, Pyro and Adze had been huddled over maps of the city and busy reading what looked like complete copies of police reports on all the missing women. Reports from the Melbourne disappearances were also piled on the seat next to Adze.

Nicor left them to it. Bloody psychopaths. Researching on a plane. Better leave the planners to it. They'd let him and the others know if they needed any help. He packed away his Switch, which had kept him distracted through the flight and pulled his headphones off his ears, tucking them safely in the top of his backpack. The sound of the engines as they revved down hit him hard.

Glancing around the cabin, he saw Adze and Pyro were packing away everything they'd been looking at. No doubt it would be pulled out again as soon as they arrived at their apartment.

Oriax and Daevas were packing up the cards and Cacus looked like he'd managed to fall asleep. Bloody psycho. Though he probably had the best idea of them all, and Nicor had a feeling they were in for a slew of long nights in their immediate future.

Daevas nudged Cacus who grunted at him. He shook his head and bitched, "Dude. Wake up, we're here."

"Fuck off," Cacus moaned.

Nicor grinned at their bickering. He found a scrap piece of paper in his bag and screwed it up into a tight ball. Nicor lobbed it at Cacus and hit him square in the face.

Oriax burst into laughter as Cacus jumped at the unexpected impact.

"Fuck you all," he groaned as he blinked open his eyes. "I know that was you Pyro."

Pyro looked up, wearing a perturbed expression. "What the fuck did I do?"

Nicor, Oriax and Daevas burst into laughter.

"Who did it?" Cacus asked.

They all shrugged, claiming innocence.

"You're all a bunch of assholes and deserve whatever is coming for you." Cacus flipped them the bird before he picked up the ball and grinned. He pegged Oriax with it.

The wadded paper ball got tossed around the small cabin several times before the plane stopped at its assigned area on the tarmac. Right then the ball went sailing into Adze's waiting hands. He looked at it then pitched it into the bin next to him.

"Hey!" several of them protested.

"Time to hunt," Adze said and stood. Everyone else followed suit, grabbing their bags from the overhead.

Waiting for the stairs to lower felt like an eternity and Nicor felt the walls closing in on him a bit.

Once the stairs lowered, he encouraged everyone to disembark as quick as possible, thankful for the fresh air outside. Unfortunately, they had to wait for the cargo hold to be opened so they could grab their gear.

All the hurry up and stop was killing Nicor.

The Sydney team had been notified of their arrival and two cars waited for them in the lot, once they were all loaded up they climbed in and broke up into teams. Oriax drove the car with Daevas and Nicor while Adze was behind the wheel of the other one with Pyro and Cacus. Two cars made it better to divide and conquer to stop the teasing everyone did—for now. Like being in different cars would stop them.

Due to their constant travel, they maintained residences in every city as it was better for their privacy while they were there. They had the money, used the properties to bring them more income, so why not? Sydney's property was located in the middle of the city.

They didn't make it very far before they ran into traffic and basically came to a standstill. Adze hadn't planned their arrival all that well. That was one thing Darwin had going for it. The lack of traffic while they were there. Their rush hour might include a five, maybe ten-minute delay in getting home, but that was about it. Not like Sydney or Melbourne where they could sit in traffic for upwards of an hour or more.

The sun was setting as they finally pulled into the garage under their building. It had been a few months since they had been in town and Nicor was surprised at how excited he felt about hunting on the streets of Sydney again. He couldn't quite put his finger on what he was feeling, but there was *something* different this time.

They each grabbed a duffle and one bag of gear out of the trunks then headed to the lift, somehow managing to cram all of them into one car. Nicor had forgotten how small the lifts were in this building. The six of them, plus their luggage, didn't leave a great deal of space left for anything else, like breathing.

The residence was clean and fully stocked when they arrived. Nicor sent a small thanks to the crew they employed to clean while they were out of town, and they had contacts they could call to stock it with only minimal notice required.

Anything for a price these days.

Unfortunately, not every residence they owned had six bedrooms. Like this one. Some of them did, but not Sydney, so that meant they had to double up most places. Nicor headed to the room he shared with Oriax. They each threw their duffles and gear on the end of their beds. The rooms were thankfully big enough that they fit two double beds. Nicor missed his king already, not to mention his massive gaming system wall. But he was used to it by now. They had been doing this for a couple hundred years.

Though maybe it was worth it to bring one of his systems down so he'd have something to do when they weren't on the hunt. Or a new system. A new one would be better. He just had to talk Oriax into it. He'd agree as long as Nicor wore his headphones. Or new headphones. Having a pair here wouldn't hurt. Darwin could use some consoles too. Could they write them off as a business expense? Did they want renters having access to them? Something for Adze or Pyro to look into. Nicor walked back out of the room with his Switch in hand.

The six of them gathered in the living room where Adze had his laptop and both files out, one which contained all the information they'd been able to gather on the mermaid and her organisation. Looked like he hadn't made it to his bedroom yet. His luggage still sat next to his feet. Adze didn't even look up from the computer when he talked.

"Let's order some food, fuel up then head out. I doubt that we'll find anything tonight. Sydney has a shit ton of waterfront property."

Nicor was all for that. At the mention of food his stomach growled, letting him know exactly how hungry he was. His mouth started watering when he remembered where he was and what restaurants were close by that delivered.

"Who's up for Vietnamese?" he asked as he pulled his phone out of his pocket. He did a quick search for the number he was after. He could totally go for a phở soup right now.

"Oh hell, yeah," Pyro agreed.

Adze nodded as did the others.

They all knew the menu off by heart. It was good

food. Really. Worth remembering and ordering any time they were in the city.

Three beef phở, one pork chops with fried egg, one chicken fried rice and a prawn with garlic and veggies, plus four serves of rice paper rolls and four serves of fried wontons would hold them over for now. Nicor disappeared down the passage for somewhere quiet to make the call. He grabbed his wallet in case they no longer had his card on file. Once the order was in, he headed back to the others.

"Food will be here in about forty minutes," he announced.

Nicor grabbed a six-pack from the fridge and made his way around the living room, handing out beers to everyone. He folded the cardboard carrier up and placed it on the coffee table. He'd throw it in the trash later. Nicor then collapsed on the couch next to Pyro and listened in. A large map of Sydney had gotten projected on the wall opposite them.

The silence in the room weighed down on them as they all studied the map—all of them frowning and shifting in their seats but not speaking to each other. The area to cover was huge. They were going to be running thin no matter how Nicor looked at it. Finally, Adze spoke up.

"Okay, here's what we know," Adze said before pausing for a second as if he needed gather his thoughts. "At least four women have gone missing in the last few weeks, around Hyde Park and the Botanic Gardens." Adze pointed to the map on the wall so they could all see where they needed to concentrate their efforts on initially. "We know these mermaids have partnered up with an incubus in the past. I wouldn't put it past them to still be working together. In fact I'd put money on them still being cohorts."

Nicor tended to agree with Adze. They had too good a thing going in Melbourne for them to have gone their separate ways.

"The incubus is luring the women, feeding from them, and then delivering them to the mermaids. They turn around and sell their victims into slavery."

There were some days that Nicor truly hated his job. This wasn't one of those days. These bloody creatures needed to be eliminated, with extreme prejudice. The sooner the better as well.

"Tonight, we'll split the city into three. We'll hunt for a few days, and then expand outward in a couple of days. As I said before, Sydney has a shit ton of waterfront property where it would be piss easy to snatch someone without anyone seeing a thing."

Adze began marking sections on the map.

"Pyro, you and Nicor take from the corner of Market and George Street. Head north to Circular Quay then east to the Botanic Gardens. Oriax, you're with me, we'll go north and west to include the Rocks, Millers point and the harbour bridge. That leaves Daevas and Cacus to head south. You'll cover Hyde Park then west to Darling Harbour."

That was three fairly decent chunks of the city covered off. Like previous hunts, they'd rotate the areas each night to make sure nothing was missed. They chatted a little longer, refining the details of the hunt as much as possible. Nicor started to get that excited feeling he always got before embarking on a mission. He couldn't wait to get out there and start searching.

The buzzer rang not long after. Finally, the food had arrived. Nicor shot up from the couch and headed to the intercom, buzzing the delivery man up.

He waited in the doorway for the elevator to arrive. When the lift doors opened Nicor doubted the kid who stepped out, laden down with bags, could be more than seventeen. Probably working to save money to go to school.

The kid looked up and down the passage until he noticed Nicor standing in the door.

"You Nicor?" he asked.

"That's me," Nicor replied. He gave the kid a bigger tip as he took the bags from him.

"Thanks, mister! Enjoy the food."

"Stay in school!" Nicor headed back inside with bags dangling from his arms.

"Stay in school?" Daevas mimicked as he sat at the dining room table while Nicor placed the bags down.

"Fuck off," Nicor laughed. A couple odd looks were sent his way and he shrugged. He had no idea why he'd said that. It wasn't like him at all. *Something* was keeping him from finding his equilibrium.

Cacus placed plates and proper cutlery on the table while Adze started unpacking all the bags. Everyone reached at once, hands getting tangled up in the foods and playful hits being exchanged. Adze held the food captive until everyone settled, then they grabbed their orders plus their share of the entrées.

The discussion in the room died off as everyone concentrated on filling their bellies for the long night to come. Nicor picked up his piping hot container of soup and opened the bowl containing the noodles, onion, chilli, sprouts and raw thin strips of beef. His mouth watered and the unsettled feeling pinging at the edges of his mind eased off a bit.

As he poured the soup, the pink beef immediately changed colour as it cooked in the heat of the liquid. Nicor leaned over his bowl and inhaled the tasty aroma of his soup. God he'd missed this. He picked up his chopsticks in one hand and spoon in the other and started eating, loving every bite. It was exactly how he remembered it.

It didn't take long before all the food had been devoured and Nicor sat back in the couch patting his stomach. He'd probably pay later for running around with a belly full of soup, but it was so worth it. He'd let it settle until they had to leave. Nicor let his Switch balance on his food bump as he zoned out while playing *Cuphead*.

When nine thirty rolled round it was finally time for their hunt. The sleepy food coma was gone and the anticipation of *something* happening rolled back in earnest. They all had their orders so the six of them headed downstairs and into a nearby dark alley where they usually shifted. They stashed their clothes in a backpack under a couple of discarded wooden pallets before shifting.

Nicor loved being in his hound form. He gave

himself a good shake to settle into his new skin then turned to face Adze.

Everyone know their orders?

They all nodded, which was something to see. Five massive hellhounds all bobbing their heads at once.

Right, as per normal, keep in touch, don't take any chances and be safe out there.

Yes, boss, Oriax replied. Nicor and Pyro huffed, as close to a chuckle they could get to in their hound form, which sounded plain weird anyway. Oriax growled, biting at them. They took off to start their recon.

They stuck to the shadows, like always, as they headed to their destination. The Botanic Gardens were huge, giving them a lot of ground to over. Once they arrived, it would be bloody easy to stay hidden while they scouted the area. It was getting there, through the lit streets and the large intersections that was the issue. They'd manage though. They always did.

Anytime someone spotted them, they were always gone by the time the person took a second look.

They crossed through the top of Hyde park, not really paying it much attention as Daevas and Cacus would cover that area. Then they passed St. Mary's Cathedral and into the grounds that surrounded the Art Gallery of New South Wales.

Crossing the M1 motorway to get to the Royal Botanic Gardens was a pain in the ass, and resulted in Pyro narrowly missing getting hit by a speeding car.

Thank fuck that's over, Pyro said as they stepped foot onto the grass lawns of the gardens.

Let's not do that again. Callum would kill me if I

called him and told him you'd been squashed under a fucking speeding Subaru.

Too right he would!

Let's head east to Woolloomooloo Bay then follow the paths right back around the gardens. After we can do a sweep of the interior.

Sounds like a solid plan to me, Pyro replied.

They took off, heading to the path that wound around the coast. They slowly and methodically patrolled their area—decades of doing similar runs defaulting into learned muscle memory. People were scarce the farther around they went. The gardens themselves closed at dusk, however, the gates remained open and a dedicated few jogged the pathways at night.

Unfortunately, due to the seclusive nature of the area, it made the perfect place for women to be snatched without any witnesses. Nicor and Pyro took their time, making sure they covered every centimetre of this place.

The night wore on, with nothing more exciting than a possum scurrying up a tree to get out of their way. They checked in every couple of hours with the others, none of them seemed to be having any more luck locating anything than they had.

It all made for a long and frustrating night that was quickly becoming morning.

The faint hints of dawn were painting the far-off sky when they rounded the corner near the Opera House. Both of them immediately spotted an incubus dragging a drugged-looking woman in workout attire away.

Nicor growled low and loud. Pyro echoed him. Both of them settled into a crouch as they began stalking their prey.

We've got something at the opera house, Pyro sounded the alarm as he reached out to the others.

The incubus spun at the sound of their twin growls and startled when he spotted the two of them. His face quickly contorted into one of grotesque rage. His sharp teeth bared as he hissed at Nicor and Pyro.

The pair of them took off, quickly eating up the distance between them and the incubus. Their prey dragged the woman to the edge, picked her now struggling form up, and tipped her over the fencing.

She screamed as she dropped while the incubus took off down the path away from Nicor and Pyro.

Fuck, fuck, fuck, Nicor swore.

The woman's screaming didn't stop though, and the drop was only about ten meters-—which meant she was clinging onto something.

You get the woman, I'm going after the incubus, Nicor said.

Adze said not to do anything stupid, Pyro replied as they raced toward the woman.

I'm not. The others should be here to help soon.

Be careful, Nicor.

Nicor veered left while Pyro went right. He increased his stride, trying to catch up to the incubus in front of him. He'd give it to the guy; he sure could run. Nicor had no doubt, however, that he would catch the guy.

What're your positions? Adze asked.

I'm at the top of the ridge, overlooking the opera house. The bastard threw a woman over the edge, Pyro replied, his voice sounding tense.

Nicor kept his eyes on his prize as he raced along the path, which soon descended onto Macquarie Street.

Heading south along Macquarie, about to go under the M1. This fucker doesn't seem to be slowing down at all.

Keep us informed, we should be with you in ten, Adze ordered.

We're on our way as well but will be a little longer, Cacus said.

How's the woman going, Pyro? Nicor asked. The distance between him and his prey had narrowed significantly. Close. So close.

Managed to get her back on solid ground. She's shaken but okay. I'm coming after you.

No! Nicor replied. *Stay with her. We don't know if there were any others close by that will come after her as soon as she's alone. See if you can get any answers from her as to what—*

Bright lights blinded Nicor. Something rammed him hard, a sudden crushing impact along his side. His entire body floated for a time in the air before he had the sickening realisation he was falling. Something hard broke his fall, but he had no idea what, all he knew was pain. So much pain.

Cool liquid surrounded him as the world went dark.

CHAPTER FOUR

Jordan yawned at he looked up at the side of the building he'd been painting. The large industrial lights he had set up to illuminate his project shone brightly in the dark alley. He was rather proud of the way the picture was coming along. Another couple of days or so and he'd be done. Working on such a massive canvas was different and challenging, but also made it a great deal of fun to work on. He used rollers and air brushes for the majority of this work, unlike the thin fiddly little brushes he had at home.

Working on the surfboards taught him how to work with spray paint and markers, and how to combine those with painting on the boards so he wasn't totally out of his depth, but this wasn't the same at all.

Checking the time, Jordan decided to call it a night. Or morning really. Working until four a.m. wasn't anything new to Jordan. There had been plenty of times in his past he'd go for weeks, if not months, working solely at night and sleeping through the day.

Jordan started to pack up all his gear, the rollers needed to be cleaned, as did the other instruments he'd used tonight. He placed them in sealed containers in the boot of his SUV to clean when he got home. He had everything already set up there. He turned off the lights, and packed them along with his small generator in the boot as well.

The first edges of dawn peeked over the horizon. He stifled another yawn as he climbed into the car and started the engine. The blast of cold air through the vents shocked his system awake. He wasn't so tired that he couldn't make it home. Jordan had seen plenty of studies that showed that driving while tired was just as bad, if not worse, than driving while drunk, and Jordan refused to do either. If he thought he couldn't make it home safely, he'd curl up on the back seat for a couple of hours and get some sleep in his SUV.

Jordan blasted his music, bouncing his head and thrumming his thumbs on the steering wheel along with the tunes. There wasn't any radio station that he listened to that played live at this time of the morning, but the music they had scheduled was decent enough. He wound his way out of the alley, soon enough he was on Bridge Street, heading home.

The lights at the intersection of Macquarie and Bridge were green so Jordan didn't slow down. He thought he saw someone running down the road, which was ridiculous this time of day. Even still, he glanced to his right, only for a second, to double-check, and that was all it took.

The crunching sound of hitting *something* was a noise Jordan would remember for the rest of his life.

He slammed his foot on the brake and screamed as he skidded to a halt. The SUV even did a little shudder. He watched in horror as whatever he hit flew through the air, only to come down on top of the horse sculpture that took up the centre island of the intersection.

The animal seemed to bounce a couple of times on its way down, before landing in the shallow pool of water at the base of the sculpture.

"Oh My God! Oh My God! Oh My God!" Jordan yelled in rapid succession. He pulled the park brake on, flicked his hazards on so he wouldn't get in another accident, not that there were many cars out here at this time of the morning but considering what just happened, he wasn't taking any chances, and jumped out of the car.

He surveyed the damage to the front of his car as he raced over to the poor creature that he'd hit. There was barely a dent to his SUV. He didn't know if that was a good thing or bad.

Jordan stepped over the brick edging and waded through the ankle-deep water. The animal lay at the base between the two middle horses. He raced to it, lifting its head out of the water, blood stained the water around the large dog.

"I'm so sorry," Jordan whispered as he checked the animal over. The dog didn't look good, cuts and gashes were seeping blood. *It* was a *he*, and his breathing seemed to be laboured and one of his back legs looked like it was at an odd angle.

"I'm so sorry," Jordan whispered a second time as he carefully lifted the animal. He grunted, the dog was huge and weighed a fucking tonne. Water cascaded from the animal and soaked him clear through to his skin. He slowly made his way back to his car, not wanting to jostle the poor thing more than he already had.

Jordan had no idea how he managed to get the door open or the place the dog on the back seat, but he had. He climbed into the front seat and pulled out his phone. He needed an emergency vet clinic. That poor dog probably belonged to someone and Jordan had nearly killed him. He had no idea what the animal had been doing running down a highway so early in the morning, but that was neither here nor there right then. It wasn't like he'd answer if Jordan asked him.

He searched his phone for a minute and thankfully found an emergency vet only ten minutes down the road.

Jordan called the after-hours number and anxiously waited for someone to answer. As he waited he took off in the direction of the clinic. He didn't want to waste any time.

Finally the call connected, a sleepy voice answering.

"Bayside Vet's emergency number."

"Hello, yes, hi," Jordan said quickly, too quickly. He needed to calm down. But his entire body was shaking, probably with shock, and he was also saturated with water and bloody cold.

"Good morning. How can we help you?"

"Morning, I've had a bit of an accident. Hit a dog with my car. He doesn't look like he's in good shape."

"Is he still breathing?" The voice sounded more alert now.

"Yes, but not very well."

"How big is the animal?"

Jordan glanced in his rearview mirror. "He very nearly takes up my entire back seat."

"How soon can you get him here?"

"I'm on my way now, should be less than ten minutes."

"Okay, we'll see you then."

"Thank you," Jordan said as he disconnected the call.

At the next red light, Jordan looked back at the dog in his back seat and thought the animal looked familiar to him. Like he'd seen him somewhere before or should know him for some reason, but Jordan couldn't put his finger on *why*.

He didn't like the way the dog sounded either. As the light turned green, Jordan put his foot down and sped the rest of the way to the vet clinic. Jordan didn't know what he'd do if this poor animal died as a result of something he had done.

By the time they arrived at the after-hours clinic, the scent of wet dog had permeated his entire car, going so far as to overwhelm the scent of all his painting products in the boot as well. He was going to need to get the interior detailed, but that could wait.

"Are you the man who called about a car accident?" a guy in blue scrubs asked him as he exited his vehicle.

"That's me. I'm Jordan." He held his hand out and the other man shook it.

"John Smith, veterinary surgeon."

"Seriously?" Jordan asked with a raised brow as he headed to the back door.

"Yeah, you wouldn't believe how much shit I get for it as well. Sometimes I wonder how high my parents were when they came up with the name."

Jordan laughed, which considering the last hour of his life, was a nice change of pace.

"Let's see what you've brought me," John said as he stepped up beside Jordan. "You weren't kidding about his size, were you? He's one of the biggest I've seen."

"He weighs a bloody tonne as well."

"Okay, Trisha, my assistant should be out shortly with a trolley we can place him on. I don't like the look of several things. Can you tell me what happened?"

Jordan took a deep breath, then recounted the events of the accident as the vet checked the dog over.

"Sounds like there's going to be some severe internal damage." The vet gave the dog a worried glance as he listened to his lungs. "We won't know how bad it is until we can get in there and check for ourselves."

A plumpish lady with flaming red curls wearing pink scrubs with blue paw prints on them came out pushing a metal trolley.

John and Jordan carefully lifted the animal from

the back seat and placed him on the cool metal. The poor thing didn't make a sound. His legs hung over the sides he was so large.

Trish and John wheeled the brute of a dog inside while Jordan locked his car then followed along behind.

"Take a seat. This may take a while. Trish will grab some paperwork for you to fill out while you wait," John said before he disappeared down the passage with the dog.

The second the animal was out of his sight, Jordan felt an immediate sense of loss. He sat down on the hard waiting room chairs and placed his head in his hands, wondering what had just happened in his life.

"Here, if you could fill these out."

"Thanks, please try and save him, money is no object. I...I can't be responsible for killing that poor dog," Jordan said, nearly in tears.

"We'll do our best," Trish replied before she disappeared down the same passage John had.

Jordan glanced at the paperwork, no idea where to start. Basically all he could fill in was his own details. He had no idea what the dog's name was, how old he was, how much he weighed or even his breed. Hell, the last thing he'd been worried about was whether or not the poor animal was de-sexed.

He placed the half-completed paperwork on the chair beside him then leaned back and closed his eyes. Maybe he should have curled up in the back seat of his car and slept for a couple of hours before heading home. He certainly wouldn't be here now if he had, feeling like he'd fucked up his life royally. For someone that was two centuries old, that was a hell of a feeling to be having, and one he didn't fully understand either.

After an hour with no word, Jordan stood up and started pacing the room. Partly because he couldn't sit and do nothing anymore and partly because his ass had gone to sleep a long time ago thanks to the uncomfortable chair.

The sun had risen at some point, and more and more cars were seen through the windows. Jordan didn't think it was going to be much longer before this place opened for the day.

Another hour later, people started trickling into the office. First came the workers in their chirpy moods, coffee in hand. Jordan wanted to kick the lot of them in the shins but managed to refrain as he paced.

As the door jingled merrily with the first customer of the day, the veterinary surgeon finally reappeared. Jordan took a deep breath for what felt like the first time since the accident.

"How is he?" Jordan asked before John could say anything.

"He made it through surgery. We had to remove his spleen, which sounds bad, but really shouldn't affect him too badly. Dogs can live a happy life without the organ."

Jordan nodded. Alive was better than dead.

"I'm sorry it took so long, we had a couple of anomalies with the x-rays. His left leg was shattered, however, when we went into pin it back together it wasn't as bad as we'd originally feared." John frowned, confusion darkening his face. "We must have read the x-ray wrong, so for now we have the leg splinted and bandaged until the incision site heals, then we'll cast it."

"That's good right?" Jordan asked.

"Yes, however, what we're really worried about is his head." John's frown thinned as he stuck his hands in lab coat's pockets. "He suffered a cracked skull and brain swelling. We won't know how much damage that may have done until he wakes up again."

"When can I see him?" Jordan asked. He didn't quite understand why he had an overwhelming need to lay eyes on the dog he'd hit, but he was like an itch crawling under his skin that he couldn't scratch.

"He's going to have to stay here for a day or two at *minimum*. Probably longer considering the shape he's in. We need to keep an eye on him, then he can go home with you."

"He's not mine!" Jordan interrupted then immediately wished he hadn't. "But if there is no owner I plan on adopting him."

"We'll put out some calls. If anyone was missing a dog like him, we'll find out." The vet finally smiled. "Right now, he's resting, but you can come back and see him if you like, before you head home."

Jordan released a heavy breath. "Thank you, for everything."

"My pleasure. It's not every day I get to work on a dog of his size."

Jordan followed the vet back through the waiting room and down the passage.

"You know, when I first saw him I thought his

injuries were a lot greater than what they turned out to be."

Jordan pondered this as John led him into a room at the end of the passage. His eyes immediately trained on the dog that was almost too big for the bed he currently lay on. The poor thing was covered in bandages practically from head to foot.

"I'll leave you alone for a minute. Stop past reception on your way out."

Jordan finally tore his gaze off the animal and turned to the vet. He held his hand out and John took it. "Thanks again. I really appreciate what you've done and I'm sorry I had to drag you out of bed in the middle of the night."

"Don't mention it." John gave another tired smile. "That's what I'm here for. I hope we'll have some answers for you soon, so we can let you take this big guy home. See you."

"You can count on it." Jordan had a feeling he'd be back every chance he could get. There was something about this animal he couldn't quite parse out. Not yet.

The vet left, closing the door quietly behind him, finally leaving Jordan alone with the dog.

He headed over to the large animal and grabbed a chair along the way and placed it by the dog's side.

Bandages covered half the dog's head, leaving only his eyes and muzzle free. His ears poked out between the bright white cloth giving the animal a mummy vibe without trying. Even so, Jordan couldn't take his eyes off the stunning animal. Now that they were together, and Jordan wasn't losing his shit about nearly killing the poor thing with his car, three things hit him all at once.

First, the animal before him was a god damn hellhound.

Second, he was the damn dog he'd been dreaming of for nearly two months.

Third, he was Jordan's mate.

What a fucking day.

Jordan reached out tentatively and placed his hand on a patch of unbandaged fur. Calm washed over him as he touched his mate. A mate. For him. The incubus. Jordan leaned in and whispered one more time, "I'm sorry."

Talk about making the fucking worst first impression.

CHAPTER FIVE

"How the fuck can a hellhound just fucking disappear without a trace?" Adze yelled at Matti, ready to toss his phone. Adze was sick and tired of the nonanswers he was getting. First from the head of the Sydney office and now from Matti.

It had been four days since Nicor had disappeared off the face of the earth and no one could tell him where the fuck his hound was. Adze and the others were worried. If it wasn't for the faint niggle in the back of his mind that told him Nicor was still alive, Adze would have completely lost his shit days ago.

"Don't take that tone with me, Adze, I haven't done anything wrong," Matti replied calmly. "I know you're worried about Nicor, but you don't need to take it out on me."

"Whatever," Adze answered, every bit as bitchy as before.

The sudden silence of a disconnected call filled the room.

Adze spun around in disbelief and stared at his offending phone. "She fucking hung up on me!"

Pyro looked an awful lot like he was trying hard to hold back a grin as he nodded.

Adze took a deep breath to calm down. He wasn't doing them any good by acting the way he was, and it definitely didn't make himself feel any better either.

He redialled Matti. The phone rang and rang, echoing loudly in his silent office. Was Matti gonna answer his call or ignore him? He was about to give up when the line finally connected.

"What took you so long?" Adze asked, his bitchiness still clear as day. He cringed.

The silence filled the office once more making Adze swear like a fucking sailor. He needed to get his shit together. He dropped into the chair and laid his head on the desk. Matti would refuse him if he tried again. But he had to find Nicor. If the mermaids had him... Adze jumped up.

"How about I try?" Pyro asked, one hand pressing against his shoulder.

Adze chose to ignore the laughter he heard in his second's tone. He waved to him to tell him to get on with it as he paced back and forth.

Pyro put the call on speaker as it rang.

"Welcome to Hunt Enterprises, this is Denise. How may I direct your call?" a perky voice answered.

"Hi Denise, it's Pyro here. Is Matti available, please?"

"Oh yes, sir. Just a moment. I'll get her for you."

"Thank you."

Atrocious hold music filled the office. Music that attacked not only the ears but the mind. Adze made a mental note to get that changed as soon as they'd found Nicor and dealt with the situation in Sydney.

"This better be Pyro."

Pyro chuckled. "It is. I do have the big guy here with me as well though. I didn't think you'd take another call from him."

"You'd be right."

"How about if he gets out of line again, I'll clock him on the jaw instead?" Pyro asked, not taking his eyes off Adze.

"That sounds bloody perfect!" Matti agreed.

"It's settled then," Pyro said.

"It bloody well is not," Adze groused. He couldn't seem to stop himself from being an ass.

"Anyway, let's just ignore him for the time being," Pyro said, flipping Adze off. "Have you had any luck on your end tracking down Nicor or figuring out what happened to him?"

Matti sighed. "I'll tell you what I already told Adze. He needs to be using the resources at hand. I didn't go to the trouble and massive expense of setting up offices in nearly every major city for you to not use them."

"Been there, done that. They didn't give us the answers we wanted." Adze growled.

"Did you really give them a chance?" Matti asked.

Silence filled the room as neither of them answered her question.

Matti sighed. "Look, I know you don't like what they're saying but they are using every resource they have to try and track down Nicor. I spoke to them this morning to get an update. They haven't heard anything from any of our contacts in the area about a hellhound abduction. Nobody can find anything. It's like he up and disappeared. But they'll keep looking. They won't stop until he's been located."

Adze growled, not happy with Matti's response. Pyro threw a stapler at him. He ducked in time. The offending weaponized office supply crashed into the wall then fell to the ground, making a racket.

"Do I even want to know?" Matti asked.

"Probably not," Pyro answered as he stared at Adze. "Anyway, were getting the same thing on our end. A big fat lot of nothing."

"I thought you guys hunted in groups so this didn't happen?"

"We do hunt in pairs, but not so much for this reason. Kidnapping a hound on a hunt hasn't happened to us before. More because it's easier to take down a lot of our foes in groups of two or more."

"Right, well, in the meantime are you continuing your hunt for the incubus and the mermaids in Sydney?" Matti asked.

"Are you kidding me?" Adze bit out. He glared as his second looked primed to say something. "One of our team is missing."

"I get that. I do." Matti's voice gentled, so unlike her normal stern and no-nonsense attitude. "I know how worried you are for Nicor. But every day that you're not out there searching for these assholes is another day where women are being abducted and sold into slavery, or drugs or god only knows what. You have a job to do, Adze."

She was right, as much as Adze hated to admit it. They did have a job to do and they couldn't stop doing it to look for one of their own. That wasn't to say they were going to stop searching for Nicor. Not at all. They'd just have to double down and do both at once. Adze wanted these mermaid fuckers and that ass of an incubus dead sooner rather than later.

"We'll continue the hunt tonight," he said as calmly as he could.

"Good. And Adze?"

"Yeah?"

"We will get Nicor back, wait and see."

"We better," he growled.

Adze stalked over and pressed the end call button. See how she liked being hung up on. It was petty, but Adze felt a little better afterwards.

The silence sat heavy in the room for a few minutes until Pyro finally broke it. "I hate that she's right."

Adze ran a hand through his hair. "I know, me too. But we need to catch these guys and put an end to this. Hopefully then we'll have a solid lead to go on in the search for Nicor."

"I hope so too. It doesn't seem right here without him."

"Come on, let's go tell the others."

Exhaustion consumed Jordan. For the last three days he'd been spending his days at the vet's sitting with his mate as he slept and healed. His nights were filled with him attempting to complete the art project for the council and make sure it looked good. Not rushed like he felt. Thankfully he'd completed the project—probably on pure adrenaline—and everyone seemed pleased. According to the vet, they couldn't find anyone missing a mastiff, an overgrown mastiff, which was the breed the staff at John's clinic all decided on, much to Jordan's amusement. Adoption papers had been signed, and Jordan could take his hound home with him tomorrow.

He'd apparently shown enough improvement that John was happy to send the hulking hound home to continue his recuperation. Why he hadn't tried to shift back did concern Jordan, but he supposed a lot of it was the trauma of being hit, then stuck in a human office. Soon. They'd be together soon.

Right now though, Jordan could barely think let alone celebrate his mate coming home with him. He was starving and not in the "I should stop skipping lunch" kind of way. His other nature needed feeding, but he worried about his hound and how it would affect both of them if he tried now, or how they would even make that work if he was stuck. Jordan needed his thirst under control before his mate came home. He'd always waited until he had to for the longest time, sometimes almost letting the thirst consume him. That, he'd learn the hard way, was never the solution. His *unique* nature often conflicted with his inborn incubus desires, but Jordan had learned how to cope through the years that satisfied both of his sexual and emotional needs.

As much as he wanted to curl up in bed and get some much-needed sleep, Jordan pulled on his tightest pair of leather pants that laced up over his crotch. He pulled on a black t-shirt that was probably two sizes too small, but showed off his body quite nicely. Jordan wasn't muscled, though he was toned and thought he looked fucking hot. Not that he was out to pick up someone or anything. This was different, he needed to fit in with the crowd. Black biker boots finished his outfit.

Jordan turned, checking his outfit out in the mirror and gave it a small nod of approval. Presentation was of the utmost importance. He grabbed his wallet, phone then after thinking about it, he took the keys to his convertible. Might as well enjoy the ride as Jordan headed to his favourite feeding ground. Where he had people who understood him and his needs.

Jordan had been through many a feeding ground over his long life, but the BDSM club he'd located on the outskirts of the city had been the best he'd found in a number of years.

It was always best and most fulfilling for incubi to feed from their own partners during sex, but that wasn't something Jordan did often. The couple of relationships Jordan had had over the years had barely progressed that far. He'd made connections, but never the deep emotional connection he needed. Let alone allow his relationships to get to the point where he could completely satisfy his hunger. Jordan was used to the constant hunger. He managed to ignore it most of the time, but there were points where it got too much, and that's when Jordan would find himself at the clubs feeding off the ambient energy instead.

For years he'd pondered why he needed the emotional connection to his partners the other incubi and succubi never seemed to want or need. When the others called him broken, Jordan only understood how he felt. Now he knew.

A demisexual incubi. The world never ceased with its surprises.

Jordan smiled as he thought of his mate back at the clinic. The hound had been another surprise. Time would tell how that one worked out.

The streets were unsurprisingly busy, even though it was closing in on eleven in the evening. Jordan enjoyed the feeling of the wind whipping through his hair as he drove. He loved his convertible, resolving now that the weather was nicer to drive it more often.

He pulled into the parking structure down the road from Paddles. If people couldn't work out what the club was all about by the name, then they certainly did within seconds of walking through the doors, if they made it that far.

A lot of humans got stuck in the doorway.

The receiving room wasn't large by any stretch of the imagination, but it wasn't tiny either. Images of men in various states of dress, bondage and ecstasy covered the walls. There were also a few open shelves with some club merchandise for sale. At the opposite end sat a young man, dressed in a long sleeve shirt with an ocean blue vest.

He glanced up as soon as Jordan stepped inside, breaking into a smile as soon as his gaze met Jordan's.

"Welcome back to Paddles, Mr. Makan. It's been a while," he greeted.

"Alex, I've told you before to call me Jordan."

"Yes, Sir," Alex replied, a slight blush colouring his cheeks.

"You're never going to do it though, are you?" Jordan asked, unable to help his grin.

"Oh no, Sir. That wouldn't be right," Alex replied adamantly.

Wanting to move past the banter Jordan asked, "How's things tonight?"

"Picking up, Sir. There's a nice crowd in right now."

"Great. Any changes I need to know about since the last time I was here?"

"Oh no, Sir. Same rules apply. There's been a couple of staff changes, but that's about it."

"Great." Jordan said as he held out his wrist for the band that would identify his intentions.

"White again, Sir?" Alex confirmed.

"Yes, thank you," Jordan agreed.

Alex placed the white band around his wrist, that signified that he was there to look, but not touch. "Have a good night, Alex."

"You too, Sir, and welcome back."

Jordan walked through the black double doors situated to the right of where Alex was seated. There was a short corridor and then another set of double doors.

Couldn't have the public seeing or hearing what went on inside here. It would scandalize some of the more uptight humans.

Groans and moans were the first thing Jordan heard as he stepped into the large club. Live versions of the pictures on wall in the reception room greeted Jordan everywhere he looked. Naked and half-naked men, stood, knelt, lay, and were strapped into just about every available implement in the room for those who liked to be on display. The more private encounters had rooms they could go to.

Alex wasn't kidding when he said things were picking up. The place was hopping. Bass heavy music piped through the speakers and the sounds of orgasm being reached by several different people reached Jordan and made him almost groan.

Jordan wasn't a Dom or a Sub. He had no issues with the lifestyle, and honestly found it fascinating to watch the interaction between loving couples or even the hook-ups. He was here as the sexual tension in the air was actually thick enough for him to feed off without him having to engage himself. It helped to satisfy some of his hunger as an incubus while protected his other nature from harm.

A perfect compromise for his two halves.

It helped that he knew the owner. Otherwise he probably wouldn't have been able to get a membership.

Jordan headed to the bar and waited to be served. He stood next to an extremely pretty older man, whose ass had been plugged and his cock caged. He also wore a stunning silver collar. Somehow he managed to convey to the bartender what he wanted without speaking a word.

Whatever Milo paid his bar staff, it wasn't enough.

He placed his order for scotch on the rocks and received a wrist band as well as his drink. Milo took the safety of his patrons seriously and if someone ordered alcohol, then he had to display the fact that he had been drinking.

Jordan slipped on his band without complaint. He wasn't picking anyone up. He wound his way through the crowd and managed to find a small table with three empty high back chairs surrounding it.

He placed his glass on a coaster and took a seat, watching the crowd.

Jordan could see the energy in the room, like a shimmer in the air. Feeding this way was like giving a grain of rice to a starving man, but enough of it could get him partially satisfied. A club like this oozed ambient sexual energy more than any of Jordan's old hunting grounds.

He sipped his drink as he sat back and closed his eyes, taking in the sounds of the place while he absorbed the energy around him.

A hand landed on his shoulder and Jordan was jolted out of his thoughts about a large dark hound.

"I heard you were here." Milo took a seat next to Jordan.

"Milo, great to see you again."

It was too. Milo was a centuries old vampire

Jordan had met nearly sixty years ago. Neither of them looked any different than the day they'd met. They'd stayed in contact over the years and when Jordan had heard that Milo had moved to the city to open the club, he'd looked his old acquaintance up. They'd become good friends over the last decade or so.

The old vamp winked. "Looking good as usual."

"You too. It's been too long."

"Whose fault is that?" Milo asked as he glanced around his club.

"I know, I know," Jordan conceded. "No boy tonight?"

Milo sighed. "Not at the moment. James and I did not part on the best of terms and I'm finding all the men I'm meeting to be a little...stale. No one is piquing my interest and hasn't in quite some time."

"That's too bad. Sorry to hear about you and James. Hopefully you'll find someone soon."

Milo waved the matter away. "It's of no matter. I do not need a man to fulfil my life. I am quite content for the time being to be alone."

"I'm glad to hear it." Jordan smiled as he finished the last of his scotch.

"Anyway, enough about me, what's brought the hermit Jordan Makan out into the light, so to speak."

"I'm not a hermit!" Jordan protested.

Milo laughed. "May as well be, with the amount of time you spend cooped up in your studio."

"That's different. I'm working."

"Of course, it is," Milo replied placatingly.

Jordan tried to wack his friend but Milo shifted out of reach too quickly, laughing as he did so.

"So, are you going to tell me what's going on with you or are you going to make me drag it out of you."

"I should make you try and drag it out of me," Jordan said, grinning at his friend. It wasn't like he could stay angry at Milo. The vamp knew him too well.

"Tell me, you know you'll feel better."

Jordan sighed, ran his fingers over his hair then waved down a waiter. If he was going to spill his guts he *needed* another drink. Instead of sipping his scotch he downed it in one go, enjoying the burn and the woodsy taste. Then he unburdened his soul to Milo about what had been happening the last couple of days starting with that dreadful night.

Milo sat quietly while Jordon talked, nodding and murmuring encouragement at the right spots. He was surprised by how much he had to say. When he finally finished and glanced at his friend, Milo remained quiet.

"Well?" he asked after several minutes ticked by.

Milo seemed to shake himself out of his thoughts and gave Jordan a sheepish smile. "Sorry."

Jordan waved his apology away. He had kinda unloaded on the guy so he couldn't blame him for taking a minute to process everything.

"First things first. You have to contact the hounds," Milo said.

Jordan sighed. He knew this was coming. He'd actually been thinking about it ever since the accident.

"You *really* think I have to?"

"I know you've been a bit preoccupied recently, but

word spread fast that the hounds are missing one of their own and are on the hunt. They should've thought to check the human veterinary practices. I bet they'll regret not considering the idea he could've been hurt and rescued by an *unknowing* person." Milo gave Jordan a sly look then shook his head. "They think he's been taken by someone or something that wishes them harm and held hostage. Don't you think they deserve to know that their teammate is safe, in a matter of speaking?"

"Don't use logic on me," Jordan groaned as he sat back in his chair and waved his empty glass at a passing waiter. "Another, thanks. I just wanted to save *the dog*. I was *flustered*. Anyone could've made the mistake in that situation."

"I'll use whatever I have to, to get you to see reason." Milo chuckled then turned serious, frowning.

"They're not going to be happy that I'm an incubus," Jordan stated matter-of-factly.

"They'll deal with it. You can't change who you are, and by the sound of it you have every right to spend time with the hound."

"Did you catch the name of the missing member of their pack?" Jordan asked hopefully. It would be nice to know what to call his mate.

Milo shook his head. "They were keeping that information close to the chest."

"Damn it."

Another drink arrived for Jordan and he gratefully took it from the waiter. This time he sipped and savoured the scotch. They lapsed into silence once again as Jordan thought things over. If the hounds were on the hunt, then him making the call could go wrong quickly. His kind weren't exactly favourites in the supernatural world. If it were him, though, he'd want to know.

"So, what are you going to do?" Milo asked, breaking the silence.

"I'm going to head home shortly. I'll make a call in the morning, and depending on how that goes, I'll either tell them where their missing member is or I'll take my hound and go visit my house in the Hunter Valley for a little while. I think he'd like it up there."

Milo raised his glass in cheers and they clinked—the sound drowned out by the pleasured cries of several young men.

For a little while longer, though, Jordan was happy to sit and take in the ambient sexual energy from those around him. It had taken him a long time to put a name to his feelings. Back when he was born there was no word for demisexual. Jordan didn't begrudge others their fun or sexual experiences, but for him, he felt no attraction or received pleasure from the act unless he felt a real connection to his partner, had gotten to know them well, and there were strong feelings involved. Now that he had a mate, he wondered how long that connection would take, *if* it would take, and what it would feel like once it was there. He had to hope fate knew what it was doing.

Jordan didn't stay much longer. He'd fed about as much as he could this way and he was wanting to get home. The sooner he got home and slept the sooner tomorrow would come. Tomorrow, he could take his adopted mate home.

He wasn't looking forward to placing the call to the hounds, but one never knew. They might surprise him yet.

Jordan bid Milo farewell and left the club. He politely declined the invitations he received on his way out from alluring subs who wanted someone to take a paddle to their asses, pleading so nicely. Maybe he'd been around too long to enthral the patrons.

"Leaving so soon?" Alex asked him as he entered the foyer.

"I'm afraid so. People to see, places to go, you know the deal."

Alex laughed and wished him a goodnight.

Ever since the night he nearly killed his mate, Jordan had been a lot more cautious while driving so late. He made it home with no worries though.

Jordan walked inside and looked around. Even with the late hour, he wasn't tired. He liked the idea of heading to the Hunter Valley house for a little while. He didn't have any appointments in the next few weeks. All he had to do was paint for his upcoming gallery showing. He could just as easily do that in the Hunter Valley as he could here.

With that in mind he set to packing up what he'd need to take with him. If he still wasn't tired by the time he'd finished collecting everything he might paint for a little while. If he was driving all the way to the Hunter Valley tomorrow, though, he'd have to get some sleep.

A little painting to set himself at ease, then some shut eye.

Jordan crawled into bed around three that morning. His alarm was set for eight. He'd get up, make a call and then pick up his hound.

With his plan firmly in place he drifted off to sleep.

CHAPTER SIX

Adze was getting more and more short-tempered since Nicor had disappeared without a trace. It grew with every passing day.

"How can nobody have seen *anything*?" he growled.

This wasn't supposed to happen. They paired up for a reason for fuck's sake. He'd made calls to everyone he could think of in the city and so far nothing had turned up. Even the local office was coming up empty. Adze couldn't even contact Nicor through their link. It was just a big blank *nothing* in response. He couldn't understand why either. His team always answered through their connection when called.

The connection wasn't cut, it still vibrated with *something*, so that gave him hope that his friend and teammate was still alive. But that was all he had.

His mobile let out a shrill sound causing Adze to jump at the unexpected noise. Everyone else in the living room turned to stare at him. They'd all been so quiet, Adze had almost forgotten they were there. It was only ten in the morning after all, and they had been out late last night—well, this morning—searching for Nicor, incubi and mermaids.

Their wanted list was growing and getting out of hand.

Adze reached into his pocket and pulled out his phone. The number was unknown. He thought about ignoring it, but he couldn't bring himself to hang up. He swiped to answer the call and pressed the phone against his ear.

"Hello," he answered, maybe a little to gruffly. There was no immediate answer.

Then a tentative melodious male voice came through. "Hello. Is this the leader of the Australian hellhound pack?"

Adze stiffened and stopped his pacing. "It is. Who may I ask am I speaking to?"

"You can call me Jay."

"Jay?"

"Yes."

"That's not your real name is it?" Adze enquired.

"That's neither here nor there. You haven't said yours."

"Adze. Why won't you tell me your name and how did you get this number? What are you?" he growled. That *voice*. It's pure sultriness. He didn't have time for this shit, he had a packmate to find and a smuggling ring to dismantle.

He had to be part of the sup community, otherwise he wouldn't know about hellhounds.

A heavy sigh down the line was all Adze received in response. Even the sigh sounded *nice.*

"Tell me," he said, his voice deepened, turning menacing.

"What I am doesn't matter. It's none of your business."

Adze was about to open his mouth to say Hell knows what when Jay continued.

"What is your business is that I know where your missing hound is."

Adze tensed and felt instant relief at the same time. Finally, they were getting somewhere.

"Where is he? What have you done to him? What do you want?" he asked all at once, his tone forceful as ever.

"I haven't done anything to him, well, not on purpose anyway."

"What's that supposed to mean?" Adze snapped.

"Would you for fuck's sake stop yelling and growling at me? I'm trying to do the right thing here."

Adze took a deep breath. His worry for his friend was making him an ass... *more* than usual.

"Tell me where I can find him."

"He's my mate."

"The fuck you say!" Adze dropped into a chair, not thinking his legs could hold him through this conversation. Except he missed the bloody chair and ended up ass down on the floor.

When he righted himself he put the phone back to his ear.

"I said he's my mate."

"What the fuck are you?" Adze asked again. The *voice* made him want to trust the man, which made him *not trust* the unknown. "And don't bother telling me it's none of my business. It just became my fucking business."

The others were all gathered around him. He had no doubt they could all hear the conversation thanks to their expert hearing, but they were leaving it to him to handle this.

"Incubus," the soft reply came nearly thirty seconds later.

"Like fuck I'm going to let you get your hands on him. Tell me where my packmate is right now."

A deep breath came followed by a soft, "*No*."

Adze growled. "What the fuck do you mean 'no'?"

"No, I won't tell you. Not like this. I told you he's my mate and you don't want to respect that due to your prejudices against my kind."

"I've got my reasons."

"I'm sure you do. But still... *fuck you* for not even wanting to give me a chance."

"I don't know you!" Adze growled.

"Precisely. Don't bother looking for us. We're leaving the city for a while."

"You're fucking kidnapping him? You're really going out of your way to prove how trustworthy you are, aren't ya?" Adze asked sarcastically.

"Not kidnapping." He paused for a moment. "I did technically adopt him though."

Before Adze could say anything else, the line went dead in his ear.

Adze growled and threw his phone against the wall. He didn't even flinch when he heard it shatter.

Now what the fuck were they supposed to do?

JORDAN HUNG UP THE PHONE. *Furious.* He'd been expecting it, but really, he'd hoped for different. He should have known better.

"Shit!" Jordan cursed when he realised he hadn't gotten his hound's name once through the entire conversation.

He'd have to come up with something soon as he couldn't keep calling him *the hound.*

Picking up the duffle he'd packed, he carried it to the car. He'd already packed everything else he wanted to take to the Hunter Valley before he'd made the phone call. Jordan placed the duffle in the back and closed the boot, his esky filled with the perishable foods he was taking with him in the front seat.

Jordan doubled-checked to make sure the house was locked up tight then closed the garage door behind him and headed to the vet clinic to pick up his pup.

An hour later, another million pieces of paper signed, and instruction on the care of his animal noted, they were finally back in the car and on the way out of the city. John might've laughed at the name Spot—those from Hell understood—being on the adoption papers but Jordan couldn't very well put the hound's real name down since he had none.

It would take at least two and a half hours to make

it to Rothbury. Hopefully the traffic would ease once they made it through the congestion in the city and hit the freeway.

Every few minutes Jordan glanced in his mirror at the large black passenger he had lying on the back seat of his vehicle. His hound seemed to be awake at the moment, but Jordan wasn't sure how long that would last.

"What am I going to call you?" he asked. There was, not unexpectedly, no answer forthcoming. However, the hound's ears did perk up slightly.

"Okay, well, let's see. What name suits you..." Jordan paused and thought about what name a hound from hell would have.

"How about Abraxis?" Jordan asked.

The hound snorted.

"I guess not then. Okay, what about Dagon?"

To this, the hound's ears drooped and he seemed to lose interest.

"Fine, be that picky. How about Balor?" Jordan asked. "That's a good strong name."

The hound growled, his teeth and gums bared, like he would take a bite out of Jordan if he didn't take back what he said right then and there.

"Okay, okay, I get it. Balor sucks."

The hound seemed to be mollified and placed his head back down on the back seat, listening as Jordan continued to rattle off name after name.

"Damn, you're picky about your name..." Jordan paused and thought long and hard about it before he finally settled on something that he thought might suit his hound. "How about Nikker?"

The hounds head popped up and he glanced at Jordan in the mirror before licking his lips then dropping his head back down again. Was that a nod? Weird.

"Okay then. I guess that's about as good as we're going to get. I'll call you Nik for short."

He didn't get an immediate growl, so it seemed he had the hound's approval.

The drive was long and smooth, roughly a hundred and sixty clicks, the radio playing softly in the background. He'd watched as Nik's eyes had drooped then refused to stay open for a second longer as the large hound had once more succumbed to sleep.

Jordan sung along to the radio quietly, not wanting to disturb his hound. He still had trouble believing that he'd met his mate and he was a damn hellhound. *And* currently seemed to be stuck in his beast form.

The scenery in this part of the country was stunning. Jordan never got sick of it, no matter how many times he made this drive. It was one of the reasons he'd bought the house in the Hunter Valley to begin with.

Jordan's muscles relaxed and he breathed easier the closer he got to his home away from home. Large properties with acres of grapevines soon bordered the roads. He really loved this area. The small towns, the people, the views. Everything spoke to the artist in him. Jordan suddenly couldn't wait to get to his house and start painting.

Jordan pulled down the long gravel drive that led to his house. The brick building with a wrap-around porch sat on several acres of land. Rolling hills covered in grapevines could be seen in every direction. Jordan broke out in a grin as he pulled the car to a stop in front of his house.

Peace and quiet settled around him like a welcoming blanket as he climbed out of the car. Everything looked to be on the up and up. Jordan hired someone to clean the house and mow the lawns on a regular basis. The fresh scent of cut grass still lingered on the air as he breathed it in deeply.

Jordan opened the back door so when Nik finally woke up he wouldn't be trapped and started unpacking his belongings.

He unlocked the door to the house and walked inside carrying the esky. Once the food was packed away in the fridge, Jordan checked the cupboards and made a note of what he needed. A quick trip to the local supermarket this afternoon would be in order. He usually called before he got to the house, but he didn't want to do that today with a hellhound in his back seat.

It didn't take long to get the rest of the car unpacked.

It was time to make the most of his escape from the city.

Jordan opened up the large bifold doors which made up most of his back wall, enjoying the cool breeze that swept through his house.

He settled on the back porch with a pad and some charcoal, a pot of tea, and started to draw. He hadn't gotten very far when his large, dark hound slowly padded around the corner, head up, sniffing.

What was the hulking hound scenting? Was he hunting? Jordan carefully placed his pad and charcoal down while he waited for Nik to come closer. His hound hadn't shifted back yet so he couldn't be too cautious until he knew what they would have to deal with.

Nik sniffed the air again and glanced about himself, his ears perking when he noticed the group of kangaroos down the back of the property under the shade of a large tree. Nik seemed to wrestle within himself, dropping into a crouch then standing at alert then dropping again, before finally deciding to let them be and headed over to Jordan. He sat down at the foot of Jordan's chair and placed his head in Jordan's lap.

Scratching behind Nik's ears seemed to be what the pup wanted. His hound sighed and grew a little heavier in his lap.

"You like that?" Jordan asked.

The huff he got in response told him everything.

They sat there for god knows how long, Jordan constantly touching his hound and Nik not wanting to go anywhere.

When his stomach growled, Jordan figured it was time to actually move. Couldn't have his hound starve. Reluctantly Nik moved so Jordan could stand and he made his way inside to the kitchen. Jordan managed to put together a sandwich with the few items he'd brought with him. He made one for Nik as well and placed the plate on the ground for his hound. Nik wolfed it down, the food disappearing in seconds flat.

Jordan took his food and headed back to the patio, resuming his earlier seat. Nik didn't follow him straight away, his hound sniffed around and explored Jordan's house a little. Jordan left his mate to it.

He resumed his earlier drawing, the charcoal lightly scratching away at the paper as he worked. The dark figure of his hound fast asleep in the back of Jordan's car came into shape on the page. When he was satisfied with the drawing, he flipped it over to the back and a fresh, blank page appeared before him.

It wasn't surprising that Jordan had drawn yet another rendition of his hound. All he'd been able to concentrate on since meeting the damn sup was him.

Jordan closed his eyes and concentrated on the sounds around him. The twitter of small birds, the occasional laugh of a kookaburra, the sound of the windchimes he had hanging in the back-right corner of his porch as the breeze flowed through them, and the click of toenails on hardwood floors as his hound explored his house.

Opening his eyes once more, Jordan took in the view. It was a view he had seen many a time over the years, and one he'd drawn just as many. He never got tired of it though. The trees, the rolling hills, the grapevines, the wildlife.

Before he even registered what he was doing, his hand was once more smoothly moving over the paper in front of him. For the thousandth time in his life Jordan got lost in his art, ignoring the world around him.

A gentle nudge to his leg broke Jordan out of his trance. He shivered as he blinked rapidly. It was like those first minutes after you wake when your brain needs time to go from sleep mode to awake.

Without thinking about it Jordan reached down and scratched Nik's head. He glanced around and realised hours had passed. The sun sat low on the horizon and would be gone in another hour or so. The temperature had dropped and Jordan realized he was quite cool.

It looked like he'd missed the shops today. They'd be long closed by now. He'd have to go in the morning.

His stomach growled loudly making Jordan notice he'd only eaten half his lunch. He hated wasting food, but this wasn't going to be the last time he'd get lost in his drawings and forget to eat. Jordan grabbed his plate and artbook.

"Come on, let's go inside and start a fire."

Nik seemed to understand and followed Jordan inside. He padded into the living room and curled up on the rug in the middle.

Jordan closed the bifold doors behind him then cleaned up the few dishes they had made. Once everything was tidy and in order, he headed to the potbelly fireplace. A small stack of logs sat to the right. He checked, finding it was already laid and ready to go. There was plenty enough wood to get them through tonight. He'd restock tomorrow.

It didn't take long before the room warmed up. The soft glow from the stove comforted him in ways Jordan couldn't explain. Seeing the fire brought him closer to his youth, his days with his mother and their tribe. Fire was life.

If the temperatures dropped in the next couple of days, and they looked like they were going to, Jordan could throw a stew on the top of the potbelly and let it simmer all day long. Those always tasted the best in his opinion. *And soups.* Jordan loved a good soup.

Thinking about food had his stomach reminding him that he hadn't gotten sufficient intake today. He was so warm and comfy though. Nik shuffled closer, laying his head in Jordan's lap. The huge hound gave him a pitiful whine.

Regretful he had to move away from his hound, Jordan gave Nik an ear scratch then managed to get out from under the hound to make some dinner. He wouldn't starve his mate, especially when he still had no thumbs to speak of. Jordan defrosted some lamb chops he had in the freezer and pulled out a packet pasta from the cupboard.

They had to make it to the shops tomorrow.

Half an hour later Jordan's kitchen filled with the scent of French onion lamb chops with a carbonara pasta side. He removed the bones before he placed a plate on the ground for his hound. Maybe he should try seating them at the table? Jog Nik's human memories. Jordan pictured the hound at his table and snorted. No, too weird.

"Be careful, it's hot," he admonished as Nik headed right in for the food.

When his hound spat the first mouthful of food back out Jordan laughed.

"I tried to warn you. Maybe next time you'll listen to me."

Nik ignored him as he concentrated on his dinner.

Jordan climbed onto the couch, his dinner resting on a lap tray. He turned on the TV and flicked through until he found something he wanted to watch. The couch jostled when Nik jumped up and joined him. The hound sat on his own square, carefully out of Jordan's way. As soon as Jordan placed his tray to the side, though, Nik scooted closer, resting his head once more in Jordan's lap.

"What am I going to do with you?" he asked quietly, not expecting an answer but wishing his mate could talk back.

Instead of answering Nik rolled over and exposed his belly for scratches. Jordan laughed. He gave gentle scritches as he ran his hand over his hound, absently watching TV.

Without being able to communicate, Jordan had no idea how much pain his hound was still in. He knew the creatures healed faster than normal. But he had no idea what that rate was, and he didn't know if that included them being stuck in their hound form or only when they were in their human form.

Jordan wasn't about to call Adze again. Not after the last phone call.

For now, he'd be gentle until it looked like his hound wasn't in any pain. Nik's back leg started kicking lightly and Jordan chuckled. Didn't seem to matter the species, if you scratched that one spot on the bellies, they kicked.

Jordan kept scratching.

When the fire dimmed, Jordan turned off the television and headed for the doors. As comfortable as he was on the lounge, he wasn't going to stay there all night, and Nik had to go out, at least for a little while. It wasn't like he could use the toilet. Jordan chuckled quietly to himself as a mental image of Nik attempting to use the bathroom flashed in his head.

Nik didn't hesitate and toddled off outside to relieve himself. Jordan left the door open and cleaned up the dishes from dinner. When Nik walked back inside and looked expectantly at Jordan, he locked up the house.

The click of nails on the wood floor followed Jordan as he headed to the bedroom.

Jordan rifled through his small wardrobe and grabbed a pair of boxer briefs before he headed to the bathroom. He kept his shower brief, too exhausted after the last few days. All Jordan wanted to do was crawl into bed and sleep for a week.

When Jordan re-entered his bedroom, clothed in nothing but his underwear, he was surprised to see Nik still sitting on the ground, staring up at the bed with desperate longing.

"What's the matter pup? Can't make the jump?" Jordan asked him.

Nik whined low in his throat so Jordan headed over to help the poor guy out. His hound placed his front two paws on the bed and Jordan bent down to lift up his back legs. Once the beast was fully on the bed, he sniffed, circled a couple of times then curled up in a ball.

"Oh, no you don't!" Jordan admonished. "That's my side of the bed, you can bloody well move over!"

Nik ignored him and Jordan growled at the damn animal. Not giving up, Jordan turned out the lights and headed to his side of the bed. He lifted the covers and scooched in, pushing Nik over as he went. Jordan had never had to fight so much for his sleeping space before.

"Stubborn bloody hound," he bitched.

Jordan received a long tongue bath for his troubles.

"Ewww." Jordan wiped his face. "Not cool dude! I just had a shower!"

Jordan laughed as Nik went to lick him again, but he was quicker and playfully pushed his hound away.

Usually Jordan would do something to wind down once he crawled into bed, whether that was watching some TV, or playing some mindless game on his iPad, or even picking up a small sketch pad and doodling for a little while. Tonight though, he didn't feel like doing any of that, instead he curled up on his side, the weight of the massive hound beside him, strangely comforting, and closed his eyes.

THE HOUND STARED at the human next to him. The man looked so familiar to him, but not, all at the same time, and he couldn't understand why. A whine escaped, low and imperceptible to the sleeping man. He felt the need to comfort him so he placed his head and a paw on the human's chest. He heard the sorrow in his voice when he talked sometimes. A voice that pretty shouldn't be sad.

Maybe he needed "Nik", as the human called him, to protect him. Deciding that was an issue for another day, the hound snuggled up against the nice-smelling human, happy to be on such a soft and cushiony surface and closed his eyes.

CHAPTER SEVEN

Jordan woke, light streaming through the gaps in the curtains and a hound laying on top of the majority of him. He tried taking a deep breath, but found the move impossible. He'd woken the same way for the last three days. Trying to move the big guy was the fun part. Jordan didn't want to disturb his sleep because the rest would help him heal, not only his physical injuries, but Jordan hoped it would help heal whatever it was that was stopping the hound from shifting back into human.

Not that Jordan was all that anxious to get the man back. In the last three days he and Nik had slowly gotten used to one another. It was peaceful having the huge hound around. Jordan's muse didn't seem to mind one bit either. He'd been hard at work the entire time.

Jordan reached up and scratched his hound behind the ears. It took a minute, but finally the big guy seemed to wake up. Once he did, he stretched out and yawned wide. The increased weight on

Jordan's chest didn't make it any easier to breathe, but the worst thing was the hot dog breath—right in his face.

"Ewww, gross!" he complained. "Do you have to do that when you're laying right on top of me? Can't you wait like two seconds?"

Nik sneezed and shook his head.

Jordan cried out in horror as dog snot landed everywhere. He attempted to push the giant beast off him. "Get off you disgusting creature. I can't believe you did that."

If Nik didn't want to move, Jordan wouldn't have much luck moving the hound. Thankfully Nik decided to allow him to escape, rising slowly up and scooted toward what was supposed to be his side of the bed. Jordan raced to the bathroom. He took a speedy shower, shuddering as he rinsed off the slime. He'd have to strip the bed and wash the sheets today.

When he walked back into the room, feeling much cleaner, Nik was still curled up on the bed, his giant head resting on Jordan's pillow.

Jordan's fingers itched to pick up a brush and start drawing the scene in front of him. Instead he grabbed his phone and took a couple of pictures for reference. He had a couple of chores he had to do this morning before he could lose himself in his art. Too bad he couldn't teach the hound how to make the bed. Sweeping hadn't worked out either.

His stomach grumbled right then, reminding Jordan that first on the list was breakfast. Maybe the smell of frying bacon might entice the hound out of bed. The big brute had a bottomless pit and made a racket when he was hungry.

The pop and sizzle of the pork strips in the frypan were soon accompanied by the click of nails on wood. Looked like the hound liked his bacon after all.

Jordan made himself a nice fresh sandwich with tomato sauce and soft fried bacon. He couldn't stand how some people cooked it to within an inch of its life. A touch of salt and pepper and his breakfast was served.

He roughly chopped up a couple of extra strips he'd cooked and placed them on the plate for Nik.

"Now, don't forget to wait a minute as it's hot."

Nik ignored him, once again, and wolfed down the food. Jordan doubted the hound even tasted it.

"You're bloody well not getting any of mine!" Jordan chastised as Nik sat up and stared with that soulful expression of his. "That look ain't gonna work on me, matey! This is mine, all mine!"

Jordan tried his hardest to ignore the creature staring at him as he ate but ended up giving in and handed the hound half his sandwich.

"You better enjoy that. I'm still hungry," he grumbled.

Jordan took his plate back to the kitchen and cleaned up. The sun shone brightly through the curtains and Jordan couldn't wait to go outside and enjoy it. The peace and tranquillity he got from coming here never failed to soothe him. There wasn't anywhere else on the earth that gave him this feeling. Jordan grabbed his sunnies and slipped into a comfortable pair of shoes as he opened the large sliding door to the back porch and called for Nik.

The hound jumped off the couch where he'd been resting and trotted over to Jordan.

"Feel up to a long walk?" Jordan asked.

Nik sneezed again and shook his head, but walked outside.

Okay, so maybe they could play some games on the iPad when they came back. His hound would be tired and seemed to love to snuggle when Jordan played games. Jordan never turned down cuddles, especially from his mate.

Jordan closed the door behind him, not bothering with the lock, and they headed off. Even with the sun overhead, the temperature remained cool. The breeze rustled the vines as Jordan and Nik walked through the rows upon rows.

The air smelled so different here than in the city. Fresh. Clean. Of the earth. Jordan really couldn't remember why he didn't spend more time here than in Sydney. Nik walked along beside him, occasionally bumping into Jordan's side. Jordan would reach down and scratch behind the giant hound's ears when he did.

Jordan didn't feel the need to fill the silence with inane chatter. Not that Nik could respond, stuck as he was. So they walked along in peace, enjoying the beautiful day and scenery. Just him and his mate enjoying the countryside. What more could he want?

Nearly three weeks had passed since Adze had received that phone call to let him know Nicor was alive and well, "Jay" refusing to tell them where he was. The second Adze had gotten off the phone, he'd given all the information he had to Matti in the hopes she and her team may have been able to trace the caller.

So far there hadn't been any luck.

As much as he hated to admit it, Adze hadn't been able to spend much time worrying about it either. There had been four more women who had gone missing in the last fourteen days. Adze was getting pretty fucking pissed off that they couldn't catch these bastards, and not for a lack of trying.

Once more they were out hunting. The problem was that Sydney had a shit tonne more waterfront than Melbourne. When they took into consideration Sydney harbour and how far in it went, then added in Botany bay as well, there was too much area for one pack to cover. It didn't help with them being a team member down either because that brought them down to two patrols instead of the regular three.

Their one stroke of luck so far was the missing women seemed to still be located in the same area as before. It wouldn't be long before the mermaids and incubi behind this expanded their area of operation. That would create more problems.

Tonight they were back in Circular Quay and the surrounding areas since the last two women had disappeared from there. So far they had come up blank once again. Adze was getting pretty sick and tired of not finding anything.

Any sign of trouble, Pyro? he asked. Pyro, Cacus and Daemon were hunting together down in Darling Harbour, while Adze and Oriax covered Millers Point to the Opera House and beyond.

Nothing over here. All quiet. How about you? Pyro asked.

Nothing. Sun should be coming up in about an hour. We'll call it quits and head back to the apartment then.

Sounds like a plan.

All the partiers had long since called it a night. The only people out and about at this time of the morning were the die-hard fitness freaks who were out in their activewear jogging or doing yoga. Adze couldn't think of anything worse. He'd much prefer to be home in his bed curled around Archie. Speaking of which, he missed his mate. This trip was supposed to be quick. Fly in, catch the bad guys, go home and get on with their lives.

Things hadn't exactly worked out that way.

Thankfully Archie and Callum had managed to fly out last weekend and visit with them. Not that Adze and Pyro had had a great deal of time to spend with them. But something was always better than nothing.

The sun was peeking over the horizon when Adze decided to call it a night.

Let's head home, he told his pack.

They all could do with a decent sleep before they came back to do it all over again tonight.

Adze and Oriax were the first back. They waited for the others before shifting and dressing, then headed up to the apartment as a group. Adze rummaged in the bag they kept their spare clothes in and pulled out his phone. He'd missed a half a dozen calls from Matti.

God he hoped there wasn't another emergency they had to deal with.

He quickly dialled her and waited impatiently for the call to connect. Adze didn't doubt she would answer. If she wanted to get a hold of him so urgently to try calling a half a dozen times while they were out on a hunt, there was no way she was going to go to sleep without talking to them first.

Matti answered on the third ring.

"Please don't let this be bad news," Adze said as the others all went quiet around him as they ascended in the lift.

Matti paused for a second then spoke the words Adze didn't think he would ever hear. "I think we've found our missing boy."

"The hell you say!" Adze exclaimed.

Matti laughed. "I'm sorry it's taken so long."

"Where the fuck is he?"

"You boys up for a drive?" she asked.

As tired and ready for bed as Adze was five minutes ago, he was wide awake and raring to go. It was time to bring Nicor home.

He glanced around at everyone as the elevator finally dinged. There wasn't a single one of them that wasn't willing to go get Nicor right that second.

"Tell me everything," Adze said as they stepped inside the apartment. They wouldn't be there for long.

Adze clicked the phone over to speaker so the

others could more easily hear. They all gathered around in the dining room, listening intently as Matti told them what they had found.

"Don't forget, Adze, if Jordan—our incubus's name is Jordan Makan, a well-known Aboriginal artist by the way—is right and they are mates, you can't go in there guns blazing as Nicor would never forgive you."

Adze sighed. "I know. But that's not going to stop us from going there and seeing what's going on with our packmate."

"I didn't for a second think that it would," Matti replied. "I'll send all the details in an email. Good luck, and bring our boy home."

"We'll do our best," Pyro said, before Adze could say anything.

"Oh, one more thing."

"What?" Adze growled. They needed to get going right quick.

"It does look like Jordan adopted him." She cackled before hanging up on them.

They looked at each other in disbelief as the phone screen flashed. It went dark for a second then a pop-up notification for an email from Matti appeared on the screen.

Oriax frowned. "How could the incubus *adopt* Nicor?"

"No idea," Adze answered, a little shell-shocked himself. "Right, let's shower, change and get on the road in thirty."

The chairs scraped against the tiles as everyone stood, the jarring sound loud in the otherwise silent space. He couldn't believe they'd finally found Nicor. A weight lifted off Adze as he walked down the passage to his room. He'd been so worried about his brother and unable to do anything about it.

Now though, now, he could finally do something.

Hopefully the supposed adoption wouldn't put a kink in their plans.

NIK WHINED low in his throat. There had been a constant buzzing in his head for the last several hours and it *hurt*. Over the past few days, it kept getting louder. He snuggled in closer to the nice human on the couch, burying his head on the man's lap. Nope, not better. Nik reached his paw up to rub at his ear but it didn't seem to make a difference.

"What's the matter, pup?" the human asked.

Not a pup. Nik whined low again in response. It hurt so bad.

The human reached for him. His whine of pain turned into a whine of pleasure as gentle fingers massaged his head and neck, occasionally scratching at his fur.

This was heaven. He scooted closer, pushing against the human.

It also wasn't the first time he had practically crawled into the human's lap. Nik just wanted to be close to him and he couldn't work out why. The human didn't seem to mind, though. Always willing to pet and scratch Nik in all the right places.

Nik loved spending all his time with this man even if he couldn't remember what he'd done before he'd found this human.

He closed his eyes and tried to block out the buzzing in his head.

Jordan massaged the back of Nik's head, his ears and neck. He didn't know what was wrong with his hound, but there was obviously something troubling him. Over the past couple of weeks Jordan had really enjoyed the time they spent together. For a big strong hound, Nik was surprisingly snuggly. Always wanting to burrow into Jordan's side when they sat on the couch and laying on top of Jordan in the bed, lung capacity be damned. Of course it never started out with Nik on him, but by the time he woke up, he found himself under a giant dead weight.

The crunch of tires on gravel outside brought Jordan out of his reverie and had his worry spiking in seconds. He wasn't expecting any visitors and no one besides Milo knew he was here right now.

Jordan was about to try to slide out from under Nik when his hound opened his eyes and leaped off the couch, making it to the front door in a couple of bounds. He stood there, ears upright and alert, his teeth showing as he growled at the door.

Not good. Though some of the panic died away knowing his hound wanted to protect him. Jordan straightened his clothes to look his best when facing an opponent.

He made his way to the door slowly. A car engine turned off then several doors opened and slammed shut.

Jordan had a bad feeling settle in his gut. *The Hounds of the Hunt.* Time was up. He wasn't looking forward to what was about to happen, especially after their phone call.

He took a deep breath, placed his hand on Nik's head to sooth his hound, and opened the door.

There, standing in his driveway with a large black SUV behind them, were five of the most menacing men Jordan had ever seen before.

Nik stepped through the doorway, growling louder than before and barked. He bared his teeth and put his head down, ready to attack. Each of the men's expressions changed in an instant.

"Nicor!" the largest of the group said.

And that would be the leader, Adze. Probably. Assumptions weren't always the best of things as Jordan had learned.

Nik, well Nicor apparently, whined low in his throat again and took a hesitant step forward. Jordan didn't try and stop him. That wasn't who he was. This was Nik's pack after all.

"What have you done to him?" one of the others asked.

The whole pack watched Nik with worried expressions.

"I haven't done anything to him...he's kinda stuck."

"Stuck?" the leader asked. "What do you mean he's stuck?"

The man finally took his gaze off Nik and actually looked at Jordan. The worried expression morphed into confusion.

"He's been like this since the night I hit him."

"Why did you hit him?" another asked.

Jordan sighed in annoyance. He couldn't really blame them. Of course they all want to know what happened to their packmate. Jordan kind of hoped that they would have a little extra time together before he had to return him to his pack.

"Look, you're here now, and I doubt you're going to be leaving anytime soon. Why don't you come in and we can discuss the situation like civilised beings?" Jordan turned and walked inside, Nik following along quickly behind him.

The others could either follow or not, he didn't really mind either way.

Jordan headed to the kitchen and put the kettle on. He figured coffee was going to be needed. Lots and lots of coffee.

When the hellhounds finally walked through his door, they all looked around like they were expecting something to jump out and attack them.

"Coffee?" Jordan asked as he started pulling mugs out of his cupboard.

"Yes, please," was the overwhelming response.

"Have you got any tea?" one of them asked.

"Sure. Take a seat, this won't be a minute." Jordan waved them to his dining room table and then set about making the tea as well as the coffee. He wasn't about to fart arse about making a half a dozen different drinks to order, instead he grabbed the sugar and milk and placed it in the middle of the table. They could all adjust to their own tastes.

"So"—he carried the tray with everything on it to the table—"you obviously know who I am, seeing as how you managed to find me."

"Jordan Makan. Incubus. Aboriginal heritage. Artist, age unknown. Currently residing in Sydney with properties all over the country."

"Nice, now that you all know who I am, can I know who you are?" he asked as he sat at the head of the table. It didn't take long before Nicor was sitting beside him, his head resting in Jordan's lap.

Everyone spent a minute or so getting their coffee's and tea to their liking then silence reigned again before the leader finally spoke.

"Name's Adze." He went around the table pointing at each of the men individually, "Pyro, Oriax, Daevas and Cacus." He paused a moment before he looked at the hound with his head in Jordan's lap. "And that is Nicor."

Jordan didn't think there was any way he was going to remember everyone's names. He would have to find a way though, if Nicor really was his mate, which he truly believed to be the case. These men sitting at his dining room table were his new family. And didn't that notion scare the crap out of him? Jordan had been on his own for such a long time, now all of a sudden more people came crashing into his world.

"Care to tell us what the hell happened?" Adze asked, a slight growl to his tone.

Jordan didn't miss the nudge the guy next to him gave Adze. The leader seemed to take a deep breath before turning back to Jordan, he raised a brow as he waited for Jordan to speak.

He looked down at Nicor and ran his fingers through his short fur and started to talk.

"I didn't mean to hit him. I would never, especially not my mate. I was on my way home from finishing up a project, when out of nowhere this one raced in front of my car." Jordan shuddered at the memory of that horrid sound his car made on impact. Nicor whined, nudging his stomach. "I didn't have enough time to slow down or stop. It all happened in a matter of seconds. One minute I'm on my way home after a long night of work. The next there's a loud crunch and crash and this guy's flying through the air and falling into a fountain." He shuddered again, having to stop Nicor from crawling up into his lap. "I managed to get him into the car and to an all-night vet clinic where they patched him up."

"We saw the report," Adze said. "It looked like he was already healing. Why did you take him to the humans?"

"I was too panicked at first to realize what he was," Jordan answered. It was the truth. They could believe him or not. "It was only after the surgery was done I figured it out. He's been stuck in this form ever since. I don't know if the accident caused something to go haywire inside him, but nothing I've said or done has resulted in him shifting back to human."

"Why didn't you bring him back to us?" Adze asked.

"Because when I called you were such an ass. I *know* he's my mate. How the hell was I to know that you would give me the time of day?" Jordan refused to apologise for what he'd done. "You certainly didn't act like you would. So, I did the only thing I could."

"Fair enough, but you didn't tell us what state he was in," Adze countered.

"You didn't give me a chance. You were too busy being angry at me for something that I can't change."

Adze sighed and then got up from his chair before he knelt down on the ground. "Nicor."

Nicor ignored his leader.

"Try Nik," Jordan said quietly.

"Why in the world would I try Nick?" Adze asked him, a confused expression on his face. "You put *Spot* on the adoption form."

"I had to give the vet *something* but because you were so much of an ass when we spoke I didn't even get a chance to ask you what his damn name was. No way in Hell I was going to call him Spot, that's taken, but I had to pick *something*." Jordan shrugged. "He seemed like a Nik to me, so that's what we've been going with. He seemed to like it, unlike some of the other names we tried."

Adze stared a moment before he turned his gaze back to his packmate. "Nik."

His hound lifted his head off Jordan's lap and looked at Adze. Did he just squint?

"Come here," he said and waved Nik over.

Nik watched his packmate for a moment before he slowly side-stepped towards Adze. His hound kept looking back at Jordan, whining and his ears moving up and down as if he didn't know what to do. Jordan encouraged him on, smiling when his hound sat by his packmate. Nik sniffed the leader's hand when he reached out, giving it a lick. Adze took Nik's big head in his hands and leaned his head forward until they were touching foreheads.

No one in the room spoke as they watched and waited.

Jordan sucked in a breath as Adze slowly started to shift, his hands still on either side of Nik's head. It looked excruciating in slow-mo, but not once did Adze acknowledge that he might be in any kind of pain.

Before he knew it there were two large hounds in his dining room, one with deep red eyes that seemed to glow eerily. Adze was also engulfed in his clothes since he hadn't undressed first. Jordan had to admit that he had no idea the hounds had to undress before they shifted. He'd assumed the clothes went to some magical place during the shift and when they transformed back again the clothes would be right back in place. Looking at it now he realised what a ridiculous notion that was.

Pyro helped Adze wriggle out of clothes then sat back down. None of them spoke, everyone focused on the two hellhounds.

Adze the hound nudged Nik a couple of times and then placed one paw against Nik's before slowly shifting back again.

"You can do it, Nicor," Adze said quietly, unconcerned for his nudity.

Adze shifted multiple times, always keeping contact with Nik when he did it. Jordan didn't know what sort of strain that would put on a hound, shifting so many times within such a short timeframe, but he didn't think it could be good.

After the fifth or sixth shift Jordan noticed a change in Nik. His hound had gotten the message, and was trying to change back. Jordan found himself holding his breath as he watched the scene unfold.

As slow as Adze had shifted the first time, Nik's shift was even slower. It certainly looked painful as well. Everyone around the table sat silently as they watched on. Jordan let out a relieved breath when suddenly there was not one naked man on his dining room floor, but two. Small graces and all.

"Adze?" Nik asked questioningly.

"Hey, buddy. Good to have you back again," Adze said with a soft smile.

He pulled Nik into his arms and hugged him. The chairs scraped against the tiles as the other hounds moved, practically as one, and descended on the two on the floor. The whole group hugged and laughed as they reunited with their lost packmate.

One big happy family.

"What the hell happened?" Nik asked.

The confused question hurt so much.

"Where are we?" Nik scowled as he looked around the dining room.

Adze and the others all turned to look at Jordan still

sitting at the table. Slowly, Nik turned to look at him too.

"Hi," Jordan said quietly.

Nicor stared for a long time without saying anything. Not even a blink. The intense gaze was unnerving and so different than the loving one his hound gave him. The man's nostrils flared and Jordan knew what he was scenting. Nicor's eyes widened and he let out a soft gasp.

"Well, I guess that truly answers that question, then," Adze said.

"Nice to know you didn't believe me when I told you he was my mate."

Adze scowled at him but didn't respond.

"What's going on here?" Nik asked again, obviously still out of sorts.

"You must be hungry," Jordan said suddenly.

He jumped up and headed to the kitchen, ignoring the question. He needed to get away from everyone for a minute. It fucking hurt that they hadn't believed him, when he'd told Adze that Nik was his mate. Mates weren't something that you fucked around with.

Bypassing the kitchen Jordan headed down the passage to his room. He needed some time to pull himself together.

CHAPTER EIGHT

Nicor's mate fled the room and raced down the passage. When he heard the door close at the other end he turned to Adze.

"What's going on?" he asked. His head hurt like a bitch and Nicor couldn't remember anything.

Adze sighed. "How about we get up off the floor?

Nicor nodded. That was a great idea. The execution, however, was a little rough. Oriax caught Nicor when he stumbled.

"What the hell happened to me? Why do I feel like I've been through the bloody wringer?" he asked no one in particular.

"What's the last thing you remember?" Adze asked as he grabbed his pants and pulled them on.

They slowly made their way into the living room.

Pyro handed Nicor a towel. God knows where he got it from but Nicor was grateful. He wrapped it around his waist before carefully taking a seat on the couch. As he sank into the cushion the feeling was almost familiar. Why would it *feel familiar*?

Nicor thought back, but his head still hurt like a bitch. The last thing he could remember was chasing the incubus through the gardens with Pyro.

"We were in the Gardens? By the Opera House," Nicor said slowly as he concentrated, trying to think back. "We had just located the incubus. And he threw a woman over the fence."

Adze sighed and sat down on the coffee table in front of him.

Nicor stared at his leader then looked away down passage. He swore the man who had walked away from them was his mate. Nicor didn't know who he was, or what he was doing here, he knew what he scented in the air and felt when he looked at the other man.

"Nicor?" Daevas asked from beside him.

Nicor shifted his attention back to his pack. It was only then that he noticed the expressions on their faces.

"What?" he asked.

"Nicor, what you remember, that was almost four weeks ago," Oriax said gently from Nicor's other side.

"Can you run that by me again? I don't think I heard you correctly."

Everyone turned to Adze. Their packmate ran a hand through his hair and sighed. "So, you've been missing for nearly four weeks—"

"Missing?" Nicor interrupted.

"Yeah."

"What the hell do you mean missing?" Nicor was having a hard time understanding any of this. "Can someone find me some damn nurofen or something? My head is fucking killing me."

Cacus stood and headed to the kitchen. "On it."

Nicor still had no idea where the hell they even were. The banging of opening and closing drawers and cupboards filled the silence before the tap ran and water filled in a glass.

"Here, this is all I could find." Cacus dropped two little white pills in Nicor's hand and gave him the glass of water.

It wasn't often that they needed medicine since they tended to heal fairly quickly, but Nicor's splitting headache wasn't getting any better on its own. He downed the pills along with the water, and hoped to Christ they worked fast.

"You okay to hear this now?" Adze asked.

"Yeah, go ahead. I'll try not to interrupt you this time," Nicor replied as he sat back and let his head rest against Oriax's shoulder.

"Pyro stayed to help the woman who had been thrown over the fence and you went after the incubus," Adze started. Nicor nodded. He remembered that much. Although everything after that was gone.

"What you don't remember is that you chased the damn incubus down the road and got hit by a car."

"I'm sorry what?" Nicor sat up suddenly at the news. He groaned from the pain the movement caused. Pyro and Oriax gently pulled him back again.

"Jordan"—Adze waved down the passageway in the general direction Nicor's mate had gone—"Was on his way home after finishing up a project. You two met at an intersection. He had right of way and didn't see you as it was dark and you were in your hound form. Hellhound versus SUV. SUV won."

"No wonder I feel like crap. But that was nearly four weeks ago you said?"

"Yeah, Jordan took you to a vet to get checked out. He was panicked at first and didn't realise what you were, but we had no idea what had happened to you. One minute we knew you were chasing the incubus, the next you disappeared off the face of the earth. No one could find you. After about a week, we received a phone call."

Pyro snorted beside him.

"What?" Nicor asked.

"Let's just say, I was less than cordial with Jordan when he called."

"Why?" Nicor asked confused.

"Because I was worried about you. We couldn't find you. Not a single sign anywhere. And all of a sudden, this guy calls me out of the blue. Says he has you, that he's an incubus and you're his mate. I may have lost my shit at him. I admit I was a bit of an ass." Adze paused for a moment before continuing, "To cut a long story short, he took you, we still had no idea where you were or who you were with because he hadn't given us any details to go on. And it's taken us until now, roughly three weeks, to be able to track you down."

Nicor tried to take in everything Adze had explained, but he kept getting stuck on one thing. "That's my mate."

"Yes, I believe it is," Adze acknowledged.

"Why did you treat him that way?" Nicor asked softly. It wasn't often that any of them went against their leader, but Adze was in the wrong here. Nicor knew it, and he bet even Adze knew it too.

"I'm sorry. I was an ass and worried about you. I heard incubus and lost my shit."

Nicor closed his eyes. "It shouldn't matter what his species is. Mate is Mate. You didn't treat Archie or Callum badly because they're human. Why treat my mate that way? He can't change who he is."

"I'm sorry," Adze said again.

"I'm not the one you need to apologise to," Nicor said as he looked around the room. Everyone else sat quietly.

"I know. I will."

Nicor knew Adze meant it. He'd never known his leader to lie about something this important. Needing a change of topic he asked, "Where the hell are we anyway?"

Daevas laughed. "The Hunter Valley. That mate of yours sequestered the two of you away in wine country."

Nicor whistled. "Oh. *Nice.*" The loud banging in his head had quietened to a dull throb. "Can someone help me up?"

Everything felt wobbly, and he wasn't sure if he could make it up on his own yet or not.

Pyro stood and helped Nicor to his feet. Once up, he stayed still for a minute to get his bearings.

"You okay?" Pyro asked.

"Yeah, I think so."

"You need a hand with something?" Pyro asked as stepped back to give Nicor room to move.

"Nah, I think I need to do this one on my own."

Nicor took it slow as he made his way through the living room and down the passage. Thankfully he could use the wall for help if he needed it as he walked down to the last door. Nicor had no idea where he was going, but something inside him, told him this was the *right door*.

Jordan hadn't come back out yet and Nicor didn't know if it was him or his pack that Jordan was hiding from. From what Adze had told him he had a feeling it was his leader in particular and Nicor couldn't blame his mate one bit.

The farther down the passage he got, the stronger the scent of his mate became. Nicor's body started to react. His whole body thrummed with the need to claim. Nicor wasn't ashamed of his body, quite the opposite. He did wish however, that he was meeting his mate for the first time dressed in something a little more than a single towel. Clothes hadn't been high on his list of priorities. Maybe they should have been.

He knocked lightly on the door. "Jordan?"

Enough time passed with no response that Nicor wondered if he was even going to get one when a quiet "come in" floated through the door.

Jordan sat in the middle of the bed, his back against the headboard with his knees pulled to his chest and his arms wrapped around them—as if he was trying to protect himself from the world outside. Or more fittingly, against the hellhounds on his doorstep. Nicor's heart broke at the expression on the man's face. Even though he didn't currently didn't remember anything of the last four weeks, this was his mate and he was obviously hurting.

Nicor closed the door behind him. "Do you mind if I come in and sit down? I'm a little wobbly on my feet still."

Jordan shook his head. It was then Nicor noticed the slight puffiness to his face and the red tinge to his eyes. Nicor wanted to turn around and go deck Adze in that instant. If he'd had the energy, and didn't think he'd end up on his ass, he might have done it. With the way he was feeling he doubted he'd even make it back to his leader.

Nicor slowly made his way around to the other side of the bed and gently sat down on the side. He scooted in, feeling like he was on the wrong side and should be where his mate was, or rather, on top of his mate. *That's weird*. He faced his mate.

"Hi," he said gently.

Jordan looked up at him and crooked a smile. "Hey, yourself."

"We haven't been officially introduced. Name's Nicor." He held out his hand.

Jordan looked at him for a long time before he reached out and took his hand in his own. "Jordan."

"It's my very greatest pleasure to meet you, Jordan."

"Really?" he asked, looking confused.

"Really. You have no idea how long I've waited to meet my mate." Nicor had never been happier than when Archie fell into their lives then soon after,

Callum had arrived. It had given Nicor hope his mate was coming.

"I'm an incubus," Jordan said out of the blue.

"I know," Nicor replied then smiled. "Thank you for taking such good care of me—"

"Wait a second. I told you I was an incubus and you just brushed it off, like it was nothing."

"It is nothing."

"Your boss didn't seem to think it was nothing."

"Yeah, well, Adze can be an ass sometimes." Nicor growled, showing teeth. "He will be apologising to you for how he treated you. That's for damn sure."

Jordan looked at him with a wary expression.

"So, back to what I was saying, thanks for taking care of me. Well, I assume you did seeing as how I'm alive and everything. I don't quite remember anything from the last four weeks apparently."

"You don't remember anything?" Jordan asked worriedly.

"Nope. Last thing I remember is chasing a bad guy through the Botanic Gardens at night then nothing until I was sitting on the floor in your dining room."

Jordan's expression sunk. Nicor reached out and placed a hand over his.

"I'm sorry," he said quietly.

"Why are you apologising? It's not your fault. I was the one who hit you with my car."

"Yeah, about that..."

Jordan chuckled lightly. "Hey, not my fault buddy. You're the one that was running down the middle of the bloody road at night, not looking where you were going. I had right of way after all."

Nicor laughed, and suddenly Jordan grinned at him. It was like the world stopped in that moment. His mate smiling was the best things ever.

"So, you really don't remember me calling you Nik for the last three weeks? You stealing all of my bacon? Or trying to suffocate me in my sleep with your massive weight?" Jordan asked him. "What about when you practically crawled in my lap when I played games on my iPad?"

Nicor laughed again. "Not even a little bit, but the bacon stealing definitely sounds like something I would do." Nicor's body reacted to the thought of laying on top of his mate and he tried to tamp it down. "And I really do like games."

That sounded nothing like what Nicor meant and he bit back a groan. Talk about cheesy. "I mean, gaming. I like gaming." Nicor was suddenly conscious of the fact that he was still only wearing a bloody towel. He needed clothes!

Jordan must have sensed where his mind went and he pulled his hand out from under Nicor's.

"There's something you need to know about me," he said quietly.

"What's that?" Nicor asked, intrigued.

"I'm unique among incubi." He took a deep breath. "But as my mate I need you to understand this. I'm demisexual."

"What does that mean exactly?" Nicor asked. "I

know I've heard the term before, but I don't want to assume I know what it means for you."

"Thank you," Jordan said quietly. He flashed another smile. "For me I don't experience sexual attraction towards someone that I haven't formed a strong emotional bond with. I'm not going to want to have sex, or even quench my thirst sexually, until that connection is there."

Nicor took some time to process what Jordan said. It sounded like he'd repeated those words plenty of times in the past. The last thing Nicor ever wanted to do was to make his mate uncomfortable in any way.

"So, that means I get to date the shit outta you!" he replied.

Jordan laughed. "You're not mad?"

"Why the hell would I be mad? I've never felt the need to fall straight into bed with someone. Yes, you're my mate and I want you, but I'm not ruled by my body. I'm more than happy to get to know the man before I get to know the body."

"Thank you."

Nicor paused for a moment before he spoke again with a little hesitance. "Can I ask a question?"

"Sure, I've never been one of those people that gets upset about answering questions. Some do. Some don't. I'm of the opinion that you can't learn if you don't ask."

"That's very astute of you." Nicor took a deep breath. "You are an incubus, yes?"

Jordan nodded and smiled, like he knew where Nicor was going with his question, but let him ask it anyway.

"Traditionally incubi are men who sleep with women and feed off the sexual energy."

"Very true. Not always, but most commonly."

"Can I ask which gender you find attractive?" Nicor wondered if trying to form an emotional connection to Jordan was going to be an impossible task.

"If I try and date anyone, wishing to form a connection with them, it is *usually* someone who identifies as male, not always, but most of the time." Jordan smiled again.

Nicor let out a relieved breath. That was something at least, then he decided he should ask for clarification. "So, you are a bi, demisexual incubus?"

Jordan winked. "That prefers masc-identifying people."

"Well, aren't you just breaking all the moulds?"

Jordan laughed. "I try my best not to be defined by stereotypes."

"Well, I think you are succeeding spectacularly."

"Why, thank you."

"Can I ask how the whole incubus part works with your sexual orientation? That can't be easy."

Jordan paused for a moment. "It's not. Thankfully I can feed partially off of others' sexual energy. There's been a lot of sex clubs in my life."

Nicor raised a brow at that unexpected comment, but didn't interrupt.

"I don't have to be engaged in the act myself. Of course, it's like eating pasta where you feel full at the time, but you're usually hungry again in an hour or so. Or in my case in a couple of weeks. On the rare occasions when it has been me engaged in the act; a good feeding can keep me going for months if needed."

"Interesting," Nicor said. He loved learning new things. "Will you be able to feed from me?"

Jordan smiled shyly and nodded.

"Will it cause any harm if you repeatedly feed from me?" Nicor asked. He didn't want to do anything would result in either one of them being hurt.

"I don't know. I hope not. I haven't ever fed from the same person multiple times...I would assume, as you are a hellhound, that you would be able to withstand more than a normal human could." Jordan paused for a moment before continuing, "I would also think that when we get to that point in our relationship I wouldn't have to be feeding in such large quantities."

"I like the sound of that," Nicor said and waggled his brows salaciously.

Jordan laughed.

"I look forward to getting to know you better, mate."

"Me too." Jordan smiled again.

Nicor figured there was something he wanted to ask, but was unsure. "You can ask me anything."

"Would you mind if I called you Nik?" Jordan looked so unsure of himself, and more than anything Nicor wanted to reassure him.

"You can call me whatever you like."

It was Jordan's turn to raise a brow at Nicor now. "How about shit for brains?"

Nicor burst into laughter, not expecting that answer in his wildest dreams. "Okay, maybe not anything."

"You did run out in the middle of the road without looking..."

"You're never going to let me live this down, are you?" Nicor asked.

"Not in this lifetime at least." Jordan chuckled, his shoulders dropping and relaxing. Comfortable looked good on his mate.

Before Nicor could respond with anything else, his stomach growled loudly.

Neither of them spoke for several seconds, then Jordan sprang into action and scrambled off the bed. "Come on, let's go make you something to eat. You're obviously starving."

Jordan opened the door before Nicor could say anything and was off down the passage. His mate moved fast. Was it an incubus thing? The one he went after in the gardens moved right quick. He should ask.

Not wanting to leave his mate in a room with the rest of the pack after the way Adze had treated him, Nicor carefully stood and made his way back to the living room. It was time he found some damn clothes.

Silence reigned supreme in the room as his pack watched Jordan bustle around the kitchen pulling things out of the fridge and freezer.

Nicor glared at Adze, waiting for his leader to make things right with his mate.

Adze stood up and walked to the kitchen, stopping on the other side of the island counter.

"Jordan?"

Jordan turned from what he was doing to look at Adze.

"I'm sorry for the way I treated you. It wasn't fair or right and you have every reason to be angry at me. I hope you can forgive me."

Everyone seemed to hold their breath as they waited for what Jordan would say.

After a moment he nodded. "You hungry?"

Adze smiled. "Starved."

Jordan looked around Adze to the rest of Nicor's mob. "What about you lot?"

They all looked at one another, gave a shrug, then back at Jordan.

"I could eat," Daevas answered, followed by nods or yeses from the others.

"How's pizza sound to everyone?"

Nicor's mouth watered. Just the thought of it had him salivating already. "It's been forever since I had pizza."

"What are you talking about?" Jordan asked. "You devoured my leftovers last week before I could stop you. Holy crap your farts were rank for the next two days! Never again, let me tell you!"

Nicor could feel himself blushing as the entire room burst into laughter.

"Fuck off," he told them all. "I don't remember so it didn't happen."

Jordan laughed now. "So that's how it's going to be is it?"

"Yep." Nicor nodded. "Cacus, would you mind helping Jordan?"

"Not at all. Happy to help," Cacus said as he sprung

up. "Ohh," Cacus said as he made his way to the kitchen. "We're going homemade, all the way?"

Jordan looked at the salt, the yeast container, then the large tub of flour he'd pulled out of the cupboard and placed on the bench. He went back for a large bottle of olive oil. "It's the only way to go as far as I'm concerned."

"Couldn't agree more," Cacus said as he started washing his hands in the sink.

Jordan started scooping out flour into a large bowl. He paused then looked around room and seemed to contemplate. He looked back down at the flour, then at everyone, then stared scooping more flour, doubling, if not tripling, what he had.

Nicor laughed.

"Good decision. This mob could quite easily eat you out of house and home," Cacus said as he went to Jordan's fridge and started gathering ingredients.

Nicor watched his mate with a happy buzz of contentment as Jordan worked silently, blooming yeast then making dough, its scent soon alive in the small house. Jordan covered the large bowl and placed it in his oven on a very low temp to proof.

"That'll take about a half hour or so," he told the group at large.

Cacus was busy chopping up meats and veggies to go on the pizzas. Jordan grabbed another bowl along with a large jar of tomato paste and a bunch of herbs. He then started putting together the sauce.

"Damn man, the pizza's aren't even cooking yet and this place smells amazing," Pyro said.

Jordan opened his fridge and frowned.

"What's the matter?" Nicor asked him.

"We might have a problem," Jordan said as he turned around.

"What's that?" he asked.

"I don't have enough cheese."

"Say no more," Daevas said as he held out his hand to Adze. "Point me in the direction of the closest supermarket and I'll go for a quick run. Anything else you need?"

"Not that I can think of, unless you guys want something specific to drink," Jordan answered before giving them directions to the local store.

"Come on then, Daevas, I'll go with you," Oriax said. "The sooner we get back, the sooner pizzas happen."

Needing to do something other than sit and watch his mate like some kind of creeper, Nicor got up and headed over to the living area where Pyro and Adze were sitting.

Before he could sit with the others the door opened and Oriax popped back inside. He held out a backpack to Nicor. "Here, I thought you might like this."

"What is it?" he asked.

"Clothes."

"You're a legend." Nicor grinned and grabbed the bag, opening it to find a ratty old shirt and a pair of trackies.

The door closed as Oriax left, Nicor wasn't paying attention though. He pulled the shirt on, the soft fabric felt good against his skin and carefully slipped into the loose trackies, trying his hardest not to flash the room as the towel slipped away.

A throat cleared behind him as he bent to pick up the towel and place it over the back of the couch.

Pyro and Adze stopped their conversation and glanced Nicor's way when he sat down.

"How you feeling?" Adze asked him.

"Better, now that I'm clothed. Head's still a little fuzzy, but hopefully that'll disappear with time."

Pyro nodded. "You had us all worried for a long time there."

"Sorry about that."

"Not your fault, man. Couldn't be helped."

"So, did you at least catch the bastard I was chasing that night?" Nicor asked, wanting to know what had been going on.

"Nah, he managed to give us the slip. Of course when we realised you'd gone missing, we were more worried about finding you than catching him anyway."

"Please tell me they're not still out there." Nicor laid back against the couch to rest his head and closed his eyes. His head really did feel quite funky right now. He hoped it didn't last too long.

"Unfortunately, can't tell you that." Adze sighed. "They've managed to elude us at every turn. But now, with a full team again, hopefully we can finally put a stop to them."

Nicor nodded, his eyes still closed, but he didn't say anything. He didn't know what to say or how to feel.

He'd met his mate. *Finally.* And now Adze was

talking about him just going back to work tomorrow like it was no big deal.

Nicor didn't know what was going to happen. He wanted to spend time with Jordan, get to know his mate. He didn't know how that was going to work. Their job was in Sydney. Jordan was currently in the Hunter Valley, and to make matters worse, their home was in Melbourne. Would Jordan pack up his life and move to Melbourne with Nicor?

Could Nicor really ask that of someone he'd only known a matter of hours?

Nicor supposed he could commute if needed. The flight between Melbourne and Sydney wasn't all that long. He could even fly commercial. But the thought of being away from his pack if they were called out on a job didn't sit well with him.

How in the hell had his life turned into a god damn soap drama in a matter of weeks?

"Here, put this on your head, it might help."

Nicor opened his eyes and stared into the pale brown orbs of his mate.

Jordan smiled and held out a cool, damp cloth.

"Thanks," Nicor said quietly. The pounding in his head seemed to have gotten worse since he sat down and started stressing over his life, not better.

Jordan placed the cloth across Nicor's forehead and pressed it down gently.

A trickle of water ran down the side of Nicor's face and gathered at his ear, annoying him until Nicor gave up and wiped it away.

The coldness of the cloth was rather refreshing, even with the currently cool temperatures outside.

Nicor drowned out all noise around him as he lay there with his eyes closed and the cloth on his head.

He awoke slowly some time later to the scent of fresh pizza.

"Holy crap, that smells good," he murmured as he sat up. The cloth fell off his head and landed in his lap. He'd completely forgotten all about it. Thankfully his head was feeling better. Not back to normal, but he thought that may take a few days.

"Tastes pretty fuckin' good too," Oriax said around a mouth full of food.

Nicor slowly stood and surveyed the room. Jordan and Cacus were busy in the kitchen making the next pizzas to go in the oven while Pyro and Oriax were at the table eating, and Adze and Daevas were getting drinks for everyone.

Seems they'd all left him to sleep on the couch for as long as he needed, which Nicor greatly appreciated.

"How you feeling?" Jordan asked, as Nicor claimed a bar stool on the other side of the island counter.

"Better, thank you."

"Anytime." Jordan smiled. "Now, what would you like on your pizza?'"

Nicor surveyed all the toppings they had cut and ready. "A little of everything sounds really good to me right now."

Before Nicor had finished talking his stomach growled low and loud.

Jordan laughed. "Okay, okay, I get the picture. Hurry the hell up."

"Sorry." Nicor's face warmed.

"No need to apologise."

Nicor watched in fascination as fresh cooked pizzas were pulled out of the oven and slid onto wooden boards ready to be cut and new pizzas were delivered to the piping hot oven. Timers were set and the cooked pizzas delivered to their owners.

Adze placed a can of Coke in front of Nicor with a large glass of ice then grabbed up his pizza Jordan held out to him and disappeared to the table with the others.

"Thanks, Adze." Nicor popped the can of soft drink. The sound making him smile as much as the first mouthful. This was his most favourite drink. He didn't know what it was, but no other canned drink came close in his opinion. He spent many a night gaming with several Cokes by his side.

His pack was silent at the table as they all devoured their food and drink like a pack of uncivilised dingos. Nicor shook his head.

Daevas was the first to break the silence. "So, what's the plan?"

Adze looked at everyone before locking eyes with Nicor. "We need to head back to Sydney after we finish eating. It's a long drive and we have work to do." Adze paused for a moment before he continued. "All of us."

Nicor saw Jordan stiffen at the words out of the corner of his eye before his mate turned away and busied himself on the other side of the kitchen, his back now to Nicor. He frowned but didn't say anything.

"I know this isn't the most ideal situation," Adze continued.

Nicor snorted at that understatement.

Adze ignored him. "But we have a job to do and it's already past the point of a bad joke. These assholes need to be stopped before they take any more women."

Nicor understood that, he did, but it didn't stop his heart from hurting that he'd finally found his mate and now he was about to be separated from him.

The oven timer beeped and Jordan made quick work of getting the food out and running the pizza wheel through it cutting it into even slices.

"Thank you," Nicor said as Jordan handed him his food.

"You're welcome."

Jordan slid the last pizza into the oven, one for himself Nicor assumed, and set the timer again.

Nicor didn't want to think about what Adze had said so he took a bite of his pizza, burning the roof of his mouth.

"Ow, ow, ow," he mumbled around a mouth full of food *and* tried to suck air in to cool the offending meal down.

Daevas and Oriax laughed as Nicor fanned his face.

"Not funny, dude. That cheese it like fucking molten lava," Nicor bitched when he finally swallowed his mouthful.

"Next time don't be so damn impatient," Pyro said as he happily took a bite of his last piece.

"Fuck you all," Nicor grumbled as he blew on his slice before taking another bite.

They bantered back and forth for the rest of lunch, no one mentioning them leaving again. And for a moment Nicor could almost forget what was coming. Jordan fit in well with his family. All they needed was Archie and Callum to make it complete.

Thinking about Pyro and Adze's mates made Nicor realise how hard it must be for the pair of them. Here he was moping because he had to get back to work when his teammates had been separated from their mates for weeks, all because of him, and all without complaint. Well, Nicor didn't really know if that last was true or not as he hadn't been there to witness it.

No. Adze definitely would have bitched.

Oriax and Pyro set about cleaning up the kitchen while everyone else finished off their food. When everything was finished and Jordan's kitchen was spotless once more everyone stood, leaving only Nicor and Jordan at the table.

"Thank you for your hospitality today," Adze said to Jordan. "Once again, I am sorry for my earlier transgressions."

Adze handed Nicor over his phone and patted him on the shoulder. "We'll wait outside."

Nicor remained quiet as his brothers all left the house.

He sat and stared at the closed door for several minutes before he turned his gaze back on Jordan. *My mate.* The man's expression was unreadable. Nicor had no idea how his mate was feeling about what was about to happen.

He opened his mouth to say something, anything, then closed it again, unsure what he should say in this moment.

Jordan didn't seem to be inclined to start a conversation either.

Nicor sighed. They couldn't sit here in silence all day. Eventually, Nicor would have to leave, and he needed to have things set with his mate before that happened. God knows Adze wasn't the most patient of men, so his time was short.

"Will you stay here?" Nicor eventually asked, his voice soft and low.

Jordan glanced at him, and Nicor thought he saw a flash of pain cross his features, but it disappeared before he could be sure. Instead Jordan broke their gaze and looked around the house.

"No," he said, shaking his head. "I don't think so. It..." He seemed to pause for a moment before he continued, "It won't be the same without a large hound to keep me company. I really enjoyed the time I got to spend with him."

Nicor wished he could remember, but the last few weeks were nothing but a blur for him. "Where will you go? Back to Sydney?"

"Probably. For now at least."

Nicor liked the sound of that, and not, all at the same time.

"Would you be interested in getting to know me better, when we both get back to the city?" Nicor held his breath as he waiting what seemed like a bloody long time for Jordan to answer.

"Yeah, I really think I'd like that."

Nicor's exhale was long and loud.

Jordan smiled slightly. "A little worried about my answer there, were ya?"

"Maybe." Nicor grinned back. He looked down at the phone he held in his hands, he hadn't thought about it once, since he shifted back. Hadn't even realised Adze had brought it with him. "Could I get your number?"

"Yeah, I think that would be a good idea." Jordan rattled off his digits and Nicor typed them into his phone contact list before he sent Jordan a quick little message so his mate had his details as well.

A muffled ping sounded and Jordan fished his own phone from his pocket and quickly glanced at it before he put it away again. "Thanks."

Nicor nodded. There was so much he wanted to say, but didn't, couldn't at this moment. Nicor could hear the car engine running outside, everyone was waiting on him.

"Thank you...for everything."

"You're thanking me for hitting you with my car?" Jordan asked with a smirk on his face and a raised brow.

Nicor laughed. "Yeah, I think I am, because without that happening, we may never have met."

Jordan seemed to contemplate that for a moment before he nodded. "Very true. Well, in that case, you're more than welcome. Any time you feel the need to get flung through the air at a high rate of speed and land in a fountain, feel free to give me a call."

Nicor burst out in laughter. "Not sure if I'll ever have that need again, but I will still call you."

Reluctantly, Nicor stood from the table, Jordan following along behind him as Nicor slowly made his way to the front door. Jordan opened it for him and stepped back, allowing Nicor the room to leave.

They stood there, facing one another for a moment. Nicor wanted nothing more than to lean in and kiss his mate. To feel Jordan's soft lips press against his own, to share breath, but he'd promised his mate to take things slow. The last thing he was going to do was break his promise.

"Thank you again," Nicor said, unsure what else he should say, then turned to leave.

To his surprise, Jordan reached out and grabbed his hand, taking it in his own and squeezing gently.

"Be safe, will you? Nik, please." Jordan bottom lip came out in a tiny pout and Nicor wanted to run his thumb over it. Instead he gently squeezed Jordan's hand back.

"I promise."

"I want to get to know you better, Nicor, and I can't do that if you're out there getting hit by cars all the time."

Nicor chuckled. "Just your car."

He squeezed one last time before he let go and walked out the door. He didn't look back because if he did, Nicor didn't think he would get in the car and leave.

The large black SUV sat idle in the drive and Nicor made his way towards it. He climbed into the front seat that had been left vacant for him and closed the door behind him. Only then did he allow himself to glance back at the entrance to his mate's house, only to find the door closed and Jordan no longer in sight.

"Ready?" Adze asked.

"Let's go," Nicor mumbled.

Adze didn't say anything, put the car in gear and backed out of the drive.

A hand landed on his shoulder as they pulled out onto the road and Nicor twisted around to see Pyro behind him. "It gets easier, trust me."

Nicor nodded, but didn't say anything. He remembered what Pyro went through when he met Callum. At least Jordan was a part of the sup community, and he didn't have to explain all that to him like Adze and Pyro had to with their mates. Nicor took a deep breath then slowly let it out. He settled down for the long drive back to the city, closed his eyes and drowned out the sound of the tyres on the bitumen and the constant chatter coming from the back seats.

CHAPTER NINE

Jordan stood there, back against the door as he listed to the crunch of tyres on his gravel drive. There went his mate. Jordan didn't do anything to stop him. Not that there was really anything he could have done, even if he'd wanted to. Nicor was a hellhound. Bound to a duty to protect the humans against the bad things that went bump in the night. Jordan had already stood in the way of that for more than three weeks when he'd taken Nicor and brought him here.

He looked around the house. There wasn't a single sign that the hounds had been there. His kitchen had been cleaned and the dishes dried and put away. Even the bowl that Jordan had been feeding Nik out of that had been on the floor had been picked up and cleaned.

He'd only known Nik the hound for a matter of weeks, and Nicor the man for a few hours. But being here now, with neither of them, his house felt empty and cold.

Jordan opened the fridge and removed the bottle of wine he'd opened the previous night. If ever that was a time to wallow and drink, now was it, he figured. Jordan emptied the remainder of the bottle into a large glass, and went outside to sit down. He looked over the rows and rows of vines and drank his wine.

He'd allow this time for his little pity party then he had shit to do. Jordan had to pack his house back up again, gather all the paintings he'd done and take them back to the city. He had to hand them over to Mandy so she could start planning his next exhibition. He still had other works he'd left behind that he had to finish as well as start new ones. And last but not least, he had to decide what the hell he was going to do with a god damned mate.

Jordan had never really figured he'd meet his mate, and now that he had, he was at a loss as to what to do. He did know that their relationship would never work unless they were in the same location.

That thought stopped Jordan in his tracks, wine glass halfway to his mouth.

"Fuck," he swore.

Jordan couldn't believe that this hadn't occurred to him until this second. The hounds didn't operate out of Sydney. They lived in Melbourne full time and travelled from there when needed. They were only in town working a case at the moment. That meant that whenever they were able to finalise whatever Adze had dragged them all back to the city to do, they would be on the next flight home.

Without Jordan.

The ache inside him at the thought alone was gut-wrenching. He hadn't known Nicor long, but already his body didn't want to be that far away from his hound.

Jordan downed the last of his wine and placed the glass on the table beside him. He didn't mind Melbourne per se. It was a nice enough city. He just liked Sydney better, and Melbourne didn't have the Hunter Valley only a couple of hours drive from it either, when he needed to get away for some peace and quiet.

His whole life had been turned upside down with the squeal of brakes and the crunch of flesh hitting metal.

Jordan lost track of time as he sat there and contemplated where his life was going now.

Before he knew it, the sun was setting and the wind had turned chilly. Now would be the perfect time to curl up on the couch with a large black hellhound for a personal heater as they watched some mindless TV together or played games on his iPad. But that wasn't to be as his hound had been taken away.

The last thing Jordan felt like right now was food, so he cleaned up the glass he'd used, locked the doors and turned the lights out and headed for bed. He had a long drive back to Sydney in the morning.

Nicor paced his room. He felt so restless he hadn't even been able to play any of his games. They were heading out for a hunt in a matter of minutes. But right now, he felt like he could quite easily crawl out of his skin. His head was feeling immensely better as he'd managed to sleep most of the drive back to Sydney. He missed Jordan, though. Nicor wanted his mate. How he was going to get through the coming weeks, hell, possibly months, was beyond him. Nicor wished he remembered the last few weeks in the valley with his mate.

A loud banging on his door, broke Nicor out of his thoughts.

"You ready?" Pyro asked from the passageway.

"Yeah, be there in a minute." Nicor didn't know what was wrong with him, but he needed to snap out of it. His brothers were counting on him.

After taking a deep breath, Nicor headed out to join the others.

Adze assigned their hunt areas then they all headed for the lift. The ride down to the basement was quiet, apparently none of them feeling the need to fill the peace with inane chatter.

Once they made it to their shifting location, everyone started to undress.

"Everyone know what they're doing?" Adze asked and was met with grunts or nods from everyone.

Brother after brother shifted, until it was he and Adze *still* in human form. He tried to call his hound to shift, but nothing happened.

"You all right?" Adze asked him, a worried expression on his face.

"I think I may need a little help," he admitted.

Nicor had never needed help to shift before, and now he'd needed it twice in one day.

"You've been through a lot. You sure you're up for this? Maybe you should sit out tonight and see if you're feeling any better tomorrow?"

As much as Nicor wanted to go back upstairs and call Jordan, he'd already let his pack go out without him for weeks on end. He needed to step up and pull his weight.

"I'm good, could you just..." Nicor didn't finish his question.

Adze didn't need him to.

His pack leader stepped forward and placed his hands on either side of Nicor's head. The other hounds all sat there patiently as they watched and waited.

The irritation Nicor had been feeling all afternoon disappeared the moment Adze touched him. Almost like the man was a calming presence or some shit. Nicor wanted to laugh at the mere thought of Adze being a *calming presence* but that was how he felt right now.

Images flashed in Nicor's mind of his hound and of his shifting in the past. He closed his eyes and concentrated on his breathing, calling to his hound. He felt Adze there as well, almost like his pack leader was inside him, coaxing his hound to the forefront.

With Adze there, his creature didn't take much coaxing. He was almost giddy to come out and get attention from Adze.

Feeling Adze's mirth inside him was pretty fucking weird, but that was something to think about later.

Right now he allowed himself to sink inside his hound, for the two of them to become one again.

When Nicor opened his eyes again he was on all fours and in animal form. He shook from head to tail to help centre himself. Nicor nuzzled against Adze, thanking him, who sat patiently in front of him in his own hound form. The others all came up and rubbed against him until Adze called a halt to their little celebration.

Let's get a move on. We have work to do.

Daevas and Nicor broke off from the pack and headed through the city. Their roaming grounds tonight were Pott's Point and Elizabeth Bay, just up from Kings Cross, but to get there they had to cross the city and through the Botanic Gardens.

It was still relatively early in the night, but that didn't mean they could dawdle. They had a job to do and they were going to do it.

Too many women had been kidnapped by this gang. It needed to stop and stop now. It was bad enough that Nicor felt guilty for slowing his team down by not being here for the last three and a bit weeks. He wasn't going to let them down again.

There was only so much of Pott's Point that they could hunt, as the point was a damn naval base, and there was no way the creatures they were looking for would be in there. The security was tight enough Adze didn't believe it warranted their attention.

He and Daevas stuck to the shadows. They'd gotten rather good at not being seen, despite their large size.

You think we should check the wharfs first? Daevas

asked him a little while later as they crossed out of the bottom of the gardens.

Seems logical to me, Nicor replied.

Mermaids were much like every other shifter species in that they could shift to a fully human shape as well. Unlike most other shifters who spent most of their time human, mermaids were different. They preferred to spend their time in their natural state and only became human if it was completely necessary.

All the women so far had been taken near water, or very close by, in the case of the Botanic Gardens—which was more than likely the work of the incubus who was working with the mermaids.

Thankfully the foot traffic out tonight was light, due to it being a Wednesday and mid-week. Things would start to pick up again from tomorrow as people started going out again in anticipation of the weekend.

Hours passed with no sight or sound out of the ordinary and only the occasional check-in from Adze.

Nicor couldn't decide if he wanted a nice and easy first night back or if he wanted this to all be over and for them to actually catch the bastards they were looking for. He and Daevas were on their way to Elizabeth Bay to check things over there when Oriax's sharp voice broke through the silence.

Boss, we got something.

Where? Adze's sharp bark answered back.

Nicor and Daevas came to a sharp halt, then turned around and started heading back the way they had come. They probably had the farthest to go so they made sure to put on the speed. Stealth wasn't so much a factor anymore. If anyone saw them, they would be gone before they could get a good look.

Fleet Steps, in the gardens, up from Victoria Lodge House, Pyro replied.

Daevas and I are on our way, we're not far, Nicor replied. They were a hell of a lot closer than Nicor had thought they would be.

What's the situation? Adze asked.

Caught the incubus injecting a jogger with something. She's unconscious. We currently have him. But there's only two of us and he's pissed, Oriax explained.

We're on our way. Be there in five, Adze replied.

Nicor and Daevas ran as fast as they could.

Traffic was light at that time of morning. It wouldn't be long though before more and more people started arriving in the city, ready to start their workday. They needed to contain this situation and fast.

Luckily, there was a road that ran all the way through the gardens to the tip of the point that would take them right to where they needed to be.

They arrived at the base of the stairs in no time flat, with Adze right on their heels. Cacus was missing, and Nicor assumed Adze had sent him to go get their vehicle and clothes since they would need to get out of there ASAP.

The road took them to the base of the stairs and at about halfway up, Pyro and Oriax circled a young man. A body lay on the stairs close by but unmoving. Why did the incubus think it would be a good idea to knock out his prey in the middle of the stairs? Surely it would have been easier to do at the top or bottom? In the middle meant he'd have to carry or drag the poor human to either end.

That obviously wasn't of high enough concern for him though. The three hounds started their sprint up the stairs, the second the incubus spotted them he turned and tried to flee. Pyro growled then leapt and tackled the guy, Oriax right behind him. The three of them struggled together, rolling up and down the stairs, hitting hard against each step.

Nicor and the others raced to reach them with Adze pulling ahead. He raced up the stairs like his tail was on fire, then joined the fray. Within seconds everything calmed down. Adze bit down on the incubus' neck. The man stilled under him. Blood trickled down from where Adze's sharp teeth pierced his flesh.

Daevas looked around then shifted, Nicor following his lead. He went to the woman lying slumped on the stairs and pressed his fingers to her neck to check for a pulse. It took a moment for him to find it, but the steady beat under his fingertips was there. He let out a deep breath. They had gotten to her in time.

"She's alive," he announced. Daevas nodded but the others were still standing over the prone form of the incubus.

"What are you waiting for? Kill me already!" the incubus rasped.

Adze bit down harder and gave his head a shake. The incubus cried out. Whether it was with fear or pain was hard to tell. With Adze it was a good chance of both.

Daevas leaned over, making sure their prey could see him. "Oh, we aren't going to kill you." He paused for a moment before smiling. "At least, not yet."

"What the hell does that mean?" the man gasped.

"It means, dear fellow, you have information and you're going to give it to us."

"Fuck off!" The incubus bellowed—well, as much as he could with massive hellhound's jaws wrapped around his throat.

It fell kinda flat. Not threatening. Not pinned down like that.

The squeal of tires on bitumen sounded less than a minute later as Cacus arrived with the car. It was quickly followed by the car door slamming shut. Cacus ran up the stairs and handed Nicor the bag with all their clothes in it. He grabbed his stuff then handed the bag off to Daevas.

As they dressed, Cacus and the others flipped the incubus to his back and zip tied his hands together.

Once the creature was bound, Adze and Pyro dragged the guy to his feet. They handed him off to Cacus and Daevas so they could get dressed too. Ready to be gone. Oriax tossed them the bag suggesting they gag the incubus too. Adze seemed to consider it as he dressed.

The hoarse bitching was annoying.

"How—" the incubus began.

Daevas gave him a shake. "We have duct tape."

That shut the bastard up.

"Nicor, Oriax. Stay and call an ambulance for the woman." Adze grabbed the incubus. "You know what to say. Head home once all is clear. I'll call the office and let them know there may be possible clean up needed with the cops if they show up with the ambos."

"You got it," Nicor said. "Thanks."

Oriax nodded beside him.

The silence was heavy as Adze and Pyro hauled the incubus down the stairs with Daevas and Cacus not far behind. They shoved him, none too gently, into the back of the car, and were gone seconds later.

Nicor knelt down next to the unconscious woman and checked her pulse again. Oriax pulled out his phone and moved away a couple steps.

"Hello?" Oriax said. "Yes. Can we please get an ambulance to the Fleet steps in the Royal Botanic Gardens? My friend and I found an unconscious woman on the stairs this morning while taking a walk."

Normally they'd call in an anonymous tip and skedaddle before anyone showed up. But with so many kidnappings, it wasn't safe to leave her here, and there was nowhere they could hide to keep an eye on her. They were stuck.

Oriax answered the operator's questions and stayed on the line as they waited for help to arrive.

Sirens could be heard in the distance, and shortly flashing blue and red lights indicated the arrival of the ambulance. As there was no traffic on the roads in the Gardens at this time, the sirens had been turned off as they pulled up. The paramedics climbed out of the ambulance and got their med kits out. They jogged up the stairs, calling out to Oriax and Nicor.

The woman showed no signs of coming around. Nicor had no idea what the incubus had injected her with. The fact he used something was disconcerting. They needed to know what was being used on the women.

The paramedics knelt down next to the woman and opened their kits, Oriax and Nicor stepping back to allow them room to do their jobs.

"You found her unconscious?" the woman medic asked. She placed a cuff on the incubus' victim.

"Yes," Oriax replied. "We were going for a morning walk and found her here like this. She wouldn't wake up, so we called you guys."

"You did the right thing." The other medic lifted her eyelids and shone a small pen torch in them.

Nicor watched as the medics located the puncture mark on the woman's neck. There was some fast talking between the two of them before the woman medic stood and hastened back down the steps.

She opened the back of the ambulance, pulling out a backboard and neck brace. Nicor groaned as he watched a police car pull up behind the ambulance and two officers clad in dark blue step out. He was really hoping for the cops not to show.

The medic and the police climbed the steps again.

The police had a quick chat with the medic, before waiving Nicor and Oriax to the side.

"Morning." Nicor said, to be polite. Just because he

was hoping they wouldn't show, didn't mean he had to be rude. That would just make things ten times harder.

"Morning, gentlemen," Officer Steadman said as he pulled out his notepad and pen. "What can you tell us about what happened here?"

Nicor watched officer Steadman's partner look over the scene, the medics were carefully situating the neck brace on the woman so they could strap her to the backboard.

"Do you guys need a hand carrying her down?" Nicor asked.

"Thanks, but we got this," the medic said, then turned to her partner. "On three."

The partner nodded. She counted down, then together they lifted the woman up and made their way easily down the stairs. Nicor was impressed.

"Nothing much," Oriax answered Steadman, bringing Nicor's attention back to the man in front of him. "As we told the emergency line dispatcher and the medics when they arrived, we were going for our morning walk, when we came across the woman. We couldn't rouse her, so thought it best to call an ambulance instead of just leaving her there."

Steadman nodded and scribbled in his pad. "You didn't see anyone else on your walk? Anyone that look like they didn't belong?"

"Just a couple of others on their morning walks. But that was on the other side of the garden. They didn't look suspicious to me, what did you think?" Nicor turned to Oriax and raised his brow.

"Nah, nothing out of the ordinary. I really wish we

could be of more help, but I'm not sure what else to tell you."

"I'll need your names and contact information in case we have some follow up questions," Steadman said.

Nicor and Oriax gave the cop their details.

"Are we free to go?" Nicor asked.

"Yeah, we'll call if we have anything further. Thanks for your help."

Oriax clapped him on the back. "Let's head home." They glanced at the cops, Steadman now chatting with his partner, and before they could be called back for more questions, the two of them started down the stairs. Oriax quietly added after they got some distance between them and the cops, "The others have probably dropped fuck-knuckle off at Marcus' and gone home by now."

"There ain't no way Adze isn't going to stay behind and have first crack at him," Nicor stated as they reached the road.

"Yeah, probably, but we have professionals to do that shit, man."

"How do you reckon Adze will go with the whole torture aspect, after what happened to Archie?" Nicor asked.

Oriax shrugged. "Who knows? It's been a minute since we've had to torture information out of anyone, not sure how he's going to react."

Nicor shuddered. He had no qualms doing the job he was tasked with. Hunting down and killing the worst of the worst, sending their souls to the underworld for all eternity. He was fine with that.

On the rare occasion that something more was required, though. When they couldn't hand out justice immediately. When information was required. There was someone else, specialised in the gathering of that information to do that job. That was where Nicor drew the line. Torture was not something he liked or could mete out himself. He couldn't imagine a situation that would arise where he'd be willing to inflict that on someone.

Jordan popped into his head then and Nicor realised he may have to revise his last thought. If something happened to Jordan, Nicor didn't think there was anything he wouldn't do to save his mate.

On the other hand, he knew exactly what torture could do to someone. Seeing first-hand what Archie went though, still went through, because of what had happened to him. Yes, the situations were completely different, one was trying to get information to save lives, the other was torturing for bloody pleasure. It didn't make what they were doing sit any easier inside Nicor. He had no idea how Adze would reconcile this within himself.

He hated what they were about to do, but he couldn't deny that it got results. Hopefully in a day or two they'd have better leads to locate and dismantle this slavery ring.

"You wanna walk or should we call an Uber?" Oriax asked him.

"Let's walk, it's not all that far," Nicor replied.

The sun had risen and traffic had started to pick up as people arrived to commence their workdays. As they left the gardens and started working their way through the streets of the city, the scent of food wafted their way. Nicor's stomach growled in anger.

Oriax laughed and clapped him on the shoulder. "Come on, let's go grab breakfast for the tribe."

Nicor wasn't about to argue. They followed their noses to a little café down the road. The smells inside made Nicor's mouth water. The café had massive toasted sandwiches, breakfast quiche's the size of his fist, and bacon and egg rolls the size of his damn forearm. There was also a fridge with fruit, yogurt and muesli as well as a juice bar.

They were so ordering multiples of everything.

It could be his stomach talking, but Nicor was sure the food was good.

"Oh my god," Nicor whined low in his throat. "How have we never been here before?"

"No idea, man, but we'll be bloody coming back. That's for sure."

"Hell yeah!"

They placed their order and Oriax tapped his phone to pay for it. Modern technology made things so much easier. They walked out of the shop with two bags full of food and three cup trays holding juices and coffees for everyone. With home only a couple of blocks away they made it back in no time flat.

Nicor's stomach growled the entire way.

Pyro was in the living room when they entered. He

glanced up from his laptop and broke out into a wide grin when he saw their bags of food.

"Breakfast is here!" he called out.

Cacus and Daevas came running down the passage at the mention of food.

"Ooh, smells good," Cacus groaned.

"Heaven," Daevas agreed. "I'll get serviettes."

Nicor and Oriax placed everything on the table and started to unpack the bags. Pyro went to grab some plates. Unable to wait, Nicor grabbed his roll, fresh pineapple and orange juice, his coffee then settled down to eat.

He needed food, a shower and bed and in that order.

Nicor wanted to call Jordan to see if he could spend some time with his mate, but he needed shut eye. Jordan probably wasn't even back in Sydney yet. Though Nicor also had some research to do. He knew next to nothing about being demisexual, and the last thing he wanted to do was hurt or offend his mate in any way. But that would have to wait until his brain wasn't filled with the need for sustenance and sleep.

"Adze not here?" Oriax asked around a mouthful of food.

"Nah, stayed behind." Pyro shrugged and gave them a look. "I'm not expecting him anytime soon. You know how he gets in these kinds of situations."

The room fell into silence.

Nicor sat back and patted his stomach once he finished. He felt sufficiently full and had no desire to move. All his body wanted to do was curl up in bed and sleep. Staying in the chair would probably not be comfortable, though. Nicor's bed called him but he wasn't ready to leave his packmates yet.

He needed their company.

"We did good today guys." Pyro broke the silence. "Hopefully this will be over soon and we can head home."

Nicor's stomach dropped and all that food wasn't sitting well anymore. He didn't want to go home. Not yet. Not until he'd had a chance to actually get to know his mate. Jordan's soft smile, his uncertainty, called to Nicor's protective instincts. His mate expected rejection, and Nicor didn't want Jordan to think that would happen.

Everyone else nodded. Nicor got it. He really did. They missed home. Their normal beds. Their stuff. Normally he'd be agreeing right there with them. Not today though.

"I'm heading to bed for a few hours." Nicor threw his rubbish in the bin then made his way to his room.

The hot water felt amazing on his skin as he stood in the shower. He was exhausted, though, so he didn't hang around. Nicor crawled naked into the cool sheets. One of life's little pleasures after a hot shower.

Nicor stared at his phone for several moments before finally gathering the courage to type out a simple text.

. . .

HEADING TO SLEEP NOW, was a long night. Would love to see you this afternoon if you're free. Have a nice day. Nik.

NICOR SWITCHED the phone on silent then placed it on the wireless charging pad he had on his bedside table.

Rolling over, Nicor pulled the dooner up to his chin, hugged a pillow close, and closed his eyes. Sleep took him immediately.

THE PING of Jordan's phone let him know he'd received a message. He stopped packing the car and glanced at his phone. His smile was instant when he saw who it was from. He didn't bother replying then as the message said Nik was going to bed, he'd reply later. Jordan shoved his phone back in his pocket and went back to packing his car. The sooner he left, the sooner he could see Nik again.

It took Jordan less than an hour to finish packing the house up before he was on his way home. He stopped at a little café in the valley to grab a to-go coffee and croissant then started his drive back to the Big Smoke.

Traffic was light thankfully, probably because it was mid-week. If he'd been on a Sunday or Monday, the traffic conditions would be vastly different.

He arrived home late morning and Jordan sighed as

he waited for his garage door to open. He was glad to be home and sad all at the same time.

Jordan wondered if he should message Nicor, and then figured against it, he'd give him a couple more hours, as his mate was probably still sleeping off the hunt from the night before. He didn't even know what it was exactly they were in town hunting. No one had mentioned that to him and he hadn't thought to ask. Maybe he should have.

He took his time to unpack his car. His house and studio were climate controlled, unlike his garage. All his completed works, he left to the side in the living room, as he'd take them to Mandy in a day or so when he finalised the last couple. They were almost done as it was.

Jordan grabbed a snack, then locked himself in his studio for the rest of the morning. He needed to concentrate to get the last little details done on these paintings. And if it helped him forget his mate was no longer by his side, even better.

CHAPTER TEN

Adze stared down at the piece of shit incubus handcuffed to the sole chair in their interrogation room. It had been bolted to the floor. Made certain...*situations* easier. A drain was recessed into the floor between the two front legs of the chair. Also making certain situations easier. Like clean up.

The room was brick with only one way in or out. Adze never liked this room. He didn't like what it represented and hated having to be in here. Having a mate who had been tortured, Adze was having difficulty reconciling what he was about to do. Years later, Archie still had nightmares about what had happened to him. Adze supposed a small saving grace was that the incubus wouldn't have to live for too long with what they did to him. He doubted the creature would see the day out. Not that that made what they were doing any less reprehensible. But he wouldn't ask someone else to do what he wasn't willing to do himself. That was the way he worked with his team, and this was no different.

"Tell us what we want to know and this will be over nice and quick," Marcus said. He was the company's Sydney interrogator. Adze had witnessed Marcus at work several times in the last decade. And every time he saw it, he hoped it would be the last time. Once again, though, he found himself standing next to this man.

"Fuck off." The incubus spat at their feet.

It always started this way. Adze shook his head. They were all so tough when they were placed in that chair. Shit changed fast once Marcus really got started.

"That, my friend, was the wrong answer." Marcus moved lightning fast.

The punch Marcus delivered to the incubus's face was so fast, Adze nearly missed it. The incubus' head flung back with the movement and he cried out in pain. Adze never had any trouble reconciling this part of the torture. It was what came later that often ate away at him little by little.

The door opened behind them and an assistant to Marcus' wheeled a small metal trolley in with a cloth draped over the top. The person parked the trolley next to Marcus then walked right back out of the room, the door closing with a sound of finality behind him.

The incubus never took his eyes from the trolley, his Adam's apple bobbing every time he swallowed, the sound loud in the small room. Sweat beaded on his forehead, and the bruise from where Marcus had clocked him earlier was already starting to show. Adze had to hand it to the guy though. He hadn't said a word.

Yet.

Marcus pulled the cloth away and tucked it into his pocket. The reveal showed a number of gleaming silver medical and construction tools, and to Adze's surprise, what looked like an iPod and a Bluetooth speaker. Adze had seen some of the instruments in play before, and he cringed internally at the thought of them being used again. There were a few though, that he'd never seen before and really didn't want to know their uses. He was also mildly curious about the iPod and speaker.

"One last chance," Marcus said as he picked up a pair of pliers. "Tell us the details of the kidnapping and slavery ring and my friend here"—he nodded toward Adze—"will kill you nice and quick and send your soul to hell faster than I can leave this room. Stay silent and I get to have my fun with you until you talk. By the time I'm through, you'll be begging for death."

The incubus spat at Marcus once more. This time right in his face. That took some serious guts... or stupidity. Adze leaned toward the latter at this point. Marcus pulled out the cloth from his pocket and wiped the spittle away.

"I'm going to enjoy this," Marcus said in a sing-song voice, too low for it to be interpreted as anything other than creepy. He walked around behind the incubus, grabbed his hand and forced one finger out away from the others.

Marcus paused for a moment then glanced up at Adze. The incubus looked as surprised as Adze felt at the stoppage in play. His chest rose and fell in quick bursts, the incubus' breathing giving away his state of mind more than anything. The incubus would probably hyperventilate if Marcus played with him for too long.

"Would you mind pressing play?" Marcus asked him, calm as ever, then nodded towards the tray of instruments.

Adze was slightly worried about what he was about to find. He picked up the iPod and had to bite his bottom lip to stop himself from laughing out loud or showing any kind of amusement. The incubus watched his every move, sweat beading on his forehead. No need to break the atmosphere they had going for them.

On the iPod there was one playlist, entitled 'Happy Fun Times Playlist of Doom'. Adze clicked into the playlist and cringed.

Talk about torture.

There in front of him was every annoying song he could think of plus a few extra. There was an original hamster dance, Baby Shark, the Frogger song—the list just went on. Adze wasn't sure how long *he'd* last in this room if Marcus insisted on this being played all day. There were several tracks of the same songs within the playlist and the whole thing was set on repeat. Someone had obviously set things up before they'd brought the trolley in.

"I really hope you enjoy this," Adze said to the incubus as he pressed play. Their prey was in for one hell of an afternoon.

Sound blared from the speaker and the incubus flinched.

The incubus started thrashing, trying to escape. Where did he think he could go? Adze stared down at their captive sup with a grin. Considering all four limbs were handcuffed to the chair and it was bolted to the floor, he wouldn't get far. If he thought he could get out of the chair and past Adze, he had another thing coming.

Marcus gripped a fingernail with the pliers and pulled the nail clean away.

Screams filled the room, mingling with the sounds of the most atrocious music known to man, Marcus making his way through the fingers on the left hand one by one. Before every nail Marcus gave the incubus the chance to talk, but the sup refused to answer. Adze had hoped the nail-pulling would be enough. Otherwise Marcus would move to more extreme measures. Knowing his Archie had endured torment at the hands of a sociopath made using these methods harder and harder for Adze. Effective, yes. Double standard, also yes.

Sups *could* handle more damage. That was why the hellhounds were needed to fight them. Normal didn't work. Plus, their thinking wasn't so... *human.* Before, Adze wouldn't even question the methods. Had he gone soft? No. Maybe Adze's thinking had changed because his mate was human.

When all the nails were out, the incubus still hadn't said anything. It almost made Adze wonder if there was a compulsion spell weaved over him.

Marcus saw the look on his face and shook his head. "No spells. We checked."

"Okay."

Baby Shark filled the room, making the incubus jerk and groan, "Will you please shut the damn music off?"

Adze turned it up louder. If he had to listen to the music, everyone did. Marcus twisted a finger, the snap obvious by the tilt of the digit but the music had covered up the sound. The incubus spat on them again.

Marcus pulled out a torch.

Shit was about to get real fast.

Blood dripped in a steady stream onto the concrete floor beneath the chair and trickled down into the drain. Burnt flesh and piss mingled with the bloody scent in the room and made for one *very* unpleasant aroma.

Adze was about at his breaking point due to the music and he was free to leave whenever he wanted. Surely their dear enemy captive had to be close to breaking. The incubus sobbed quietly where he sat, snot and tears running down his face. He'd long ago screamed himself hoarse.

Marcus stood and took a step back, surveying his handiwork. He winked at Adze, then reached out and turned off the music.

Silence fell on the room, apart from the continued sobs from their guest.

Marcus got into the incubus' space and crowded him. "Are you ready to tell us what we want to know yet?"

The incubus ignored them, head down, chin against his marked chest as he cried. Adze and Marcus waited patiently, neither of them saying anything as they stood there and watched the pitiful sight before them.

"Wha..." The incubus swallowed several times, trying to get some lubrication back into his throat. It probably wouldn't help. Adze figured with the way the sup sounded, he probably damaged something with all his screaming. "What... do you want... to know?"

"Everything," Adze replied.

The incubus nodded and quietly started to talk.

JORDAN HAD HONESTLY worried when Nik walked out of his house and had to go hunt. They had just started to build something as Nik the hellhound, to not know his person half created unease and tension within Jordan. But his hound had been attentive as a hound, so maybe Jordan could believe in the person too. He thought long and hard about what he wanted to reply to Nik's message from that morning before finally sending the text.

HOW ABOUT A LATE LUNCH? Say 1:30-2:00? I know a great place. Let me know. If I don't hear from you before then, I'll assume you're still asleep.

. . .

Message sent, Jordan shoved his phone in his pocket, it was already closing in on midday, he knew he wasn't giving Nik much time, but Jordan was hungry and didn't want to eat without giving Nik the opportunity to join him. He grabbed a cuppa to try and tide him over for now and then headed back to his studio to finish working on his latest piece.

The stretched piece of canvas held a lot of signature Jordan. Traditional aboriginal with a twist. Like him. Seeing it nearly completed sent his brain into overdrive. The desire to finish hit him hard and he was mixing paints to get the colours right before he could even think about it. The brush teased him with its flair of bristles and coat of colour. He twisted the brush, enjoying the flair and lifted it the canvas.

Bold sun-yellow flew across his painting.

Joy. Life. Warmth.

His phone buzzing in his pocket broke Jordan out of his concentration. Jordan made a face and looked back at his canvas. How rude of it to interrupt him when he was so close to finishing. He ignored the buzz and went back into his space of colour. One final stroke and Jordan stepped back to make sure he was happy with the results. He breathed a heavy sigh of relief when he liked what he saw. That didn't always happen. Now it only had to dry.

Jordan placed his brush in the jar of turps, his used pallet on the workbench and pulled his phone out of his pocket, uncaring if he got paint on his clothes. Paint clothes were supposed to be messy.

. . .

Lunch sounds great. Let me know where and when.

Jordan blinked a couple of times. His eyes were a little dry from staring at his canvas for what felt like hours on end. Who... Nik! It was his Nik saying he wanted lunch. Jordan checked the time at the top of his phone then swore when he saw that it was ten past one. He quickly typed back. Would Nik the human be mad? Would he not respond? Jordan lost himself in his art so often it had been a bone of contention in the past. He hoped his mate would be okay with his late reply.

Café Amici in 30?

He didn't have to wait long. As soon as he sent the message, a text bubble with three dots appeared under his message, letting him know that Nik was typing a response already.

See you there.

Jordan sent a little thumbs up emoji as he was the least cool person that he knew, shoved his phone back in his pocket then rushed to clean up. He had to clean his brushes and palette off, as paint was a bitch if left to dry on his instruments and this painting was done. No more tooling around and making it look worse because he wouldn't stop fussing. Looking at his hands and arms, a shower wouldn't go astray either *and* a change of clothes.

Presentation mattered, *especially* for the first date with one's mate.

It was a good thing the café he suggested wasn't far from his place. Jordan often stopped in and grabbed some takeaway on his way home from the gallery, or called up and placed an order if he was working from home. The café did sensational pastas and pastries as well as paninis and pizzas in the evenings. The coffee was bloody delicious as well.

A whimper escaped from him and Jordan's stomach growled, reminding him to get going if he wanted to see his mate. Right, right. It was going to be his quickest shower known to mankind. He had to at least try to be on time for his mate...Jordan checked the time. At least *close* to on time. If not for Nik, then who?

JORDAN WALKED into the restaurant only ten minutes late. He scanned the tables, half of which were still full with people eating and drinking. It wasn't hard to spot Nik, the man stood out as easily as his hound did. Six and god knew what foot frame, wide shoulders, short brown hair and what looked like a five o'clock shadow—the man was *pretty*.

There was no other word for it. Jordan hadn't gotten to appreciate it when the hellhounds had taken over his Hunter Valley home. Now he could.

Nik's face lit up when he spotted Jordan making his way through the other patrons to the table where he sat. The happiness there shone so hard Jordan wondered if Nik thought he was going to stand him up. His expression gave that impression. Nik's smile almost split the man's face. His hound didn't have their memories together so it really was starting over for them. A piece of Jordan ached at the loss of their time already spent together.

"I'm so sorry I'm late," he said as he neared the table.

Nik stood to greet him, he reached then stopped and dropped his hands. "It's okay. I understand you're busy."

"Apparently when I paint, I like to get a lot on myself. That shit takes forever to clean off," Jordan explained.

He shrugged out of his light jacket and placed it on the back of the chair before taking a seat.

Nik sat opposite him and they both sat there grinning like idiots for several seconds before Nik cleared his throat.

"So, what's good here?" he asked.

"Everything." Jordan shrugged when Nik squinted. It was the truth. "I've yet to have a bad meal. There aren't a lot of places I've eaten at over the years I can say that about."

Nik gave him another brilliant smile. "Challenge accepted."

"You can't possibly eat everything off the menu."

"Have you seen me eat?"

The image of Nik the hound wolfing down dinner

popped in his head, making Jordan laugh. "Okay, I take it back. You could."

"Why are you laughing?" Nik offered the shyest smile Jordan had ever seen. A man looking like his hound shouldn't be able to do that. It was illegal. It almost made Jordan's fingers itch for some charcoal.

Jordan cleared his throat. "I remember how a certain *hound* was always impatient to eat and gobbled up his food."

"Oh." Nik's gaze dropped momentarily.

That ache came back. "Sorry."

"No, don't apologize." Nik reached for him again but paused.

"It's okay." Jordan offered his hand. "Hand-holding is nice. So is cuddling."

"I want to know all about our time together. It frustrates me I can't remember."

Jordan smiled back this time. "You mean like how you liked to pee on my fourth bush from the back?"

"Well, that's helpful," Nik laughed.

Jordan shrugged and picked up his menu with his free hand then put it straight back down again. He already knew what he was going to order. As soon as he'd replied to Nik's message, Jordan knew exactly what he wanted for lunch. He'd then proceeded to forget everything when he worked. Now that he was here, smelling all the enticing aromas of the place, his mouth salivated for their pasta.

The restaurant, even though only half full at this time of day, sounded like it was full. Cutlery clattered against crockery, people chatted with vigour among their friends or acquaintances. Laughter scattered through the room, and to the side in the open-air kitchen, chefs yelled back and forth. The sizzle of food joined the sounds of the rest of the place. Jordan loved the atmosphere here, he'd never tire of it.

"Would you like to split a garlic bread?" Jordan asked. He knew people tended to stay away from garlic when on a date, but Jordan had no plans on kissing Nik today, or any time in the near future really, so he didn't feel the normal rule applied to either of them.

"Oh, hell yeah," Nik replied enthusiastically. "Garlic bread is probably one of the best things ever invented."

"I might have to agree with you there." Jordan chuckled. Like hound, like human.

A server came over and introduced himself. "Can I start you gentlemen off with some drinks and bread today?"

"Can we get a garlic bread to share?" Jordan asked. "And I'll take a glass of your house Chianti, thanks."

"I'll take a Great Northern if you have it, thanks."

"Are you ready to order? Or would you like a few more minutes while I get your drinks?" the server asked.

Jordan glanced over to see if Nik was ready or not.

"I'm good to go if you are?" Nik said.

Jordan nodded.

"We may as well order our mains now. Can I please have the Penna alla Boscaiola?"

"Very good choice." The server turned to Jordan. "And for you?"

"I'll take the Linguini Amatriciana. Thanks."

"Very well. I'll get these orders placed. Your food shouldn't be too long. I'll be right back with your drinks."

"Thanks," Nik replied.

The waiter walked away and slipped behind the counter, leaving them to their date. Now what? More talk about their time at Hunter Valley? Though the public space would be precarious.

"So," Jordan said into the silence that fell over their table. "You guys have a good night? Or no?"

"Yeah, we caught a break. Finally found the incubus bastard that we've been hunting for months."

Jordan flinched at Nik's wording. He knew it wasn't aimed at him, but still. Also, probably not the best public conversation either. He needed to calm down and stop being so nervous. This was his mate. He could believe in his mate, right?

"Oh yeah? That's great news." His voice came out a little flatter than he meant it to.

"Yeah, Pyro and Oriax cornered him in the Botanic Gardens this morning in the middle of attempting to kidnap another woman." Nik's voice had lowered, obviously not wanting to be overheard. "You flinched?"

Or maybe not. Most people would've ignored the elephant.

"It's hard. Another"—Jordan gestured to himself—"like *me*."

"I'm sorry." Nik paused, his brows coming together. "I'll find a better way to talk about the hunt."

"Thanks." Jordan squeezed Nik's hand and his

hound's smile came back. So the smile was his hound happy in *human*. "So, what now?"

Nik paused and waited while their drinks were delivered. Jordan picked up his glass and took a sip of his wine. The fruity flavour was pleasing to his pallet, helped take the edge off. He relaxed and focused on his mate. This was about them. He fervently hoped like hound, like human was consistent. Jordan already loved the hound Nik. Hopefully he could find that connection with the human side of his mate.

The amber liquid frothed slightly in the bottle as Nik drank his beer. He smiled—that smile—was pretty as Jordan's hound.

Nik sat for a minute, a thoughtful expression on his face, before he continued, "Adze is currently with... *our suspect*. Hopefully, tonight, we'll have a lead on where their base of operations is and we can go in and dismantle the damn thing."

"Sounds like you have another long night ahead of you."

"Yep." Nik took another drink of his beer. "How about you? What have you been up to since coming back from the Hunter Valley?"

"Nothing too exciting. Finishing off some pieces for my next exhibition."

Nik sat up straighter at that. "How is that not exciting? When's your show? And where?"

Jordan shrugged. He'd never liked boasting about himself in the past, now was no different. "I've got a gallery downtown. Once the pieces I finished today are completely dry, I'll drop them off. Then Mandy, my manager, and I can go through and arrange them how I want. The show isn't for a couple of months."

First for the city council art project and then the trip to Hunter Valley, Jordan had pushed back the opening day. Jordan picked up his wine and took another sip, trying hard not to fidget under his mate's scrutiny.

"Sounds interesting?"

Jordan shrugged. "It's been in the pipeline for a while now. Mandy wanted to murder me when I stole you away to the Hunter Valley, and delayed the opening a second time in as many weeks."

"Stole feels like a strong word."

"True, technically I adopted you, so it was a rescue mission? Of course Mandy only knows I wanted more time to work on my projects, so she doesn't know that."

The arrival of their garlic bread interrupted Nik's sputtering and the scent of it had Jordan's mouthwatering for a bite.

"Ohhh. This smells delicious," Nik said as he reached for a slice. "What do you mean you adopted me?"

"Since no one claimed you as their missing dog, I had to adopt you to get you away from the surgery." Jordan shrugged and bit into the bread as his mate worked through several expressions.

"I'm not sure how I feel about you owning me," Nik said finally.

"Technically I adopted the hound. So more like I'm your doggy daddy."

Nik choked on his piece of bread and grabbed for

his beer. Jordan grinned, his eyes locking with his mate's as he swallowed. He took another bite into the garlic-y bread of goodness, groaning. Nik squinted, looking an awful lot like his ears perked up and he was trying to figure Jordan out—much like his hound.

The bread was hard and crunchy on the outside and soft and fluffy on the inside. Carbs like this didn't count. The amount of garlic with the bread had the perfect balance. Just the way a good garlic bread should be. The flavours burst on Jordan's tongue as he took his next bite. Talk about perfection. Only cake topped carby goodness. He motioned for Nik to join in.

"This is so good," Nik mumbled around a mouth full of food.

Jordan grinned. If Nik thought this was good, he was in for a real treat when they got their mains.

Their server reappeared at their side to clear the empty board for the garlic bread. "Can I interest you gentlemen in another round?"

Jordan glanced at his almost empty glass and nodded in agreement. "Yes, thank you, that would be lovely."

Nik also agreed and the server hustled off to his next table.

"So, do you follow any sports?" Nik asked.

"I love my NRL. Sydney Roosters all the way."

"Is that because they won for the last two years? Or were you a fan before that?"

Jordan scowled. "I've been following them since inception."

"Oh yeah?" Nik asked. "When was that?"

Jordan lowered his voice and glanced around to make sure no one would overhear him. "Nineteen oh eight."

Nik looked shocked for a second before he chuckled. "A long-time fan then, a bit like me."

"What about you?" Jordan asked.

"I'm a Melbourne boy, which means AFL all the way."

"Let me guess." Jordan grinned wide. "The Melbourne Demons."

Laughter burst from Nik as he grabbed his near-empty bottle of beer and finished it off. "What gave it away?"

"You'd have to be a long-time fan of theirs in order to still barrack for them. They haven't won a premiership in a bloody long time."

"Since nineteen sixty-four. The longest-running team to have not won a premiership. We beat St. Kilda by two years."

Their meals were delivered then, along with their second round of drinks.

Jordan wanted to pick up his fork and dig in, instead he lifted his wine glass and hovered it over the table.

"To the Melbourne Demons, may they forever continue to break the hearts of their fans, and may the Roosters continue to reign supreme."

Nik laughed loudly, picked up his beer, and clinked it with Jordan's wine glass.

"Next year will be our year," Nik said as he picked up his fork.

"Wishful thinking," Jordan said, pretending to cough to cover his words.

Nik chuckled and shook his head then glanced down at his large bowl filled to the brim with pasta.

"Thank you for suggesting this place. Everything has been amazing so far, and I see no reason that this won't follow trend."

"You're welcome. I'm glad you could make it."

"Anything to spend time with my *mate*."

Jordan took his first bite and closed his eyes as the flavours of bacon and tomato mingled in his mouth with the remnants of the Chianti. The heat of the chili tingled on his tongue.

"Though maybe you want to be alone with your food?"

"Maybe a minute or two. If you don't mind."

Nik's rumbly laughter filled his ears.

"So FULL." Nik groaned and pushed his bowl back towards the centre of the table. "I couldn't eat another thing."

The hound then proceeded to contradict himself and pick up his third beer to take a sip.

"Are you sure?" Jordan asked. "They make homemade chocolate croissants on premises here."

"Oh my god, you're trying to kill me." Nik patted his stomach. "Maybe give me ten minutes then I should be good to go."

Jordan shook his head and chuckled. He'd only made it halfway through his pasta. He'd get the rest to take away so he could warm it up for dinner tonight. Nik had somehow managed to finish his off. No wonder the man was full as a goog. One more thing the man and the hound had in common.

The restaurant had slowly emptied around them, new patrons arriving the later it got. At no time, however, were they the only ones in there. This place was super popular and had been for quite some time.

Jordan finished off his fourth glass of wine and looked at the man sitting opposite him. He'd been pleasantly surprised by how easy their interaction had gone today. There'd never been that uncomfortable silence when you didn't know what to say next. They'd just talked. Getting to know one another. It had been nice.

Nik glanced at his watch and winced.

Jordan looked at his own and blinked. Was it really five o'clock?

"Where the hell has the afternoon gone?" he asked.

"No idea. But I had a wonderful time." Nik smiled.

"Yeah. Me too," Jordan agreed.

"I should probably make a move, though. Need to get home and find out what the plan for tonight is going to be." Nik raised his hand and signalled for the check.

Jordan's stomach suddenly roiled at the thought of the hell hounds finishing their job, then packing up and leaving. That wasn't what Jordan wanted. He hoped that Nik might choose to stay, so they could continue to get to know one another. Only time would tell if Nik wanted that as well.

"Do you live far?" Nik asked him as he checked the

bill, then tapped his card against the portable machine the server held.

"Not far, why?" he asked.

They stood from the table and started shrugging into their jackets.

"Would you permit me to walk you home?" Nik asked. "I understand if you would prefer I didn't."

Jordan nodded. "I'd like that, thank you." He paused for a moment then continued, "It's a shame we didn't get a chance to spend any time here before."

"Wish I could remember it," Nik said as they walked towards the door. Jordan felt the warmth of Nik's hand on his lower back, even through his clothes as they left the restaurant. "Maybe if we talk about it enough I will."

"Shame you can't remember. I rather enjoyed my time with your hound."

"Really?" Nik waggled his brows and grinned. "Because you were my doggy daddy?"

Jordan groaned.

"You said it first."

"I take it back. I take it back! Yeah, you know, until I'd wake up with a face full of dog snot from you sneezing on me."

Nik roared with laughter. "Oh my god," he said between his sputtering. "I'm so sorry."

"Sure you are," Jordan said with a wink.

Nik chuckled. "I do like to play games."

"You said that before. You like gaming? *Oof.*"

The wind had picked up and the temperature had dropped in the time they'd been inside. Jordan pulled his jacket closer around him and shoved his hands in his pockets. If it had been Nik the hound he'd lean in for a cuddle, but it didn't feel right, not yet. It would hurt if Nik expected more than Jordan could give him yet so it was better if he didn't send confusing signals... but it was hard.

"Gaming?" Jordan prompted again.

"Right, I prefer FPSs most, uh, that's first-person shooters, but I usually have some kind of game going. It's how I relax."

"By shooting things up?"

Nik shrugged. "It's a different kind of challenge. Half-Life 2 hooked me bad when it first came out. Then you got COD, uh, the Call of Duty franchise, C.S. Go, wait, that's Counter-Strike Global Offensive, the Overwatch games...well, let's say there are a lot. Some are better solo, some you need a team. There are some heavy competitions that happen with some of the games but my duty here has kept me from going to anything like building a team so we can try to compete at TI, uh, I mean The International...I'm boring you, aren't I?"

"No! No!" Jordan shook his head, hair bouncing around. He should've tied it back. "You were so quiet as a hound, and I did most of the talking at dinner, it's nice to see you so happy and energetic. No wonder you crawled in my lap when I played on the iPad. You'll show me sometime?"

Nik chuckled. "Yeah, I'd like that."

They fell into a comfortable silence as they walked along the footpath home. Nicor never once took his hand from the middle of Jordan's back, despite the streets being crowded with the afternoon commuters desperately trying to get home as fast as they could. The warm, solid presence of his mate felt good against him. Before Jordan knew it, they arrived at his home all too fast.

"This is me," he said, coming to a stop in front of his townhouse.

"Well, thank you for today. I had a wonderful time." Nik flashed that beautiful smile of his. "I can't wait to do it again."

"Me too."

Jordan held his breath as Nik leaned down like he was about to kiss him. No. Oh no. He wasn't ready for that step and the date had been going so well. Seconds away from taking a step back and pushing them apart, Jordan's mate surprised him by turning his head and giving Jordan a light peck on the cheek. Sweet. Innocent. Nothing like he expected. None of the energy read like lust, though he could tell his mate wanted him. *Affection*. That's what it was. A kiss showing his mate's affection. Nik quickly straightened, giving some space. His mate *had* listened. Possibly?

"Uh..."

Nik offered one of those shy smiles. "I hope that was okay? I got a little ahead of myself. Sorry if I overstepped. Just say so. I wasn't sure how best to show I enjoyed our date. I should've read up more or asked."

They were interrupted by the ringing of Nik's phone before Jordan could answer.

"Sorry," he muttered. Nik pulled the phone out and glanced at the screen. "I need to get this."

Jorden nodded and took a step back to give Nik his privacy.

Nik, however, reached out and grabbed Jordan's hand, squeezing it gently as he answered the call.

"Hey, how'd you go?" Nik asked then fell silent.

Jordan's hearing was good, but he tried not to eavesdrop. He did hear words like "assault" and "rescue" and assumed Adze had gotten the information needed. If so, that meant his hound would be on the hunt again soon. His mind raced with all the "what ifs" that came after. They had one date. Only one.

Nik finished up the call quick, then turned back to Jordan. "I have to go."

Jordan had known that the second the phone rang. "Be safe."

"Thank you for a wonderful afternoon. I look forward to being able to do it again with you soon."

"I do too," Jordan said, and meant it. He'd had a great afternoon getting to know Nik and wanted more. Would they get more? The hound hadn't been much different than the man. Kind. Gentle. A little pushy but always aware. "The kiss on the cheek was nice, as long as it stays there. It was *affectionate*. Hugs are welcome too."

"Good to know." Nik squeezed his hand one last time before he let go. His mate turned and walked off at a fast pace. "I'll let you know how it goes!"

Jordan stood there and watched as his mate disappeared around the corner. He sighed and unlocked his door. Looked like he was in for a long night of worry. Shame he didn't have a large black hound to keep him company and snuggle on the lounge with.

Funny things, hearts.

CHAPTER ELEVEN

Nicor made his way to the downtown building that held their offices. Every major city in Australia had one now. They all consisted of on-ground resources and the people to help with tracking and the extermination of the sups the hellhounds were tasked with hunting down.

Their main contact, Matti, worked out of their Melbourne office. She had decided there needed to be more permanent bases throughout Australia and managed the whole empire. It was times like this that reminded Nicor of that. Adze should really give her another raise. It wasn't often they actually stepped foot in the offices, preferring to work from home, but this was a special case.

Nicor listened to the god-awful lift music as he ascended to the ninth floor. When the door finally opened and Nicor stepped out, he stopped short at the utter chaos surrounding him. He hadn't expected the multitude of people scurrying across the place or the phones ringing and not being answered.

The receptionist who usually sat out front and dissuaded anyone who wasn't supposed to be there was even missing.

Nicor dodged around the chaotic people scrambling every which way to the large meeting room they had in the back. The blinds were up and through the glass windows he could see they had a large cluster of people talking with the rest of his pack. A number of them Nicor had never seen before.

All eyes turned to him as he stepped inside the room.

"Did I miss anything?" he asked, choosing an empty seat next to Daevas and sitting his ass down.

"Not much. Haven't started yet. We're waiting on a few others before we begin," Adze replied then he continued his chat with some chick with bright purple hair and a nose ring. Several more women sat on the opposite side of the table, all closely watching the woman talking to Adze.

Nicor turned to the rest of his pack. "What do we know?"

"It's not as easy as us just going in there and getting the bad guy," Pyro said.

"Why the hell not?" Nicor asked.

"Because there isn't only one bad guy," Oriax answered quickly.

"We've known all along the mermaids were behind this." Daevas said. "We just didn't know how many there were. Well, not only are there a larger number than we anticipated, they've also teamed up with some other sups for protection."

"Fuck," Nicor swore.

"You got that right," Oriax said. "There's also god knows how many victims on site. Plus we need to be able to track those that they've already sold off."

"It's a frickin' nightmare. Give me a good ole fashioned Nephilim murderer any day," Pyro said then paused, seeming to think about his remark twice. "Not that I want people to get killed or anything."

They all burst out into laughter.

Pyro shook his head. "You know what I mean."

"Yeah," Nicor agreed. "Unfortunately, as technology advances, so do the fuck-knuckles we have to hunt down, making it harder for us to do our jobs." Nicor looked around the room, then turned back to his team. "Who are all these people?"

The others shrugged. Okay, so not everyone had been introduced yet. Hopefully that would be happening soon.

More men and women filed into the room as they waited. Oriax stilled, watching the unknowns warily with a persistent growl. Cacus nudged him but he shook his head. Yeah, Nicor got it, they were all mad about needing to call in help. Seemed like they couldn't catch a break these days and were traveling nonstop, some baddie sup making problems after another. Australia was a lot of ground to cover.

Look at how long it took for Nicor to find his mate and they'd both been here a long time. Nicor shifted in his seat, noticing the deepening hue of gold in the room. Orange-hued light filtered through the windows as the sun outside started to set. It would be dark in another hour or so. Part of Nicor whined, his hound, wanting to snuggle with his mate. This time of day was meant for cuddling. The flash of something, a partial memory of sitting on a porch guarding his mate, caught him off guard and had Nicor rubbing his chest.

Was Jordan missing him right now? Like how Nicor missed his mate? It had been so hard leaving Jordan on his doorstep. Something in his mate's expression hurt him, like he was missing something or had done something wrong. The loneliness there called to him. All he had wanted to do was comfort his mate. Though he'd actually been going in for a *lick*. Nicor had been relieved to know he hadn't screwed up with the kiss to Jordan's cheek. His brain took over before he could stop himself. Luckily his human brain kicked in.

Had he given Jordan *doggy* kisses during their escape? Had Jordan felt alone then? Something deep inside Nicor said *no*. Too bad he couldn't remember any of it.

Adze cleared his throat and all the chatter in the room died, almost instantly. It was almost funny, if the situation wasn't so serious.

All eyes fell on Adze as he started to speak. "Thanks everyone for coming, and on such short notice. I understand what a pain it was for many of you to drop what you were doing and to get here. I appreciate it. Now, to the matter at hand.

"I've asked you all here today as we have a situation that is unlike anything the sup community has dealt with before. As you all know, my team is called in to take care of and clean up any sup that thinks this world is their own personal playpen to do anything they like within."

Several people in the room glanced at Nicor and the others, before turning their attention back to Adze.

"We came across a situation in Melbourne last year, where a small group of mermaids were working in conjunction with an incubus and kidnapping women to sell them into slavery."

Several people growled at Adze's pronouncement, however they quietened down just as quickly.

"When we got too close to shutting down the Melbourne operation they packed up and moved locations. We got word through the police about a month ago that it looked like the same people had set up shop here in Sydney, but on a much larger scale.

"My team and I have been on the ground since then trying to track these sups down and put an end to this once and for all.

"Last night we finally got the breakthrough we needed. Two of my men"—Adze nodded in the pack's direction—"managed to locate and apprehend the incubus the mermaids had been working with. He was in the process of kidnapping yet another woman. This afternoon the incubus gave up the location of the headquarters of the operation."

Adze pressed a button and the ceiling mounted projector lit up the blank wall behind him.

Someone close to the switches flicked the lights off.

A large schematic drawing of the building covered

the wall, which Nicor assumed was the headquarters for this mob. Something about it was odd.

Several people around the room gasped then started gesturing animatedly at the schematics, angrily hissing at the others standing next to them.

Nicor didn't know what the big deal was. He glanced back at the building. It took him longer than it should have. Oriax whistled from beside him. Adze had to ask people to settle down and call attention back to him. He sounded way annoyed when he spoke up next.

"As you can see from plans we have available, the bastards chose to set up shop right in the middle of Circular Quay. Their property backs onto the water on one side and the Botanic Gardens on the other."

"Talk about your easy access," Daevas muttered as the room burst into angry hisses again.

"*And* easy escape," Adze said loudly over the noise. He slowly swept his gaze around the office, his big stature and glower leaving the impression he was probably going for—annoyed and hungry.

All chatter in the room died and attention was once again trained directly on their pack leader.

"According to the information we were given, they've taken over three apartments on the ground floor. There are currently six women being held within, awaiting the next auction, which is scheduled to take place tomorrow at noon."

Several people gasped. Yeah, Nicor agreed. That wasn't a whole lot of time.

"If we want any chance of getting these women back then we need to go in tonight before they disappear altogether." Adze switched to the inside building schematics. "The information about the auction has already been sent to our man in the force. He is liaising with others to try and track down the scumbags that are planning to be in attendance.

"We'll need a coordinated breach of all three apartments at once. I know it won't be easy. But we *cannot*, under any circumstances, let a single mermaid get to the water. If they do, then they're gone and free to set up shop in a different city again. We don't have anyone who can track them in the water."

"What if we had a selkie to help?" a red-headed woman asked.

"Do you know any?" Adze asked hopefully. "I wasn't aware there were any in Australia."

"Let me make a call," she replied then stepped outside the office.

"How are we supposed to negate their song?" someone asked from the back of the room.

The purple-haired chick Adze had been chatting with when Nicor arrived snorted derisively. Nicor swore he heard her mutter "Fucking wannabes" under her breath. He smiled because she was the kind of cool attitude that he liked working with on these hunts. The confidence she exuded probably matched Adze's cool exterior.

Adze grinned like the question was no big deal. "Let me introduce you to Olympia and her team." He paused for an obvious dramatic effect. "They're sirens."

Pyro whistled. "You brought out the big guns, boss. The true songstresses."

Olympia nodded in acknowledgement, then turned her golden eyes on the rest of the gathering. "Thank you. We will easily be able to deal with whatever the mermaids try and throw at us. Their songs are pale imitations compared to ours. We will give you the time you need to apprehend the sups behind this."

Adze smiled. "Thanks to you and your flock for agreeing to help."

"It is our pleasure."

Nicor glanced at the other women then, paying attention to them for probably the first time. They were all beautiful with sharp features—model-like. The kind one saw in magazines trying to sell makeup that never really worked. These ladies did. While Olympia had her bright purple hair, the others were no different. Shocks of intense blue, blonde, black, and the redhead who left to make her call. The colours were incredible. Nicor also noticed that every single one of the women had nails that had been filed to a tip.

Or maybe not.

Sirens were half-woman, half-bird. Those nails could easily be talons, and there was no way Nicor wanted to be on the receiving end of them. Over time, the sirens had evolved to be able to hide their wings and bird features when not required. Some features they couldn't hide. Like those '*nails*.'

Nicor couldn't remember the last time they'd had any dealings with sirens. They were usually a peaceful race, so the hounds had no reason to hunt them.

The woman who had stepped out to make a call

earlier came back inside, pushing her phone into her pocket as she closed the door behind her.

"How'd you go?" Adze asked.

"I have three selkies who are willing to help. I need to call them back once we're done here with the plans. They'll guard the boardwalk and, in case anyone gets through, the ocean too."

"Fantastic news. Thank you, Gemma," Adze said before continuing, "With the mermaid's song being taken out of action, and their incubus friend already taken care of, we shouldn't have any problem with rounding them up."

"What if they have back up? Surely they have someone guarding their victims," one of Olympia's flock asked.

Adze gestured towards the back of the room and the group of men that hadn't been introduced yet. "We will have our own back up. As soon as we caught our incubus, I sent a Hell runner down below for reinforcements. Thankfully the nearest entrance is only a couple of hours from here."

"I didn't know there was an entrance to Hell nearby!" one of the other women asked, looking around like the entrance was in the room with them.

Nicor shook his head.

"There's nothing to worry about, the entrance is well guarded. Nothing is getting though that shouldn't," Adze assured her, then addressed the rest of the room. "Speaking of, two teams of hounds, who were in need of some in the field training, answered the call. Tonight is the perfect opportunity for them to prove themselves."

"Glad to be here," one smaller hound said. "Team Leader Aamon of Beta Group."

"Likewise," a bulky hound said. "Team Leader Seth of Theta Group."

All the other men grinned like bloody idiots.

"Right, now that that's all sorted"—Adze clapped his hands together—"I will need my men inside each apartment as we need to be able to call forth the hellfire and send these creatures souls to the depths of Hell for all eternity. My team, and my team only, will be the ones to do this."

The room fell deadly silent at Adze's pronouncement. He glanced around the room but no one questioned him. By the looks of the other hounds this was no surprise to them, which Nicor was grateful for. The last thing he wanted was to get into a pissing match over this. They had enough on their plates and they had bigger priorities.

Nicor understood, it wasn't that the trainee hounds couldn't call forth the hellfire. They could. It was that Australia was under Adze's jurisdiction and their team was responsible for everything that happened here. They didn't want any mistakes. This was the easiest way to make sure of that.

Adze nodded then said, "There will be two sirens with two of my hounds per apartment. The other two hound teams will split evenly and join us as back up.

"We also have some lower-level angels who have agreed to come and help us with the women." Adze continued.

Three women raised their hands in greeting. Nicor

had known what these people were as soon as he laid eyes on them, their soft features and ethereal glow gave them away as far as he was concerned.

"God only knows what those poor women have been through and what they've seen." Adze shook his head, his hands fisting at his sides. "Unfortunately, we can't just call an ambulance and let them go to the hospital. They've no doubt seen and heard too much. Their memories will need to be altered slightly before they can be released home. This shouldn't take too long. The women have been through enough already, and the last thing we want to do is add to their trauma."

Nicor knew how much Adze hated needing to have any human's memories modified. None of them liked it. That was the number one reason why the hounds were so careful when they hunted. The mind was a complex organ and even the best of intentions could lead to disastrous results if not done correctly. It was better off to avoid modifying it at all costs. This situation couldn't be avoided unfortunately. Angels weren't the only sup that could modify a human's memories, but they were the best at it and had the lightest touch. That was definitely what was needed here.

"What about local authorities?" Nicor asked.

"Callum has already made a call," Pyro said. "The police are on standby and will be called in once it's clear."

"Who's Callum?" Olympia asked, her voice sounding suspicious.

"He's my mate—"

Several of the hounds at the back gasped and made

other noises, causing Pyro to glare at them due to the interruption.

He continued "—and a police detective in Melbourne. He's the one that got the tip that the operation had been moved to Sydney."

Olympia nodded, seemingly satisfied with Pyro's answer.

"Everyone know what they need to do?" Adze asked. When everyone nodded, Adze checked his watch then continued, "We'll meet at the Conservatorium of Music in four hours, at ten thirty, go over the plan one last time before we head in."

Taking that as the dismissal it was, everyone started talking and moving all at once. Nicor wasn't sure he was happy with the downtime. Waiting for the hunt was always the hardest part for him, and he didn't even have his Switch on him because of his date with Jordan—no need to freak out his mate with his gaming yet.

Maybe he could FaceTime his mate for dinner? Or talk. Nicor yearned to hear Jordan's laughter.

The sirens left as a group, the angels not far behind them. That left only the hounds in the conference room. All of them wore that young, eager look on their faces. Nicor knew that had been him once. He suspected some of the energy might be from Pyro talking about his *mate*. They spent the next ten minutes or so introducing themselves until everyone was acquainted.

"Aamon. Seth. I want to thank you and your men for coming to help out," Adze said as everyone gathered closer.

"It's our pleasure, Adze. As you said earlier, we're looking forward to getting a little field experience and testing how the team works in a non-controlled situation," Seth answered.

"Well, we're glad we could help with that." Pyro shrugged casually.

"Do you really have a mate?" Seth asked.

The rest of the newbies nodded in unison. Like bobble-heads. Nicor pushed down a laugh. They had waited longer than he thought they would.

"I do." Pyro chuckled and threw everyone under the bus. "So do Adze and Nicor."

It was like seared steak was on the menu, except it was Pyro, Nicor and Adze being grilled every which way to Sunday about meeting their mates.

"Seeing as how you're all new here, how about we all head back to the apartment and order some pizza to fuel up for tonight," Nicor suggested. Maybe food would divert their attention.

"What's pizza?" Aamon asked.

Jackpot.

Oriax laughed. "Man, do we have a treat for *you.*"

He slung his arm around Aamon's neck and walked him out of the conference room, everyone else following along behind.

Hopefully the newbie teams would be so focused on discovering pizza Nicor could slip away for a call to his mate.

Seth angled next to Nicor and shoulder bumped him. "How long did you have to wait to claim your mate?"

A hound could hope.

THEY GATHERED on the edges of the Botanic Gardens at the Conservatorium of Music. Traffic had started to slow down because of the late hour. Tomorrow, Friday, would be a different matter altogether. But tonight people were most likely already home to rest for their last workday. By the time midnight rolled around there should be fewer people on the streets and on the road.

Meaning an easier hunt for the hounds. Probably.

They split into their teams, making sure they had the right number of hounds, selkies, angels and sirens on each.

Adrenalin pumped through Nicor's veins at the prospect of what was about to happen. They were finally going to be able to put a stop to this damn smuggling ring. It had been a blight hanging over them for the past year, and for it to be finally lifting helped wash away the dreary feeling.

It didn't hurt that Nicor managed to sneak in a call to his mate. Jordan took him on a visual tour of his studio but was stingy on sharing his art. Nicor hoped he'd get the chance to stay and see it in person.

Adze patted him on the shoulder and Nicor gave him a nod in return. How did Adze handle his time away from Archie? All Nicor wanted to do was curl up in Jordan's scent and never leave. Nicor huffed then shook himself out.

Now was the time for focus.

Nicor, Adze and their team would take the first

apartment. Daevas and Oriax were on apartment two. Cacus and Pyro with their team would infiltrate apartment three. If all went to plan they'd be able to call in the police by one, two at the latest, depending on how long the angels took with their rescues.

The teams split up. The hounds needed to find some privacy within the gardens to shift. The selkies and sirens were staying in human form unless necessity required them to shift.

Sneaking up on a property in the middle of Circular Quay with eighteen hellhounds was no easy feat. It was hard enough when two of them were on a hunt, but having three groups of six, all converging on the one place, was a damn nightmare.

One or two hounds could be explained away. A dozen and a half drew attention no matter what. There were only so many shadows to hide them.

The trek to the building was slow going since they didn't want to tip their hand too soon.

The selkies had it nice and easy. They could just wander down the boardwalk and take up position on any of the numerous benches, pretending to fall asleep or look at their phones.

Once shifted, the hounds kept to the shadows as they made their way through the gardens down to Circular Quay. They came to a halt opposite the building they wanted, hidden by the trees. No humans. They had a clear path across the road to the entrance doors of the apartments in question.

Everyone in position? Adze asked.

When in hound form, only Adze could

communicate with the other pack leaders. They could then disseminate the instructions to their own packs. Nicor looked around him. The other four guys that had been assigned to them stood poised to go as soon as they were given the word. The two sirens and the angel nodded in readiness.

Good to go here, Daevas responded.

Ready here, Pyro said.

They had to wait until Olympia signalled the selkies were in position.

The buzzing of her phone sounded loud in the silence of the night. She pulled it out of her pocket, glanced at her screen, quickly tapped out a reply then shoved the phone back in her pants and nodded at Adze.

"Ready when you are."

Let's end this for good. Adze growled through their link.

Adze took the lead and headed out. Nicor was right behind him, the others close on their heels. They ducked between the parked cars on the side of the road and across the wide footpath that ran down the side of the building. When they arrived at the front door, Adze and Nicor stood poised on either side of it. The others were heading round to the side entrance that doubled as a fire exit. They would all meet inside before branching off to the individual apartments.

Olympia stepped up, dressed in a singlet, jeans that look like they could have been painted on and combat boots. She glanced once at Adze then took something else out of her pocket and went to work on the electronic lock mechanism of the front door. They last thing they wanted was to smash the large glass door and alert the entire neighbourhood.

Time stood still for Nicor as they waited for Olympia and the blue-haired siren to get them inside.

The click of the lock sounded loudly as the light above the door handle turned from red to green. Olympia held the door open with a wide smile as they made their way inside. They bypassed the elevators and mailboxes, heading down the passage to the units they were after. Olympia took up a stance in front of the door to apartment one. They waited. Moments later the others filed in from the other direction. Two more of Olympia's team took stances similar to her own, hounds poised on either side, the angels behind everyone else.

Olympia glanced down the long passage at her girls. Held up one finger, then a second, then a third. She leaned back on her left leg, lifted the right and kicked the door, next to the handle, with so much force the damn thing splintered as it crashed inside. Similar sounds filled the passage farther down as the other teams moved out, but Nicor focused on his hunt.

Adze shot through the door, quickly followed by Olympia.

The sound of glass breaking shattered the quiet, and he bounded in after his packmate.

Nicor was third into the dim apartment.

We've got a runner. I'm going after her, Adze said.

Everything happened so quick. They'd managed to take the merpeople by surprise. Men and women jumped up from where they'd been sitting, watching TV or playing what looked to be a board game at the dining room table, and yelled in alarm.

They took one look at the hounds streaming into their apartment and chose to flee.

Nicor wasn't about to let another mermaid get away. He leapt and landed on the back of some black-haired chick, tumbling them both to the ground. She screamed as Nicor bit through her flesh. Even with Nicor's fangs buried in her body she fought for her life. Nicor had bad news for her.

Glass shattered, sending shards all over. Nicor shook the woman's arm with his mouth. More yells filled the room around him. Grunts and thwacks mixed in as the two forces brawled. Nicor couldn't concentrate on anything other than the woman he had under him. Nicor didn't give a fuck that the person under him was man or woman. They would all pay for the parts they played in the slave ring.

Nicor ignored the hits the woman rained down on him. He might be a little sore later due to them, but they weren't enough to make him let go. Instead, he bit down harder and shook his head again. The woman screamed.

In a last-ditch effort, she opened her mouth, Nicor assumed to try and lure him to stop with her persuasive voice. Before she could even get the first notes out, Olympia knelt down beside them and shoved a dirty rag in the woman's mouth.

Nicor would've laughed at the complete surprise on the woman's face, if his mouth hadn't already been full.

He glanced at Olympia though and cocked a brow, well, as much as he could in hound form. Olympia shrugged and then grinned. Stuffing mouths worked just as well. Nicor couldn't argue that.

Olympia stood and placed one of her combat booted feet on the stomach of the woman, pressing down hard enough the chick grunted through the gag in her mouth.

Nicor let her go and stepped back before he shifted.

Blood covered her torso, shoulder and arm, none of that seemed to matter to her though as she stared at them with open hatred and defiance. Nicor shook his head.

"You have been sentenced to die for the part you have played in the kidnapping and sale of innocent women. Do you have anything to say before I carry out your sentence?"

Her eyes hardened, and Nicor could have sworn she spat "Fuck you" but the rag muffled it. Good riddance. It was time for her to go.

Nicor called for the bright green hellfire from within and flung it at the mermaid. It engulfed her within seconds. The dim room glowed with the green and yellow flames as her soul was ripped from her body and sent to Hell for all eternity. When the flames died out all that was left was an empty shell that looked like the woman had died of natural causes.

"Well, that was something to see," Olympia said, still staring at the husk.

"Thanks for your help." Nicor glanced around the room. As only he and Adze were allowed to call the hellfire in this apartment, they had some work to do. Nicor didn't see Adze anywhere but he wasn't worried. His leader would be somewhere close, no doubt kicking ass.

Nicor made his way over to where two hounds had a burley looking bloke trapped in a corner. The guy swung a lamp at the two hounds, who maintained enough distance not to get hurt.

"Let's end this shall we?" Nicor asked as he stepped up between the two hounds. A small ball of flicking hellfire balanced on his palm.

"You won't get us all," the guy said as he swung the lamp at them.

"Yes, we will," Nicor said. He doused the man in flame, then turned his back on him, ignored the screams and headed to the next bad guy to mete out justice.

Noticing everything was under control in here, for now, Nicor shifted back to his hound and went through the sliding glass door to find Adze. As he stepped out onto the back porch the mermaid, with flaming red hair and porcelain white skin disengaged from her battle with Adze and vaulted over the low fence. She took off down the boardwalk, a trail of blood behind her. Adze leapt the fence easily and chased after her. In this form, Nicor didn't doubt that Adze could catch her. He just hoped he did it before she reached the water.

They had the selkies out here keeping watch, but that was no guarantee that she wouldn't escape.

She was about five meters ahead of Adze when she went to round the small kiosk on the water's edge. An arm struck out from behind the small building at roughly neck height. The mermaid hit the arm bang on and was flung into the air and landed hard on her back on the paving. Johan, one of the selkies, stepped out from behind the building as first Adze, then Nicor skidded to a stop beside them.

The mermaid clutched at her throat, working to breathe but not doing so well. The selkie grabbed her by the hair and dragged her into the little space beside the shop. She tried to cry out but failed, then started kicking and scratching at Johan.

She was trapped and knew it.

Adze shifted back to human form. He looked down on the mermaid they'd chased across two states and spent countless hours hunting.

"You're a real piece of work, you know that?" Adze said as she still struggled for breath.

The mermaid simply flipped him the bird. Nicor snorted. How stupid was this chick? Then again, her life was already forfeit, she had nothing more to lose.

Adze grinned. "I don't usually enjoy this part, but tonight, I'll make an exception for you."

"I'm flattered," she rasped.

"Don't be," Adze spat. "Let her go."

"Got it!" Johan took a large step back.

Before she could say anything else, or even attempt to flee, Adze engulfed her entirely in hellfire.

Johan jumped a few more steps away. Arms windmilling slightly as he nearly ended up in the water.

"It's okay. It's contained to her. You could be standing on top of her, and it wouldn't harm you," Adze let him know. "I told you to let her go more so you wouldn't freak out."

"Huh. Well, you learn something new every day."

"That you do. Thanks for your help. That was very timely back there."

"It's what you called me in for. To stop any of them from making it to the ocean."

"Even so, I appreciate it." Adze glanced back down at the now dead mermaid and then at himself. Nicor saw the small grimace on Adze's face and knew his leader was contemplating his sudden nakedness. Adze recalled the hellfire within him, then looked at Johan. "Are you okay to take her back to the apartment while I shift? I need to get back and check on how things are going."

"No worries," Johan said then stepped forward, reached down and picked the dead mermaid up, flinging her over his shoulder. Adze shifted back to his hound form and the three of them quickly made their way down the walk and to the porch of the first apartment.

Update report, Adze said as he leapt the railing again, Nicor hot on his heels. Adze would be focused on clean-up now that their rooms were cleared and needed someone at his back.

One left to go in here boss, Daevas said. *Oriax is dealing with it now. Four women in total. The angel is currently in there with them.*

Good let me know when you're all done, Adze replied. *Pyro how's things in apartment three?*

All clear here, Adze, Pyro replied. *Had one attempt*

to flee, but he was caught before he could get to the water. Three women, all with the Angel at the moment. Shouldn't be much longer.

Glad to hear it. Let wrap things up as quickly as we can so we can call the police in to come and get the women.

They would need to dispose of any dead that weren't human first as they couldn't allow an autopsy to be performed on them.

Johan dumped the woman on the floor unceremoniously when they all re-entered the apartment.

Adze shifted back to human and grabbed up the bag one of the others had carried inside. They contained their phones and an item of clothing each. He tossed the bag to Nicor, then snatched another for himself. They both began dressing as his pack leader called the local office. Nicor took up guard near the open sliding door, it never hurt to be careful.

"How'd it go?" Matilda, the head of the Sydney office, asked with no preamble. Nicor heard her from where he was standing, and even though it was well past midnight the woman sounded alert and ready for action.

"Everything is secure here. We need removal of roughly a dozen bodies before the authorities can be brought in."

"They'll be there in five minutes," Matilda replied shortly.

"Thanks," Adze said as he hung up the phone.

Nicor glanced around the apartment. The high-end

furniture and fittings annoyed him as he doubted any of the women who were abducted by these creatures got to enjoy them. The others had piled the dead, ready for extraction.

There were four men and women in one pile and two men who had been left where they'd fallen. The two men on their own were humans and as such were the jurisdiction of the human police. Nicor didn't know if the men were there willingly or if they had been coerced by either the mermaids or the incubus to be there. It didn't matter now. They had paid the ultimate price for whatever involvement they played.

Seeing everything under control in the living room, Nicor and Adze made their way down the long, tiled passage to what Nicor assumed were the bedrooms.

The farther along the passage he walked the worse the smell became. The overwhelming scent of urine almost made him gag.

How had these poor women survived?

Adze knocked gently on one door before opening it slightly, they both glanced inside. What Nicor saw made him want to head back to the living room and kill that mermaid bitch all over again.

Three women in torn and dirty clothes sat huddled on the floor holding each other. Three pathetically thin mattresses were scattered across the floor with no blankets or pillows. Each of the women had a shackle around her left leg which was chained to a bolt that had been driven into the centre of the floor. In the corner there was a bucket, which Nicor didn't even want to think about.

The women had all coiled back when Adze opened the door. The youngest of the three was clearly crying. Christ, the girl didn't even look old enough to vote yet.

Adze put his hands up to show he meant them no harm.

"It's okay," he tried to reassure them. "We're not here to hurt you."

The women's grip on each other seemed to tighten. Not wanting to cause them any more pain or suffering, then they'd already been through so they stayed in the doorway.

"We're gonna get you out of here just as soon as we can."

One young girl whimpered as she continued to sob.

"Police and an ambulance will be here shortly, then you can go to the hospital. Your families will be contacted to let them know you've been found."

Adze stepped back and went to close the door when he heard the soft, "Thank you."

"You're very welcome. I'm going to send a colleague in shortly who will be able to help, she's a counsellor of sorts."

Adze saw the woman in the middle nod, as she rubbed her hand up and down on the youngest's back, trying to soothe her. He closed the door and stepped back. Nicor wanted to punch something or someone. He had half a mind to bring that damn mermaid bitch back to life just so he could have the pleasure of killing her all over again.

Nicor took a deep breath then let it out slowly in the hopes of trying to get his mounting anger under control.

Adze stood there for several moments next to him, breathing deeply as well, when the door to the room next to theirs opened. Christy, the Angel for their group, stepped out and gently closed the door behind her.

"There's more than just these three?" Nicor asked, motioning to the door directly behind where he and Adze stood.

Christy nodded sadly.

"How many?" Adze asked.

"Seven in this apartment. Eighteen in total."

"How are they?" Adze asked.

"They have a long road ahead of them. They've been through one hell of an ordeal. We're lucky we got here when we did."

"Will they remember anything?" Adze asked her quietly.

"Unfortunately, yes. The only thing I could obscure was the supernatural element. Everything else, faces, voices, what they've been through, remains unchanged."

Adze nodded beside Nicor. He wished it could be otherwise, but that was not allowed.

Nicor watched Adze clenched his fists, his knuckles turning white. He too wanted to hit something so badly. They'd allowed these scum to operate for far too long. Had failed too often in their hunts to track them down and put a stop to this sooner.

Christy placed her hand on Adze's shoulder and squeezed gently. "This is not your fault."

Adze didn't say anything. Nicor knew his leader

would be blaming himself for what these poor women had been though.

"I mean it Adze," Christy told him sternly, moving from his gaze to Nicor's. "This isn't your fault. Neither of yours. You are not to blame, nor are you responsible for the actions of others. This..." Christy motioned around them. "Is due to the actions of some very sick and twisted individuals. You did everything you could to bring this to an end. You and your team should be proud of the work you've done here. What we need to do is focus on the victims here and now. This is about them. Not you."

Adze nodded, Nicor knew there was just no arguing with damn angels. Not even for his pack leader.

"If you'll excuse me, I have to check on the women inside the second room now, so we can get them all to the hospital."

They stepped out of the way and let Christy do what she needed.

"Adze?" one of the sirens startled them out of his thoughts moments later.

Adze spun around to face her.

"What is it?" he asked.

"The cleaners are here."

Adze nodded. They followed the siren back down the passage and into the living room space. The cleaners were already hard at work packing up the bodies, ready for removal.

"Make sure you get any security footage from the

camera I saw in the lobby on the way in," Adze told one of the men in white coveralls.

"Already have someone working on that as we speak," he replied.

"Good to hear."

Nicor remained quiet, guarding Adze's back as they surveyed the damage. Adze looked around at the hounds who had helped to make this rescue possible, then spoke.

"Thank you for your help. You can fall back to the gardens and shift when safe. Your team leaders should be proud you all executed your tasks with precision and poise."

The four hellhounds nodded before turning and heading out the door.

"How're you holding up?" Olympia asked as she walked up beside Adze and Nicor. The other siren left with the hounds, no doubt waiting for Olympia and the rest of their team in the gardens.

"As good as can be expected." Adze shrugged. "This has been a long time coming."

"These bastards deserved what they got."

"No arguments here," Nicor agreed.

"Look me up next time you're in Sydney and find yourself in need of some help," Olympia told them.

"Thank you for everything. We couldn't have done it without you and your team."

"You would have found a way. I have no doubt."

Adze held out his hand and the two leaders shook, before Olympia turned and left the apartment as well.

The cleaners carried out the last body, then made a

thorough sweep of the apartment to make sure there was nothing left behind that could implicate the supernatural community in the slightest.

Christy walked out and joined them in the living room.

"All done?" Adze asked.

"Yeah, they're all sleeping. When they wake they won't remember any of the events of today, or anything to indicate supernatural involvement," Christy informed them.

"Thank you for all your help, along with your sisters."

"We're always here if you need us."

"Appreciate it. Hopefully we won't require your services again any time soon," Adze commented.

"Amen to that." Christy shook Adze's hand before she, too, left the apartment.

Adze glanced around one last time before he clapped Nicor on the shoulder.

Let's clear out, Adze communicated to his team.

He and Nicor left, closing the door gently behind them.

Adze pulled his phone out and dialled Callum.

"Adze?" Callum answered before Nicor could hear a single ring tone.

"Yeah, make the call," Adze advised.

"You got it."

Adze shoved the phone in the pocket of his shorts then jogged across the road and disappeared into the trees.

"Local authorities have been notified," he said as

they came across the other members of his team. Everyone else had cleared out, not wanting to be caught in the vicinity should the police go looking for witnesses.

They all headed back to the edge of the gardens where they could keep an eye on the building without being seen by passers-by. None of them were about to walk away fully until they knew those women were taken care of.

It didn't take long for the police to arrive, their blue and red flashing lights bright in the darkness of the night. Thankfully they didn't have any sirens blaring. Three cars all converged at once, from two different directions, the police parking the cars on angles in the middle of the street.

Six men and women gathered out the front of the building, their dark blue uniforms looking black at this time of night, their vests weighed down and bulked out with numerous items. POLICE, shone brightly in reflective material across their chests. Handguns were strapped to their thighs and large M4s were held, pointed down across their chests.

Nicor wondered what they were waiting for before he realised they needed someone *to let them into* the building. A very sleepy and bedraggled man stepped out of the lift, wearing nothing but a pair of boxers and a threadbare shirt.

He seemed surprised to find fully armed and decked out police on his doorstep, but he opened the door. He spoke briefly with one of the officers before turning around and heading right back to the lift.

More police cars arrived and the officers joined the others as they entered the building in single file.

The six of them watched until officers came back out to clear room for the ambulances to arrive, and set a perimeter, blocking off the street and walkways surrounding the building. Once the first ambulance arrived on scene, Adze turned to the others.

"Our job here is done. Let's head home."

They quietly made their way through the gardens until they were well clear of the perimeter, before turning and making their way through the city to their building.

Home, sweet home. Kinda.

Nicor felt immense relief that this hunt was finally over as he stepped under the shower spray a half hour later. He also felt sadness for what those women had been put through. He couldn't dwell on either though. This was his job and before too long, there would be another creature and another case.

The last thought that drifted through his mind before sleep took him, was that he would get to see Jordan tomorrow.

CHAPTER TWELVE

Nicor woke to the smell of frying bacon. Followed by his stomach protesting its lack of food quite loudly. The phone read nine thirty-two when he checked it. It had been close to four in the morning when he'd finally been able to fall asleep.

The call of the bacon was too much, though. As much as Nicor wanted to roll over and go back to sleep, the *God of All Food* was crying out for him.

Nicor pulled on a pair of sweats then walked out to join the other idiots awake so damn early in the morning. He yawned and scratched the small patch of hair he had scattered on his abs as he stepped into the kitchen.

"Morning," he yawned.

Oriax hummed away as he cooked. Nicor headed right for the coffee machine, stealing a strip of perfectly cooked bacon on his way.

"Ow!"

Oriax slapped his hand with a spatula again. "No stealing!"

"Too late!" Nicor didn't care. He had what he wanted and took another exaggerated bite for good measure.

"See if I let you have any more!"

Nicor crunched away on the bacon as he placed his cup under the machine and pressed the buttons for what he wanted. The scent of coffee soon filled the air to fight with those of the bacon and eggs.

"Why the hell are you up so darn early?" Nicor asked around another yawn.

"Gotta be. Heading home today."

Pyro and Adze walked into the kitchen then, both showered and dressed like they'd been awake a lot longer than Nicor's five minutes.

"Can you make me one of those?" Adze asked him as he pointed to the coffee machine.

"Sure." Nicor pulled down a mug for Adze and grabbed up the pod he liked best. He eyed the bacon but Oriax was guarding it with more awareness now. Not worth a third spatula hit. When Nicor's coffee was finished, he disposed of the used capsule and set the machine to making Adze's.

"Why wasn't I told we're heading home today?" Nicor asked, still half-asleep. He took his first sip of java and almost groaned with pure joy at the taste, but managed to hold back.

"Because you're staying while the rest of us go home."

It took Nicor longer than he would have liked to

process what Adze had said. When it sunk in he stared. Nicor's heart started beating faster at the thought of being able to stay and spend some time with Jordan.

"What do you mean I'm not going with you?"

"You need time with Jordan. *Human* time." Adze said.

Nicor grinned at the prospect.

"I don't know how long we can give you, as it's out of our hands, so make the most of it. Get to know your mate, bond with him, then bring him home."

Nicor nodded. Absolutely elated that he wasn't going home today, his mind already trying to figure out what he could do next with his mate. He'd been dreading the end of the investigation for this exact reason. He should have known Adze wouldn't force him to leave without his mate.

"Thank you. I'll be home as soon as I can. If you need me before then, call."

"Have no doubt. I won't endanger my team," Adze said pointedly as he grabbed his cup from the coffee machine and headed for the table, stealing a piece of bacon on his way out.

"Out!" Oriax chased Adze with his spatula. "All of you, get out of my kitchen!"

"What's going on out here?" Daevas asked as he and Cacus joined them.

"Fuckers keep stealing my bacon! If they're not careful they won't be getting any breakfast at all."

"Now, now, Oriax, no need to be hasty," Pyro said gently as he stepped towards the kitchen.

"Where the hell do you think you're going?" Oriax

asked brandishing his spatula, little drops of oil flinging all over the place. His voice didn't have its usual amused tolerant acceptance. "I am trying to cook here."

"Tea. I won't touch the food. I promise," Pyro placated.

"You bloody better not."

Wow. What had him in such a mood? Oriax went back to cooking with a huff. They all shared confused looks and silently decided to stay out of his way. Nicor escaped as the others rotated through the kitchen one at a time to get their morning drinks.

Nicor sat at the table and sipped his coffee, working to wake up his muddled brain. Being able to make complete sentences was hard before a cup or two. He'd have to try anyway. Nicor typed out a quick message to his mate.

Busy today?

There. That counted as a sentence.

Soon Oriax had the table loaded up with all the goodies, eggs, bacon, mushrooms, grilled tomatoes, hash browns and toast.

"This looks awesome, like always."

"No thanks to you mob," Oriax bitched as he sat down.

"You know you love us," Cacus said around a mouth stuffed with hash browns. The man didn't even have anything on his plate yet. Talk about no impulse control. He'd get a spatula before brekkie was over. Nicor loaded his own plate up and started to eat, when his phone vibrated.

WHAT DID you have in mind?

NICOR THOUGHT QUICK THEN REPLIED, *Dinner and a movie?*

NICOR KNEW it was the most boring date option available, but after last night, he just wanted to spend time with Jordan with no pressure. A movie seemed like the perfect idea for that. He didn't have to wait long to see what his mate wanted.

SOUNDS FUN. Let me know when and where.

Awesome. Will do.

WITH A DATE SET, the anxiousness Nicor hadn't even been aware of faded away from his chest, his heart more settled than it had been since he came back from Hunter Valley. He couldn't contain his smile as he went back to eating his breakfast. He would look at movie theatres and times this afternoon once the others had left.

Breakfast was the usual noisy affair as they talked over the previous night's happenings.

"Adze, have you heard anything about the women we rescued?" Cacus asked, then proceeded to make a sandwich so thick Nicor worried the man would need to dislocate his jaw to eat it, then drowned it in tomato sauce and siracha. He picked up the behemoth in front of him and asked, "Were we able to get them placed?"

"Matilda called earlier," Adze answered between bites. "All the women have been split between St. Vincent's and Sydney Hospitals. Their families were contacted and they're being looked after."

"What about the ones that were taken from Melbourne last year?" Daevas asked as he took a drink of his OJ.

"The police confiscated all digital equipment from the apartments." Adze frowned. "Hopefully they'll be able to locate the women who were sold and track them down. Matti will keep an eye on things. Once they find a solid lead, she'll inform the hounds of whatever country they now reside in, and hopefully, the women can be brought home."

Silence fell for the next several minutes as they all digested what that meant and the horror those poor women were probably experiencing.

Adze turned to look at Nicor. "I've let Matti know that you're staying on for a little bit, so the cleaners won't be needed at the moment."

"Thanks," Nicor answered.

He appreciated not having anyone poking around while courting his mate. It was always nice to have cleaners come through and tidy up after they left, as they never knew how long it would be before they came back again. When it looked like they were headed back somewhere, she sent them in again for a quick clean and to stock the fridge with the essentials.

"I'll let her know when I'm on my way home."

They finished up their breakfast chatting about the weekend's footy game, which derailed into flight times. The others went to clear the table but Nicor stopped them. They needed to get going. Who? Him? Pushing his packmates out the door. Nope.

"Leave the dishes, I'll do them while you all go pack," Nicor said.

"Thanks, man." Pyro clapped him on the back then hurried to his room.

Nicor finally understood how much Pyro and Adze were looking forward to going home and seeing their mates. They'd been away from them for over a month. That one short visit over the weekend they had couldn't have been enough. Nicor didn't know how they managed. It had been less than a day for him. The mere thought of heading home today with the others made him feel nauseous at the idea of leaving Jordan behind and they weren't even mated yet.

Nicor took his stacked dishes into the kitchen and he packed the dishwasher. He attacked the benches next, wiping them down. Bacon grease got everywhere. His pent-up anticipation had to go somewhere. Waiting for the guys to leave meant he had nothing to do. Empty hands were never a good thing. Starting a game now wasn't an option, though. He had to plan.

After making himself another coffee, Nicor settled on the couch to look up cinemas and movie times for this afternoon. Since he was usually here for work and not pleasure, he kind of knew the area but not well... food joints, yes, the pack knew those. Anything else? It was up for grabs. Nicor googled nice restaurants within walking distance of the theatre. Walking meant more time with his mate. Sue him.

One by one the other hounds came out carrying their bags and settled on the couch next to him as they waited for the rest to finish up. Oriax was still grumpy, coming out last, complaining about the fridge's state to Nicor. Why was he so fixated on what food Nicor had? It wasn't like Nicor would burn down the building if he tried to cook...*maybe* an order of to-go meals were in order. Oriax needed someone to look after so he'd stop fretting about the rest of them so much.

When everyone was ready, Nicor drove them to the airport. Usually they would leave the car there and someone from Matilda's office would swing past to collect it then they would take it back to the apartment, but as Nicor wasn't leaving he got to drive. Wasn't that a weird feeling to have? A car to himself and to escort his mate around with.

"Take care and have fun," Cacus said as he hugged Nicor before stepping back to make room for the others.

"You got this, bro," Daevas said, clapping Nicor on the shoulder.

"We'll see you, and hopefully, Jordan again soon,"

Adze said. He picked up his duffle and threw it over his shoulder.

"Don't do anything I wouldn't do." Pyro winked then followed Adze.

"The way to a man's heart is through his belly. Shame you can't cook." Oriax laughed and jumped out of the way from the playful swipe Nicor took at him. Relief flooded Nicor seeing his friend back to his usual self.

It was strange watching the others walk across the tarmac and up the stairs to their plane without him. Nicor waited and watched as they all stepped aboard, taking all the noise with them. The sounds of the airport were one thing, but being without his pack? It felt lonely and bloody quiet.

Then again, when he'd changed back in Hunter Valley, this feeling hadn't been there with him. Was it because of his mate being there with him? Nicor grunted, trying to remember anything as the plane taxied down the runway.

Butterflies suddenly dive-bombed in his stomach as Nicor realised he was there by himself, trying to woo his mate. He really was all on his own. No team to back him up for this. No game to get lost in because he had someone else to rely on. This time, it was all up to him to level up and find a way to help his mate fall in love with him.

Nicor messaged Jordan with a time to meet him at the Event Cinema on George Street and climbed back into the car to head home.

The wait might be too much for his heart. But it

wasn't just his he had to worry about. Nicor needed to show Jordan, as mates, they could work through anything. Real life didn't have med kits stashed in empty bookcases to fix whatever damage they got along the way.

Nicor paced as he waited for Jordan to show up. He should've brought his Switch, then he'd have something to occupy him so he couldn't think about all the things that could go wrong. Still, showing up to a date with his games was probably too soon in their relationship. Next time he'd have to plan better.

He might have arrived a half hour early just to make sure he wasn't late. But also because being at the apartment, by himself, with no one to distract him, was driving him crazy. Normally he could get lost in *Call of Duty* or *Overwatch*, but this wasn't home and he didn't have his system. Nicor could only beat his *Cuphead* game so many times. Maybe it was time to work through and see how well he liked *BioShock* on the Switch.

No, now was not the time to panic. A snip had Nicor checking out his hand. He'd already bitten the nails on his left hand down to the quick. He cringed. He hadn't meant to do that. But he had nothing for his hands to do. No enemy. No games. He was about to start on his right hand when someone stepped up behind him.

"Hey stranger, looking for a date?"

Nicor grinned as he turned around and took in the

sight of Jordan. His mate wore tight black jeans that hugged his legs paired with a T-shirt with a comic book character on it and a dark jacket. His hair had been pulled back into a ponytail, and it didn't look like he'd shaved since Nicor had last seen him. The dark stubble on his face made him look rugged and handsome.

Deciding to play along, Nicor let his gaze linger on Jordan as he slowly moved it up and down. "Depends on what you're offering."

"Wouldn't you like to know?" Jordan replied, his dark brown eyes lighting up. "I even made it here on time. Presentable and everything."

Nicor leaned down and lightly kissed Jordan's cheek. "You look wonderful."

"Thank you. You don't look too bad yourself."

Nicor practically felt Jordan's gaze scorching him as he took in what Nicor wore. Blue jeans, black boots and a button up, open at the collar.

"So..." Jordan started and then turned to look at the large board listing all the movies and their times. "What movie did you have in mind?"

"I didn't." Nicor gave him a smile, worried it hadn't been the right call, as Jordan glanced at him and raised a brow. "I thought we could decide when we got here. Don't know what you like yet. I chose this time as it had the most movies starting within a half-hour period. Figured there'd be something we'd both want to see."

"Very sound and logical thinking." Jordan nodded, his eyes warming, then turned back to the board. "So, what will it be?"

They stood there and debated the movie choices for

a couple of minutes until they settled on one that they both wanted to watch then lined up to get the tickets. People crowded around them as they waited, so much noise. Nicor glanced at his mate wondering if he could hold his hand, but the ticket seller interrupted him before he got the chance to try.

They settled in their seats with a large box of popcorn between them, a bag of plain M&M's that Jordan had insisted on getting, and a large soda each.

Being this close to his mate and not touching him was making Nicor a little twitchy. Slow and steady, that was what his mate asked for. To combat that he opened the box of popcorn and grabbed a small handful.

The buttery, salty taste of the popcorn made his stomach growl. He hadn't realised how hungry he had been. He hadn't been able to eat anything since breakfast that morning with his pack. Waiting for his mate, to get this chance, had consumed Nicor.

The date had to be perfect. Had to.

"You want to know the perfect way to eat popcorn?" Jordan asked him as he ripped the top of the brown bag of M&M's.

"There's a perfect way to eat popcorn?" Nicor asked sceptically.

"Yep." He fished into the chocolate bag and pulled out two little M&M's. "You get two, and only two of these. Place them in your mouth, then grab a small handful of popcorn." Jordan demonstrated the small clump of kernels he held between all five fingers. "Then add that to your mouth and eat. Thus, the perfect way to eat popcorn has been achieved."

Joy shone on his mate's face as he added the popcorn to the chocolate and ate.

"I'm game." Nicor shrugged and fished for two pieces of chocolate before going for the popcorn.

He was pleasantly surprised by the burst of flavour as the two ingredients melded together. The sweetness of the chocolate married perfectly with the butteriness and saltiness of the popcorn.

"Not bad, not bad at all," Nicor said while Jordan watched him. "I wonder if peanut M&M's would work?"

"No. You don't mess with perfection. Plain, and plain only. And only ever two. You start messing with the chocolate to popcorn, sweet to salty ratio. You may as well just throw it out the window then."

Nicor chuckled. It escaped before he could stop himself. He'd never seen someone so serious over a snack combo. "I'll take your word for it. Two plain M&M's only."

Jordan nodded, obviously please Nicor had seen the light, then went back for seconds.

The lights dimmed and adverts started playing on the screen. Nicor settled back to enjoy the movie. He couldn't think of anyone else he'd rather be here with than Jordan. For the first time in a long time, he felt entirely content.

Twenty minutes into the movie, Nicor felt Jordan's hand slide into his own. Not wanting Jordan to feel self-conscious about the move, Nicor didn't react other than to link his fingers with Jordan's. They stayed that way for the rest of the movie. Both of their hands more than a little hot in the cool theatre but Nicor was loathe to let his mate go.

"What'd you think?" Jordan asked him as the credits started to roll.

"I really enjoyed it. You?"

"Yeah, I liked it more than I thought I would."

Reluctantly Nicor let Jordan's hand go as they stood and packed up their rubbish. Snuggling in a dark theatre seemed like a whole lot more fun than trying to find an empty bin to toss their stuff.

Back in the lobby of the cinema, Jordan looked at Nicor. "I believe dinner was also promised to me."

"You would be correct. How do you feel about Indian?" Nicor asked. He liked everything, but realised some people didn't like the spiciness of Indian cuisine.

"Love it. What did you have in mind?"

"There's a place not too far from here," Nicor replied.

"Lead the way."

Without a word, Jordan slipped his hand back into Nicor's as they walked out onto the street. The sun had set some time ago, and the streets were full of people. Every single one of them seemed like they were in a hurry to get somewhere. The heat had disappeared with the sun and the air had a slight chill to it as they walked.

Those butterflies Nicor had visit him earlier today were back, with a vengeance, while he led his mate to the Indian restaurant he'd found online that day. The cool air helped him from overheating as they made their way to the restaurant.

When they stopped in front of Indian Harvest, Jordan let out a rumble of excitement.

"Ohhh. I love this place," Jordan said as he squeezed Nicor's hand gently.

"That's lucky. Was a completely random choice off the internet." He laughed.

The little bell on the top of the door jingled as they walked into the restaurant. The aroma hit them all at once, making Nicor's stomach growl, even after his healthy serving of popcorn at the movies. The spices in the room teased his tongue. Nicor gulped, anticipating the foods he could chow down on.

"Table for two?" a young woman wearing a teal and gold sari asked as she approached them. Her long dark hair was braided down her back and she had a bindi on her forehead between her brows.

"Please," Jordan replied before Nicor could.

"Right this way."

The hostess picked up two menus, then showed them to a large booth on the other side of the restaurant. The place was fairly full, food covering the tables and animated discussions going on, which Nicor took as a sign that not only the food here was good, but the atmosphere let people relax and enjoy.

"Can I get you something to drink?" she asked as they sat opposite of each other. The high-backed red booth seats gave them an impression of privacy in such a busy restaurant, for which Nicor was grateful. He wanted time with his mate.

"Do you drink wine?" Jordan asked him. "I know you like beer, but what's your stance on wine?"

"I enjoy a good red."

"Want to share a bottle?" Jordan asked.

"Yeah, I think I like that idea. You choose." Nicor picked up his menu but didn't open it. Instead he watched Jordan as his mate quickly perused the wine list then made his decision and ordered their bottle.

"Your server will be right back with that," the hostess said.

"There's two types of people in this world," Jordan said seriously as he too picked up his menu.

"Oh yeah?" Nicor asked.

"Yeah. Those that share their Indian food. And those that *do not*. Which one are you?"

Nicor laughed. This man continued to surprise him.

"Definitely a sharer." Nicor leaned forward and lowered his voice. "Living in a house with five other hellhounds, you gotta learn to share your food, otherwise there would be multiple fights a day."

"Fights you say?" Jordan asked, his brow cocked in question.

"Yeah, unless you're Oriax. He don't share nothing while he's cooking. God forbid you steal something from him while he's in the kitchen."

Jordan laughed. "I'll have to remember that."

Nicor's stomach flipped then at the implications of Jordan's words. Not wanting to push the subject he cleared his throat. "What about you—sharer or non?"

"Same." Jordan smiled. "Now that we've got that out of the way, what are we going to feast on?"

They perused the menu and volleyed back and

forth with the dishes that stood out to the both of them. By the time their server arrived at their table with the wine, glasses and a jug of ice water, they'd settled on their order.

She poured Jordan a small amount in his glass, which he tasted. When he nodded his approval she filled both glasses partially and set the bottle on the edge of the table with a napkin folded neatly around its neck.

"Are you ready to order, or would you like a few more minutes?" she asked as she tucked the drinks tray under her arm and held a small note pad and pen at the ready.

"I think we're good to order now?" Jordan confirmed.

Nicor nodded.

Jordan opened the menu again and pointed at each dish as he tried unsuccessfully to pronounce some of the dishes.

The waitress read their order back to them and once they were satisfied she had everything down correctly, she left.

Nicor picked up his glass of wine and took a sip. The pleasant fruity taste lingered on his tastebuds.

"Very nice," he told Jordan.

"Glad you like it." Jordan paused and seemed to take a deep breath before he continued, "So, now that your mission here is complete, are you heading back to Melbourne tomorrow?"

His mate looked down at the table, his hands fiddling with the stem of his wine glass. Nicor reached out across the table and laid his hand on top of Jordan's.

"I'm not going anywhere. At least not yet, hopefully."

Jordan looked up, hope in his expression. "But what about your team?"

"They all left this afternoon. Drove them to the airport myself."

"Really?"

"Yeah. Adze allowed me to stay behind in the hopes that we could spend time together. I don't know how long I have, because if the team needs me, I have to go. But for now, I'm all yours."

"That was nice of Adze."

"Yeah it was. He knows what it's like to find your mate. He and Archie had some difficulties in the beginning."

"What sort of difficulties?" Jordan took another sip of his wine, their hands now rested, one on top of the other in the centre of the table.

Nicor took a deep breath. "It's not something we talk about much. Archie still has trouble dealing with it sometimes. He was kidnapped and tortured by a crazed nephilim we were hunting at the time."

"Holy crap."

"Yeah. It wasn't a good time. Archie's strong, though. He's come a long way since it happened." Nicor paused a moment, before continuing. "It's something we've never had to deal with before. The ramifications on a human. We're so used to doing our job and walking away. This time we couldn't. Seeing what it did to Archie affected us all."

"I can see how that would have been hard on you all, after so many years alone, and not having to deal with it."

Nicor nodded, then released a loud breath. "Can we talk about something happier?" he asked, wanting to change the subject.

"Of course, what about the others? Any of them mated?" Jordan asked.

"Just Adze and Pyro. I'm the third of the team to find their mate."

"How'd Pyro find his mate?"

Oh, Nicor was going to enjoy this. "Callum shot him!"

Jordan choked on his drink and spat it all over the table. Nicor had to stop himself from bursting into laughter. Instead he picked up his napkin, shook it out and handed it to Jordan. His mate coughed a couple of times, trying to clear his airway as he wiped at the drops on the table. Jordan's eyes were watery as he looked back at Nicor.

"Seriously, dude. You can't tell me something like that when I'm drinking."

Nicor laughed. "I'd say I'm sorry, but it was kinda fun watching your reaction."

Jordan threw Nicor's napkin back at him in mock outrange, but he snatched it out of the air, flattened it out then placed it in his lap.

"Pyro's mate really shot him?" Jordan enquired.

"Yeah," Nicor leaned closer and lowered his voice

again. "Callum's a cop. Both he and Archie are human, so when Callum investigated something he shouldn't have he saw Pyro shift, then advance on him, so he shot him. Knocked Pyro clear out with the hit too!"

"Holy crap!"

"Yep."

"And here I was thinking it was weird that I technically own you."

Now it was Nicor's time to choke. Unfortunately for him he'd just taken a sip of his wine and that shit burned as it went up the back of his throat and into his nose.

Nicor grabbed up his napkin and cleaned himself up. When he could breathe again he looked at Jordan who sat quietly with a smug expression on his face.

"Holy shit, how did I completely forget that?" he asked as he wiped his watering eyes.

Jordan shrugged, his expression saddening all of a sudden. "Do you remember anything about that time?"

Nicor's heart ached at the obvious pain his lack of memories caused his mate. He hated that he couldn't remember the weeks they'd spent together. "Tell me something."

"Tell you what?" Jordan asked in confusion.

"Tell me about our time together. I hate that I can't remember it. I'd like to know, if you're willing to tell me." Nicor reached out and placed his hand over Jordan's where it rested on the table.

"I think... I think I'd really like that." Jordan smiled tentatively at him.

This wasn't how Nicor saw their conversation

going when they'd started talking, but he was really happy they'd gotten here.

"Well, what can I tell you?" Jordan thought for a moment. "You are the world's biggest bacon thief."

Nicor laughed. He already knew that. "That doesn't surprise me in the slightest. I love me some bacon." He winked and Jordan grinned.

"You were always right under foot the second the meat hit the frypan. I can't tell you the number of times I nearly went ass over head."

"Sorry."

"No you're not." Jordan laughed.

"Nah, I'm really not, but it seemed the polite thing to say."

"Dog breath, drool and snot, first thing in the morning is disgusting."

Nicor winced. "Now, that I am sorry about." He racked his memories trying to remember something, anything.

"I think the kangaroos were pleased to see the back of you when you left."

Nicor raised a brow at that.

"We used to walk in the afternoons, through the vineyards at the back of my property. Nothing too strenuous at first, but as you healed, they lasted longer and longer. Every time you'd see a roo, you crouch down into this kinda protective stance and start growling, teeth bared. If I didn't know how much of a big softy you were, it would have been kinda intimidating."

Him, a softy? Nicor didn't get a chance to correct Jordan before his mate continued.

"Roos being roos, completely ignored you, which you hated. As soon as you were well enough, the chase was on. Nothing I said or did would dissuade you from your duty to protect me from the horrible roos that were sleeping in the shade."

Nicor laughed. "That sounds totally like something I would have done. Kangaroos are a bloody pest."

Jordan lowered his voice before he continued. "You are the best snuggle companion I've ever had."

Nicor's heart broke.

"I'm sorry," Nicor replied just as quietly.

He closed his eyes, called out to the beast within him. His hound was a part of him, always, two halves of the one whole. His animal came surging forth, and Nicor had a hard time not shifting then and there in the middle of the restaurant. Something flickered across his mind. A feeling? A memory maybe. He tried to grab it and concentrate on it before it disappeared.

"Did I..." he trailed off, then asked uncertainly, "Did I ever fall asleep on top of you while we watched movies on the couch?"

Was it a memory? Or something he hoped had happened? He didn't know if what he'd just remembered was real or not. Jordan looked at him intently before the biggest smile Nicor had ever seen appeared on his face.

"Did you just remember that?" Jordan asked, hope clear in his voice.

"I don't know. I think so?"

"Well, to answer your question, yes, you did that several times. You loved stretching out beside me on the long couch, head in my lap. You used to growl every time I stopped patting, or scratching your ears."

Nicor's cheeks flushed.

Before either of them could say anything else, their waitress arrived loaded down with their entrées. The two large triangular samosas took up most of their plate, only leaving enough room for the small dish with the green dipping sauce. The charcoal tandoori chicken and the masala lamb cutlets looked and smelled divine. The heat sizzled off the dishes, enriching the aromas around them and made Nicor's mouth water.

A man stepped up beside the server and handed them the last of their entrées. She took the cone-shaped lid off and placed the clay plate with their trumpet mushrooms on the table.

"This looks great. Thank you," Nicor told her as she stepped back.

"Enjoy, gentlemen," she said then walked away.

"Where to start?" Jordan asked as he eyed the food.

"I'm going for one of these," Nicor said as he picked up his fork and scooped out one of the whole, stuffed mushrooms from the small divot it resided in on the clay plate.

"Good choice." Jordan followed his lead.

Nicor, not wanting to burn his mouth with molten mushroom juice, did the sensible thing and cut the thing in half before eating it. Heaven. His mouth had found heaven. The noises Jordan made seemed to be in agreement too.

"Oh, God. This is so good," Nicor muttered before eating the other half.

"I told you they were to die for."

"I'm glad you suggested them. Not sure I would have ordered them myself." Nicor picked up a lamb cutlet next, cut a piece and popped it into his mouth. He moaned again as the spices used to tenderise and flavour the meat burst on his tongue. Holy crap that was delicious!

When he finished he thought he'd get back to their previous conversation. "So, getting back to this whole adoption thing. Just how adopted am I?" At Jordan's confused expression, Nicor tried again. "Well, what I suppose I'm asking is, is it legal? Or just something the vet made you sign to say you'd take care of me?"

Jordan smiled. "I have the official certificate at home if you'd like to see it?"

"Oh, God," Nicor said in pure horror. "You can never let the guys see that. Or know that it even exists. I'd never live it down."

"About that...." Jordan trailed off and laughed.

"They know?" Nicor asked, the horror of moments before coming back full force.

"Ummmm. I maybe had to tell them when they showed up on my doorstep and demanded an explanation."

Nicor groaned as he closed his eyes. He could understand why none of them had mentioned it yet. But he didn't hold out hope for his future. They were probably too focused on getting him back then the hunt. He'd gotten a pass, now that their mission was over he bet it was game on once he got home to Melbourne.

"You might want to know..." Jordan winced.

"What?"

"I didn't have a name so I put Spot on the adoption form."

Nicor groaned. "That's going to bite me in the arse."

"Sorry." His mate wore a sheepish grin.

"You didn't mean any harm."

They finished off their entrées and the server topped up their wine glasses when she came back to clear the dishes.

"Your mains will be out shortly," she told them.

"Thanks," Jordan acknowledged.

They sat and drank and chatted their way through the mains, and well into the night, ordering a second bottle of wine at some point. Nicor had completely lost track of time until their server came back and broke the spell he'd fallen under.

"I'm sorry, gentlemen, but we're closing," she said quietly.

Being secluded in the high-backed booth, Nicor hadn't even realised that the rest of the restaurant had already been cleared out, and reset for service tomorrow.

"We're terribly sorry," Jordan said as he scooched to the end of the booth then stood. Nicor, too, stood and they made their way to the register where Nicor pulled his wallet out to pay.

He placed his hand over Jordan's, who was opening his own wallet. "My treat. Please."

"Thank you." Jordan nodded.

Within a few minutes they were back outside in the chill night air, their bellies full of good food and wine.

"Can I walk you home?" Nicor asked.

"I'd like that."

It was a nice night and the walk would do them some good. Plus, it wasn't all that far. The cool breeze was a change to the warm restaurant they'd been in for the past several hours. Nicor, feeling emboldened by the events of the night, reached out and took Jordan's hand. His mate smiled shyly up at him and linked their fingers together.

They continued to chat about anything and everything as they walked through the city. The streets had cleared as it was closing in on midnight, leaving them plenty of room. And before Nicor knew it, they were standing out the front of Jordan's house. Their date had officially come to an end. Nicor's heart already protested leaving his mate alone. He wanted more time. His human half didn't have the memories of their time in Hunter Valley and he wished they could seclude themselves to start new ones. Tonight gave him hope that they might return, in time.

"Thank you for a wonderful night," Jordan said as he smiled up at Nicor. "It'll be my treat next time."

"Well, that sounds like fun." Nicor smiled.

"Would it be okay...?"

"Yes."

Jordan laughed. "You don't even know what I was going to ask."

"I don't need to know. Whatever you want is okay with me."

Jordan seemed to take a deep breath before he stepped forward, right up close and personal, then wrapped his arms around Nicor's back and snuggled in close.

Jordan's head rested perfectly in the crook of Nicor's shoulder. Loving the feeling of his mate pressed against him, Nicor wrapped his arms around Jordan and held him, never wanting to let him go.

There was nothing sexual about the contact and Nicor thanked Christ his body didn't react. The last thing he wanted was to have that happen and to scare Jordan away. He leaned down and breathed the wonderful scent of his mate in, his body relaxing completely as that wonderful aroma soothed him. He placed a soft kiss to the top of Jordan's head. Taking his lead from Jordan, Nicor lowered his arms and stepped back when he felt Jordan's grip on him relax.

"Thank you," Jordan whispered.

"You're very welcome. I hope you know, that I'm just as good a snuggler in human form as I am in hound form."

Jordan smiled.

"I'm not sure that's possible."

"We'll just have to put it to the test then."

Jordan nodded, then turned and hurried down his drive and into his house.

Nicor stood there on the footpath staring at the now-closed door. His arms felt empty without his mate in them. He loved that Jordan had felt comfortable enough with him to ask for a cuddle. Nicor couldn't wait to do it again. They fit well together. Tonight couldn't have gone better. Jordan was something else and Nicor looked forward to unravelling the mystery that was his mate.

He shoved his hands in his pockets and whistled a happy little tune as he walked home.

CHAPTER THIRTEEN

You busy tonight?

Nicor grinned as soon as he saw the message from his mate. Things had been going well between them, at least Nicor thought they had. It was a nice change of pace, to take things slow, get to know someone without jumping straight into bed. Nicor had never been the type of person who enjoyed one night stands all that much, but this time he was spending with Jordan, he was so grateful Adze had given it to him.

That wasn't to say that Nicor didn't feel guilty as hell for letting his team down and staying behind, because he did. It had only been a couple of weeks, and every night Nicor stressed that his team would come across something they couldn't handle and it'd be his fault one of them would be injured.

Adze had told him that he'd call Nicor in if they got anything too bad on the docket, and he could come right back to Sydney afterwards, but it didn't stop Nicor worrying.

Wanting to get his thoughts back on happier things Nicor typed out a quick reply.

That depends. What did you have in mind?

Nicor practically held his breath as those three little dots appeared on his screen.

Dinner, my place? That enough to drag you away from your other plans?

Nicor stared at his new gaming system that he'd set up in the living room. Figuring if he was going to be here a while he may as well have some creature comforts. He had a lot of spare time on his hands these days, with not hunting every night.

Dinner at your place sounds wonderful. What time?

How about 5?

Nicor glanced at his watch and realised it was already nearly four. That would give him enough time to finish this level, have a shower, and make it to Jordan's on time.

Great. See you soon.

Nicor placed his phone back on the coffee table where it had been and picked up the controller he'd put down when he saw Jordan's initial message pop up. If he thought too much about getting to see his mate and spend time with him in his own space, Nicor would be too keyed up to concentrate on anything.

The picture on the television un-paused and Nicor once more tried to lose himself in this world before him. Unlike other days though where Nicor could just play for hours and not realise the passage of time, today, he was very conscious of the passing minutes.

At five o'clock Nicor found himself on the front porch step ready to knock on Jordan's door, when it swung open in front of him.

His mate looked relaxed in a worn shirt and paint-stained pair of shorts. Nicor smiled when he spotted flecks of paint in his mate's hair as well. He hoped he'd be seeing his mate this way for years to come.

"You look wonderful," Nicor said, thankful that he'd decided not to dress up.

"Seriously?" Jordan arched an eyebrow. "I look like a mess. I was hoping to shower before you got here, but lost track of time."

His mate stepped back and waved Nicor in.

Accepting the invitation, he crossed the threshold and walked into Jordan's home. The place was warm and inviting, red brick walls and comfortable looking furniture. The living area was separated from the kitchen by a large island bench that had a pot rack dangling from the ceiling.

Nicor loved it immediately. The entire area just screamed Jordan. A tight knot formed in his belly. Why would Jordan ever want to leave this place?

"Hey, you all right?" Jordan asked as he stepped up beside him and placed a gentle hand to Nicor's arm.

No... Not at all, I've seen two rooms of your house and I don't know if I could ever compete. "Yeah, sure. Why?"

Jordan stared at him quizzically for a moment. "You

just had this look on your face like you'd lost something."

Nicor swallowed the lump in his throat. "I'm fine."

He tried smiling, but even to him it seemed half hearted. Nicor's gaze danced around the room again, taking in even more this time, trying to find something to talk about that would break that sudden awkward silence that had just fallen around them. Then he spotted it.

"Oh my god, are you cooking rack of lamb for dinner?" His mouth started watering just looking at the uncooked cut of meat sitting on the kitchen bench.

"I take it my choice is okay with you?"

"Oh hell yeah, I just have one question."

"And that is?"

"Do you have mint sauce to go with it?"

Jordan walked over to his fridge and pulled out a mug with a teaspoon still in it. Nicor had followed behind him, curious about the silence. Jordan held the mug out to him and the smell of mint and the vinegar pungent. He moaned.

"Homemade too. Jesus. Where have you been hiding all my life?"

Jordan chuckled then placed the mug back in the fridge. "Let me just finish wrapping the bones and then I'll show you around."

"Sounds great. Anything I can do to help?"

"Nope. Potatoes are already on the stove parboiling. Sauce is made. Carrots and broccoli are cut and ready to be cooked. Just need to roast the lamb, and make the gravy when it's all done."

"Excuse me while I sit here and drool," Nicor said as he pulled out one of the bar stools sitting under the island bench overhang.

Jordan laughed then pointed. "Tissues are there."

Nicor snorted as he watched Jordan rip off smaller pieces of alfoil and wrap the exposed bones like a pro. "Done that a time or two, yeah?"

"Just once or twice." Jordan winked.

He placed the rack of meat on a tray ready to go in the oven and let it rest to bring it up to room temp.

Jordan washed his hands. "Wanna see the rest of the place?"

No! Not if it's anything like this. "Sure," he said even though his heart was hurting at the thought. Jordan belonged here. He could practically feel his mate's presence soaked into the brickwork.

The artwork on the walls was incredible and Nicor wondered if it was all his mate's own. He'd have to ask later, or investigate for himself.

"It's not much, but it's home."

Nicor nodded, even though he wanted to cry with those words.

"It was a three-bedroom, two bath, but as it's just me, I knocked down the wall between the two largest bedrooms to make my studio. I spend more time in there than in my bedroom anyway, so as long as there was enough room for my bed and somewhere to store my clothes, that's all I needed."

"That makes sense. Living with five brothers, our rooms need to be a little bigger than normal as they're our sanctuaries." Nicor wondered if their place in

Melbourne even had room for Jordan. There were so many of them now. Where would he create his art? "Places for us to get away from everything and everyone and just decompress. My room has an entire gaming set up in it, including a standing desk with PC and couch with TV for the console systems..."

Nicor stopped talking as soon as they stepped foot through the door to Jordan's studio. Two large windows allowed the light to stream into the room, lighting it well, on the ceiling, light tracks hung to make sure Jordan would have sufficient light to work by when the sun wasn't up.

Three easels sat in the middle of the room, two of them with half-finished canvases resting on them. A bench ran along one wall, with all the paintbrushes lined up in paint-splattered glasses along the top. Nicor figured all the paints were stored in the cupboards.

What really caught his eye though, was the number of paintings of his hound staring back at him from every wall. Some of the paintings had been hung on the walls. Others were just stacked on the floor leaning against the wall.

Jordan cleared his throat. "I thought about trying to hide them, but there's just so damn many, that I didn't have anywhere to put them."

"I'm flattered?" Nicor kinda asked as much as said at the same time.

Jordan laughed. "You should be. Your bloody image has been haunting me for months. Even before that fateful night, I couldn't get you out of my head, and I couldn't understand why I was so obsessed with drawing a damn dog,"

Nicor growled.

Jordan laughed. "Hound. Sorry. It got so bad that you nearly ended up on the side of a six-story building in downtown Sydney."

Nicor coughed. "I *what* now!"

"I told you how the council commissioned me to paint the side of a building, that's what I was doing the night we met."

Nicor nodded.

"Anyway, all I'd been able to concentrate on for the couple of weeks leading up to that project was you. You were one of the sample ideas that was submitted to the council for consideration. They thankfully chose one of my other submissions."

"I'm not quite sure what to say to that." Nicor thought about everything Jordan had just told him. "I wonder..."

"What?"

"I wonder if your obsession with me started when we arrived in town. I wonder if we investigated if they would line up."

"Huh," Jordan thought about it for a moment and then shook his head. "I think the times are close, but still out by more than a month or so, from what you've told me. I think it may have been my incubus nature wanting to get me used to the idea of a mate and I just didn't realise what it was trying to tell me." He shrugged.

"These are really very good," Nicor said as he walked around the large room and looked at the paintings his mate had done. Not all of them were of him. There were others scattered in amongst the hounds.

"Would you..." Nicor trailed off, not sure he actually wanted to know the answer.

"Would I what?"

Nicor bit the bullet and asked his question anyway. "Would you consider painting the human me as well?"

His mate smiled shyly at him. "I have tried. I just can't seem to get them quite right." He waved around. "The hounds are easy. You're proving just a little more difficult."

Nicor nodded, uncertain whether he was glad he'd asked or not.

Jordan showed him the rest of the home before they ended back up in the living room. His mate moved into the kitchen and placed the potatoes into a pan of hot oil and put them in the oven alongside the rack of lamb.

"Want to watch a movie or something?" Jordan asked as he motioned Nicor over to the large sectional couch.

They settled down, getting comfy, and searched through the various streaming services until they found a movie they wanted to watch. His mate had curled up in the corner of the couch, his feet stretched out on the cushions in front of him. He was a picture of contentment.

Nicor pulled his gaze away from his mate and

towards the movie. They lapsed into a comfortable silence as they sat there and watched the movie. At some point their fingers ended up entwined again, making Nicor content.

Jordan got up to attend to dinner halfway through. The scent of the roasting lamb permeated the entire living area and Nicor's stomach growled at the delicious smell and the thought he'd soon get to eat it.

Dinner was just as amazing as it had smelled. The lamb was perfectly cooked, juicy and tender. The mint sauce added that little bit extra to the meal. Jordan had opened a bottle of red to go with dinner and Nicor enjoyed the wine. The bold fruity flavour complimented the meal well.

Plates cleared, they settled back on the couch again, both their glasses refilled with the remainder of the bottle.

Another movie went on the TV and they both settled in to watch. After a while, Jordan placed his glass on the small side table next to his end of the couch.

"Would you mind if I sketched you?" Jordan asked out of the blue.

Nicor smiled. "You can draw me anytime. No need to ask."

"Thanks." Jordan disappeared down the passage then returned a couple of minutes later. He had a large notepad and a small metal tin.

Jordan resumed his seat, once again in the corner of the sectional, this time his feet were flat on the cushion in front of him, his knees up, the now open pad resting against his legs. He placed the small metal box on the side table next to his glass of wine and opened it.

Inside the tin housed all sorts of different shapes, shades, and sizes of charcoal.

"Not pencils?" he asked, curious.

"Pardon?" Jordan asked him.

Nicor nodded to the little box on the side table.

"Oh. No, I love charcoal. There's just something about it. Reminds me of a much simpler time. It was the first medium I ever used to draw with, and I've just stuck with it over time. That's not to say that I haven't used pencils, and I do love paint and all the various colours. But charcoal just resonates with me."

Nicor nodded. He hadn't expected that, but it made a kind of beautiful sense to him. He loved learning all these little pieces about the man who was fated to be his.

"Doesn't your hand get dirty?" Nicor asked, still curious.

Jordan laughed. "You have no idea. I have to be very careful what I touch when I'm using it. I've found charcoal handprints in the weirdest places before. And don't even get me started on having to go to the toilet!"

Nicor burst out laughing, glad he hadn't had a mouthful of wine, or he'd have sprayed it everywhere. "Now that's one hell of an image."

"Sorry." Jordan blushed slightly, which Nicor found the burnt umber adorable on his dark skin. "Just relax and watch the movie."

"But you'll miss it?" Nicor questioned.

"It's okay, I can always watch it again later."

Nicor didn't want to take his eyes off his mate. He wanted to watch him get lost in his art. But that wasn't what Jordan wanted, so Nicor turned his attention back to the television and tried to concentrate on the movie. Tried. He sipped his wine slowly, still enjoying the fruity bouquet, but ended up watching his mate out of the corner of his eye.

"I can see you watching me." Jordan broke the silence that had fallen between them.

"Sorry," Nicor said, even though he really wasn't. That famous scene in Titanic, between Rose and Jack, where he drew her completely naked on the couch sprung to mind and Nicor wondered if Jordan would ever consider drawing him that way.

It was something for him to look forward to, in the future.

The scratch of the charcoal against the thick sheet of paper soon lulled Nicor into a relaxed state as he settled back into the couch and got comfortable, drinking his wine and watching the TV, just hanging out with Jordan.

Life really couldn't get much better than this.

"Thank you for choosing to fly with Qantas, we hope you have a pleasant day."

Nicor stood the second that damn seatbelt sign disappeared. He groaned as he stretched and straightened. The flight from Adelaide had only been a few hours, but it felt like forever. Flying commercial was certainly something he was glad he didn't have to do very often.

He wriggled as he waited to disembark. Nicor couldn't wait to see Jordan again. It had been nearly a month. A month of hunting one creature after another across Australia's vast plains. A month of dealing with a cranky Oriax who snarled at everyone, their normally easy-going packmate causing everyone to tiptoe around him as they got buried under sup case after case. First it was up to Broome in the Kimberly, then down to Launceston in Tassie, Newcastle in NSW, then Adelaide in South Aus. It had been one after the other, which was unusual. They weren't used to having so many sups to go after, and it seemed like it wasn't going to slow down any time soon. No rest for the wicked and Adze had had no choice but to call Nicor back for help.

He was exhausted. The whole team was. Unlike the others who all took the private jet back home to Melbourne, Nicor boarded a commercial flight and headed straight for Sydney. He had no idea how long he'd have before he was called up again, but any time he could squeeze in with Jordan was worth it.

FaceTime and Messenger chats had been his friend this last month.

Finally, the plane door opened and they were able to disembark, being in business class did come with a couple of advantages. Exiting first was definitely one of them.

Nicor slung his pack over his shoulder and made the long walk up the gangway. He hadn't taken much with him so he wouldn't have to wait around at the carousel for any luggage. Not expecting anyone to be waiting for him, Nicor ignored all the eager loved ones and looked around for the exit sign.

"Nicor!"

Stilling at the astonishing sound of his name being shouted over the noise of all the passengers milling in the area, Nicor looked around and grinned when he spotted Jordan. His mate was currently trying to squeeze his way through a densely packed group of people. His hand was raised and waived, and his eyes were locked directly on Nicor.

Nicor stopped and dropped his bag to the ground as Jordan made his way to him through the crowd. He held his arms out and Jordan didn't hesitate, stepping close and wrapping his arms around Nicor's back.

A relieved sigh escaped him as he breathed in the wonderful scent that was his mate.

"What are you doing here?" he asked softly, wishing this moment would never end.

"I missed you."

Nicor's heart beat a little faster at that confession. He'd missed Jordan like crazy while he'd been gone. To the point that he'd never thought it was possible to miss someone so much. He had a whole new appreciation for what Adze and Pyro went through.

They were bumped and jostled as people tried to move around them so Nicor loosened his hold and stepped back. His wide grin, however, he couldn't get rid of. He couldn't believe that Jordan had come to meet his flight.

"How did you even know what time my flight was

getting in?" he asked as Jordan slipped his hand into his. Nicor grabbed his bag with his free hand and they headed off.

"I texted Adze. He was more than happy to give me all the details."

Nicor needed to thank his brother.

"Did you drive?" he asked as they made their way through the airport.

"No, caught an Uber. Figured you had a car in long-term parking, and if not, we could just catch another Uber."

The idea that Jordan had thought that much about it, and that he wanted to be with Nicor, however they travelled, made him happier than he could remember.

They left the terminal and headed towards the short-term parking.

"Not long term?" Jordan asked when he saw the direction Nicor headed in.

"No, the office we maintain here knew I was flying back in and dropped a car off, they come and pick it up when we fly out, too. Saves a fortune on parking fees. Do you have any idea how expensive it is to park at airports these days?" Nicor asked.

Jordan laughed. "I have a vague idea."

He stopped and looked around, trying to spot the car.

"I think it's this way." He led Jordan to the left, only to find nothing and for them to have to backtrack. Nicor ignored the little snicker beside him as they headed back the way they had come.

"There it is!" Nicor announced proudly.

Jordan patted his arm. "Very nice, dear."

"Smartass," Nicor muttered under his breath, but Jordan still heard him and burst into laughter. Nicor shook his head. This was not how he saw his day going when he woke up this morning. He was not mad at this turn of events though.

Nicor pressed his finger to the door and waited for the car to unlock, then threw his bag in the backseat and they climbed in. Nicor fished the keys out of the centre console and he started the engine.

"Where to?" he asked.

Jordan shrugged beside him as he buckled his seatbelt. "I figured you'd be exhausted after your time away and flights so we'd just head back to your place so you could shower and relax."

"That sounds wonderful." It really did. Nicor would love to shower and just veg on the couch. The fact that Jordan thought about what Nicor would want after so long away, had his heart racing.

JORDAN CHECKED the contents of the fridge and realised it was completely empty. He doubted Nicor had done that before he'd left, as the departure was so sudden. Jordan figured someone had organised for a cleaning crew to come through and tidy up.

He pulled out his phone and opened up the Uber Eats app. He changed his delivery address, then clicked through and ordered a couple of different things from one of his favourite restaurants. The food would take a little while to be delivered. Order made, Jordan tucked the phone back into his pocket. His eyes were drawn to a small pile of goodies on the table. He stepped closer to investigate.

Jordan couldn't believe it when he realised what he was looking at. There in the middle of the table were three different sized spiral bound artist pads, with tins of charcoal sticks of varying kinds on top, some of the charcoals were even colours.

His hand trembled slightly as he reached out to touch them.

"They're for you." Nicor's voice came from behind him, startling Jordan so he jumped and snatched his hand back.

He turned to look at his mate and his breath hitched.

Nicor stood there in nothing but a pair of sweats that hung low on his hips. Droplets of water still glistened on his chest as they dripped from his head. He had a towel in one hand, his head tilted to the side as he vigorously rubbed his hair, trying to dry it.

This wasn't the first time Jordan had seen his mate nearly naked, and it probably wouldn't be the last. He could definitely enjoy the view. His muscled abs were well defined, which didn't surprise Jordan considering what he did for a living. The little happy trail of dark hair that meandered its way from his bellybutton to below the waistband of his pants drew Jordan's attention.

He shook his head and lifted his gaze back to Nicor's face, his mate smiled shyly at him. "Sorry, I can go and put some more clothes on, if that would make you more comfortable."

Jordan loved that Nicor was always wanting to do what was right for him. Never pushing.

"It's fine. As long as you're comfortable."

Nicor smiled at him, then nodded again to the table as he draped the towel around his neck. "Those are for you."

Jordan turned back to glance at the table, almost having forgotten the pile on the table. "What? Why?"

"I got them for you just before I had to leave. Was going to invite you around, and didn't want you getting bored. Thought it might be nice if you could have something that you enjoy doing here. I hope they're the right sort. I can return them if they're not."

"No, they're perfect," Jordan said as he did reach out this time and ran a finger over the cool metal tin of the charcoal. "Thank you. That was very thoughtful of you."

"It's nothing." Nicor shrugged him off, but Jordan could see the happiness in his eyes that Jordan had liked the gift.

"Hungry?" Nicor asked as he headed to the kitchen. He opened the fridge and then swore. "Okay, so I forgot that the cleaners would have cleared the place out."

"It's okay. I've already ordered food. Hope that was okay. But I saw the fridge was empty and thought I'd get a jump on things."

"You're amazing," Nicor said.

Jordan stood there and chewed on his lip as Nicor settled on the couch and picked up the remote to the television. He had been surprised at just how much he'd missed Nicor while he'd been gone and wanted to be close to his mate, but he didn't know if Nicor would take his wanting to cuddle the wrong way and think he wanted more.

"Come here," Nicor said as he held his arm out to Jordan.

He didn't hesitate. Jordan climbed onto the couch and snuggled into Nicor's side. His arm rested around Nicor's waist and Nicor's large arm went around his back, his hand resting on his side. Jordan could swear he felt the heat of Nicor's hand through his clothes but dismissed it as silliness.

He sighed happily.

"How are you?" Nicor asked him quietly. "I missed you while I was gone."

"I missed you too." Jordan admitted. "And I'm good. Been keeping busy getting ready for the show."

"I hope you're looking after yourself, and by that I mean both of your natures," Nicor said.

Jordan stilled for a moment not sure how Nicor would take his answer, then decided to just bite the bullet. "Yeah, I went to a club not long after you were called away."

Below him Nicor tensed, only for a moment, but Jordan still felt it.

"I'm glad to hear it." Nicor said softly then leaned down and lightly kissed the top of Jordan's head as he turned on the television. They cuddled closer then settled in to watch some mindless TV as they waited for their delivery. It wasn't quite the perfect homecoming for his mate he'd been hoping for, but it would do. Except Sydney wasn't home for Nicor. Something Jordan had to think about.

He *had* missed his mate.

CHAPTER FOURTEEN

Jordan's entire body ached as he lay in bed a week later. He and Nicor had been out on two more dinner dates since Nicor had arrived back in Sydney and Jordan could see himself falling for his mate. He'd been surprised at how much he'd missed the hound while he was gone. It gave him hope for their future. Nicor had been patient and never pushed for anything other than Jordan's company. Attentive, sweet—Nicor was just a big puppy in human form. Jordan only had one problem—right now he was in pain. Lots of it.

He'd been so wrapped up in his art and Nicor he'd forgotten to take care of himself. Knowing he now had a mate, but not having a strong enough emotional connection to him to want to feed from him was anxiety inducing. He didn't want to hurt his mate, but at the same time Jordan wasn't ready to go there yet with Nicor. He had to trust that the mate bond knew what it was doing pairing them together and that Nicor would understand.

Jordan had broached the subject of how he fed with Nicor several times since they had met. But talking about it and having Nicor actually witness it for real were two totally different things. He guessed he was about to find out how Nicor would react.

It had been well over a month since the last time he'd visited the club when Nicor was called away, and managed to feed. He was running on empty, which was why he hurt so much. It also felt like bloody awful timing since he was only now getting to spend quality time to know his mate.

Sure he liked his mate, but they still hadn't had time to develop the strong bond Jordan needed to feel any attraction, which left him in a conundrum.

Jordan glanced out the gap in the curtain and thanked fuck the sun was going down. A Monday night wasn't the best time to visit the club, but Jordan hadn't been paying attention to his body on the weekend, otherwise he would have gone then.

He also didn't *want* to go to the club, but he needed to, his sup nature once again at odds with himself. Jordan groaned in pain as he sat up and picked up his phone. He swore when he saw three missed messages from Nicor. Not wanting to delay whatever conversation they would have next, he dialled his mate and waited for him to answer.

"Jordan? Everything okay?"

"Sorry. Kinda not feeling well. Slept most of the

day," Jordan said, even he could hear the pain in his own voice.

"What's going on? Anything I can help with?"

"Yeah, can you come pick me up? There's somewhere I need to go."

"I can be there in fifteen minutes, twenty tops, depending on traffic."

"Thanks. I'll see you then." Jordan hung up the call and threw his phone on the bed nightstand. Movement would help loosen his body up, but wouldn't get rid of the gnawing ache. Only one thing would help with that. If he didn't feed soon things would get worse. Fast.

Jordan forced himself to move and ran a shower. The hot water felt wonderful on his aching body. The pain of having delayed his feed to the point where he wanted to pass out was mixed with the stress Jordan felt over what was about to happen. How would Nicor react to Jordan having to feed from other's sexual energy? Would he be mad that Jordan wasn't feeding from him? Jordan contemplated calling Nicor back and telling him not to worry, and just taking a cab out to the club himself, but he didn't want to feed without Nicor again. They both had to see if they could do this.

After much umming and ahhhing, he decided not to call Nicor back. If their relationship had any hope in hell of lasting, Nicor would need to know and understand this side of him. It wasn't like Jordan could just ignore it. Look where that had gotten him, in only a month.

God he hoped this didn't all blow up in his face.

Jordan kicked himself for forgetting to tell Nicor the dress code, but he hoped it would be okay. Jordan pulled out several outfits from his closet, not happy with any of them. How would Nicor react to seeing him in these kinds of clothes? Would he get the wrong idea and expect more from Jordan than he was ready to give?

Fuck! His stomach was in god damn knots. His body ached, his hands trembled, and his forehead was covered in sweat and he'd only just taken a damn shower. Why did everything have to be so damn stressful!

Leather always felt good against his skin, so he settled on his favourite pair of pants. Jordan leaned against the wall, breathing hard, as he then stepped into his black boots.

A tight red shirt finished his outfit, to contrast the dark leather. Both colours went well with his dark russet skin and black hair.

Presentation was key, especially when he was in such a sorry state. He was a firm believer that dressing up when feeling sick made one feel better.

As Jordan finished getting ready there was a knock at his front door. His stomach clenched and Jordan had to decide if he was going to be sick or not. He breathed deeply for a few heartbeats, before making his way to the door.

Nicor whistled as he took in Jordan's outfit, hunger blazing in his eyes as they landed on his own. Nicor's reaction to how he looked did not fill Jordan with confidence they would make it through tonight unscathed.

"You look good enough to eat." Nicor growled, his voice low and deep, before he cleared his throat and shook his head. "Sorry."

Jordan bit his lip, not sure what to say. He should just tell Nicor to go home. It wasn't too late.

His mate did look delicious, as always. Such a pretty, pretty man. Jordan appreciated how nice Nicor looked. His mate appealed to him aesthetically on an artistic level, making his fingers itch for charcoal. Nicor was easy on the eyes. Everyone looked. Jordan noticed how often people eyed his mate when they were out and about.

Nicor shouldn't have any trouble getting into the club. His jeans hugged him in all the right places. A few well-placed tears gave the viewer tantalising glimpses of his flesh below the material. He wore boots and a loose shirt.

"You may need to lose the shirt," Jordan muttered as he looked Nicor up and down.

"Oh yeah?" Nicor asked, his expression showing confusion at Jordan's suggestion. Jordan was pleasantly surprised his mate hadn't cracked a joke or offered to remove his clothes right then and there. Nicor really was trying to do everything he could to make Jordan comfortable and happy. "So, where are you planning on taking me that I'm going to need to go topless?"

Jordan didn't want to tell him, but there was no getting around it. He didn't like the idea of Nicor walking through Paddles without his shirt on either. All eyes would be on Jordan's mate, and he didn't like the thought of that.

"I need to feed," he said quietly, looking at the ground.

"Sure. Let me know what restaurant you want to go to and we'll go. That doesn't explain the shirt though," Nicor said happily.

"No, Nicor. I need to *Feed*." He looked Nicor in the eyes, waiting until his mate understood. It didn't take long before Nicor whistled.

"Ohhh. You're not... I mean.... You're my...." Nicor couldn't seem to finish a sentence.

Jordan, wanting to reassure his mate, placed his hand on Nicor's arm and squeezed gently. "No, I'm not going to touch anyone else. You're it for me... But, I'm sorry, I'm not there yet and I'm drained." Jordan practically whispered the last. "I left it too long and I'm in pain... So much pain."

Nicor let out a heavy breath then straightened his shoulders and took a step back. "You ready to go?"

Relief flooded Jordan at his mate's words that he was stunned still for a moment. "Ahh, let me grab my things."

Jordan ducked back inside to grab his keys, wallet and phone, then closed his door and locked the deadbolt. He moved slowly, his body still in considerable pain from being so drained. Nicor had waited until he got back outside, then walked with him to the passenger side. He opened the passenger door to the large SUV for Jordan to climb into.

"Thank you." Jordan buckled himself in and patiently waited for Nicor to round the car. He couldn't believe they were about to do this. He never in a million years thought he'd have a mate, so the idea of going to a sex club with them while he fed off others had never even crossed his mind. Nicor was being so good about it though. He couldn't believe how hard his mate was trying.

"So, which club? Sorry, I can't remember if you mentioned one by name or not?" Nicor asked as he started the engine.

"Have you heard of Paddles?" Jordan couldn't remember if they'd gone into specifics in one of their long talks. He'd just been so wrapped up in getting to know the man, that he'd let out all the actual details.

"Nope, but that doesn't surprise me. I'm not aware of a lot of the clubs in Sydney. Now, if this was Melbourne, that would be another matter. I know those streets like the back of my hand. Where is it?" Nicor asked.

"On the outskirts of town. I'll direct you."

Nicor nodded and put the car in gear. The drive was pleasant, the radio playing softly in the background.

"It's a Monday night, are there going to be people there?" Nicor asked suddenly about halfway through the drive.

"Yeah. The best time's obviously Friday and Saturday nights. They're closed on Tuesdays. But Mondays there's quite a number of people that like to head there to blow off some steam after the first day back at work after the weekend. I should be okay."

"Huh. I didn't think about that. Interesting."

"I know this isn't exactly an ideal situation," Jordan

said softly, breaking the silence that had descended on the car.

Nicor reached over and squeezed Jordan's hand gently. "It's fine, Jordan. I understand that this needs to happen and that you're not ready for it to be from me. I'm not going to hold this against you. I am, however, glad that you trust me enough to allow me to accompany you."

Jordan swallowed the sudden lump that had formed in his throat. He hadn't expected his mate to be so understanding. If Jordan wasn't careful, he could really fall for him. Then again, they were mates, which was kind of the point.

Nicor pulled into the half-full car park, and Jordan climbed out of the car the moment they stopped. A small groan escaping him when a sharp pain raced through his body as he stepped down.

His mate was at his side in seconds. "You okay?"

"Yeah. Left it far too long between feeds." He paused for a moment before continuing, "I've kinda been a little distracted lately?" He grinned at Nicor.

His mate frowned down at him.

"Don't do that," Jordan admonished as he rubbed at the crease lines in Nicor's forehead.

"I don't like the thought that I'm to blame for you being in pain," his mate said softly.

"It's not your fault. It's my own. I was the one that wasn't paying enough attention to my own body." He stepped back and took Nicor's hand, leading the way to the entrance to the club. "First time at a club like this?"

Nicor coughed and blushed, which Jordan found kinda adorable.

"I take it that's a no?" he asked.

"Well, I have been on earth for a couple hundred years. So... you know. I may have checked out a club or two in my time."

"What'd you think?"

"Not really my thing, but to each their own."

"I agree. If it wasn't for my constant need to feed, then I wouldn't go either."

Jordan pulled the large door open and held it for Nicor to enter, before walking in behind him.

"Welcome back, Mr. Makan," Alex said from where he sat at the reception desk in the back of the room.

"Thank you, Alex. I have a guest with me today. I hope that's okay."

"Of course, Sir. If I can get your guest to sign in, that would be greatly appreciated."

"Of course," Jordan said as he and Nicor walked over.

"Will you or your guest be participating in any of the activities going on tonight?" Alex asked them.

"No, I don't think so, thank you though."

Alex opened a drawer in his desk and pulled out two white wrist bands and handed them over. "Please wear this on your right hand. It lets the others know that you're not there to play."

"Thank you," Nicor said as he fastened the band around his wrist.

"Enjoy your evening, Sirs."

"Thank you, Alex."

They stepped past to the double doors and down the short corridor, making their way into the club.

"And I didn't even have to lose my shirt," Nicor joked.

"Good thing too. Don't think I would have liked all the boys being able to see what belongs to me."

Nicor seemed to falter momentarily in his steps at Jordan's pronouncement, but righted himself quickly.

"Would you like a drink?" Jordan asked as they entered the club. The sounds of groaning could be faintly heard over the thump of the music.

"Love one."

Together they found a free table and sat down, waving over one of the waiters, wearing nothing but short shorts and boots. They ordered their drinks, then Jordan relaxed back into the comfortable chair, closed his eyes and breathed. He was feeling slightly better already and he'd only been here for a few minutes.

It didn't take long for their waiter to come back with their drinks—a scotch on the rocks for Jordan and a bourbon and Coke for Nicor. Along with the drinks they were both handed a red wrist band.

"What's this one for?" Nicor asked him.

"Milo, the owner, takes the safety of his guests very seriously. It's to let people know that you've been drinking."

"What a good idea." Nicor slipped the red band on next to his white one and picked up his drink.

"I agree. One can never be too careful in this day and age," he said, and secured the band around his wrist. He took a sip of his scotch before placing it on the coaster on the small table.

His mate glanced around the room, watching the men in their various states of dress or undress as it may be. Personally, Jordan was more interested in the ones who were on their knees, strapped down to any flat surface available or over their dom's lap.

The sound of so much pleasure being dished out really was a heady thing. He sat back and took it all in. Feeding off other people's pleasure this way wasn't anywhere near as good or filling as feeding off his own. But it would do.

Nicor sat quietly and let Jordan absorb the energy around him.

"I was wondering when, or *if*, I would see you here again," Milo said as he stepped up beside Jordan's table.

"Milo. Great to see you again." Jordan smiled up at his friend and waved at the spare seat. "Please join us."

"Thank you, don't mind if I do." Milo sat down, glanced over at Nicor, then back at Jordan and raised his brown in inquiry.

"Shit, sorry. Nicor, meet Milo, the owner of Paddles, and a very old friend of mine. Milo, my mate, Nicor."

The two shook hands.

"A *very* old friend indeed," Nicor said grinning.

Milo chuckled. "Not that old, thank you *very* much. I prefer to think of myself as still in my prime." He glanced back at Jordan. "I see you took my advice and things turned out?"

"Eh." Jordan shrugged. "They kinda went to shit after the phone call. But it all worked out in the end."

"I'm glad to hear it." Milo turned to Nicor. "Congratulations to you and your team on bringing down the smuggling ring a while back. It was all over the sup news networks for a while. I figured that's why you guys were in town."

"Thank you. We couldn't have done it without the help of several different groups. It was definitely a team effort."

"So I heard." He turned back to Jordan. "Will this be your last visit to Paddles?"

Jordan was a little caught off guard by that question. He was nowhere near being attached enough to bond with Nicor yet, which meant he'd still need the use of Paddles for a while longer.

However, Nicor would have to permanently go back to Melbourne at some point. The man couldn't live here, away from his pack, which meant Jordan was going to have to pack up and go with him. He wasn't ready to jump into bed with the man and fully bond with him, but that didn't mean he wanted them to live in different states and never see one another. He wanted to reach the point where he was comfortable with Nicor to mate with him fully, and he could only do that by spending time with him and getting to know Nicor.

Jordan mulled that idea over in his head for a few moments and found he didn't hate the idea of leaving Sydney as much as he thought he would. He'd have to talk to Mandy about it, obviously. But there was no reason why he couldn't ship his art to the gallery here, or hell, set up another one in Melbourne.

He glanced at Nicor who smiled reassuringly at him.

Before Jordan could answer, Nicor started talking. "No, we'll be back again, as often as Jordan needs."

Jordan's heart felt lighter at the understanding his mate was showing him.

"Well, you know you're always welcome."

"Thank you, Milo," Jordan said as Milo stood.

"Nicor, it was lovely to meet you. I look forward to seeing you again soon. Make sure you take care of this one. He's something special."

"I know, and I will." Nicor and Milo shook hands, before Milo excused himself as he had work to do.

Nicor waved over a waiter and ordered another round of drinks for them. His mate was obviously in no hurry to leave.

Jordan relaxed again and the two of them settled down to chat and pass the time while he silently fed on all the ambient sexual energy in the room.

CHAPTER FIFTEEN

The ringing of his phone broke Jordan out of the trance he'd been in. He made a face then ignored the blasted thing, Jordan glanced back at the painting in front of him, taking it in once more. His eyes watered suddenly and Jordan had to blink to clear them. He glanced at his watch and cursed when he realised it was three in the afternoon. He'd had an appointment with Mandy at the gallery at two to go over the final pieces for his upcoming show.

He'd been working on this piece for the last eight hours. As he'd woken up in the early morning hours with idea for it and hadn't been able to get back to sleep without putting brush to canvas. The arid landscape of central Australia started back at him, the reds and ochres blended so seamlessly. The image was one from his childhood that he hadn't thought about in years, but suddenly couldn't get out of his head and had to get down on canvas.

Jordan placed his brush in the glass bottle of turps

to clean the paint and cleared up his work surface. He then glanced at himself and realised he needed a shower before he went anywhere. Forever, perpetually, having to run for a shower before meeting someone.

No, that wasn't true. He managed for Nicor most days. Not always. But he definitely managed for his mate better than anyone else.

On his way to the bathroom, Jordan remembered the missed call and went back for his phone. He unlocked it and found four missed calls from Mandy and two from Nicor. He called Mandy back first. Nicor would understand. *She* might actually kill him this time. Amanda had to be psychic. Had to. Maybe the hounds would look into her lineage for him so that he could figure out whom to appease so she wouldn't accidentally kill him on purpose.

"Yes, I know, I'm late," he said as soon as she answered the call.

"You better be in the car and on your way here right now." She sounded annoyed. Jordan couldn't blame her. Really. Lucky for him she never stayed angry at him for long.

"I'm just getting into the shower," he told her truthfully, knowing, from past experiences, that lying to her would only make things worse.

She sighed heavily down the phone.

"I'm sorry. But I really think you'll like the reason behind why I'm late," he told her honestly.

"I bet I will. Hurry the hell up. I have shit to do this afternoon," she said then hung up. Someday she really would kill him. Not today, though.

Jordan didn't think twice before he dialled Nicor, put the phone on speaker and placed it on the bathroom counter while he undressed.

Nicor answered almost straight away, as if the man had been hanging out for his call. Then again, his mate was probably playing one of his games. No noise came through the phone so he must've paused it.

"Everything okay?" Nicor asked as Jordan started the shower to warm the water up.

"Yeah, sorry, got caught up in a piece."

"Ahh..." Nicor went quiet for a moment before he asked quietly, "Jordan? Is that the shower I can hear? Are you naked?"

"Ummm." Jordan blushed. "Maybe?"

"Would you like to come over this afternoon?" Nicor asked, his voice a little huskier than normal. "We can watch some Netflix and order delivery for dinner. Like a real dinner. I'm not asking for Netflix and chill."

"Sounds wonderful, but I'm late for a meeting at the gallery," he told Nicor regretfully. He really would like to curl up on the couch with the man and zone out to some movies. That sounded wonderful.

"Oh." That one word conveyed so much disappointment.

Jordan didn't even think before he opened his mouth. "Would you like to come with me to the gallery? We can go back to your place afterwards."

"Really?" Nicor asked. "You don't mind me seeing your work for the exhibition?"

Jordan thought about that, and realised he really was okay with Nicor seeing the exhibit before everyone else. "No one is supposed to see the new stuff until the show opens to the public, but you're not just anyone. I'd like it if you came with me."

"I'm on my way."

"Wonderful. I'll see you soon." Jordan disconnected the call then stepped into the shower to wash all the little splashes of paint off.

Jordan was waiting out the front when the large SUV pulled up in his driveway. He climbed into the passenger seat and gave Nicor's hand a squeeze. His mate chuckled.

"What?" he asked.

"You missed a bit." Nicor leaned over and scratched lightly at his Jordan's right cheek. He pulled his hand back to show a fleck of deep red paint that he'd managed to miss.

"Thank you. You wouldn't believe how often I find flecks of paint on me in places I have no idea how they got there in the first place."

"I look forward to finding out someday." Nicor winked, then pulled back out into traffic. "Point me towards the gallery."

Jordan told him the way, then relaxed and enjoyed the company as Nicor navigated through the busy city streets.

"I'm in trouble," Jordan muttered as they turned onto the road with his gallery.

"Why?" Nicor asked him confused.

"You see that woman standing over there?" Jordan pointed.

"Yeah. What about her?" Nicor asked.

"That's Mandy. My agent, remember? She only ever waits outside for me when she's not happy."

Nicor laughed, found an empty parking spot on the side of the road and parked. "You ready to face the music?"

Jordan groaned but got out of the car anyway.

As soon as Mandy saw him walking towards the gallery she crossed her arms over her chest and yelled to him. "What time do you call this?"

"I said I was sorry," he told her as he stepped up in front of her.

Mandy harrumphed, the scowl on her face making her look rather cute, or so Jordan thought. Nicor's large hand slipped into his own as his mate stepped up beside him on the walkway.

He didn't miss the shocked expression that replaced Mandy's anger in an instant. Her eyebrow raised and she looked at Jordan with wide eyes. "And who is this large specimen of man?" she asked, then furrowed her brows. "Haven't I seen him somewhere..."

"Mandy, this is my boyfriend, Nicor. Nicor, my agent Mandy," Jordan interrupted her before she could say anything else. Jordan didn't know why he did that. It wasn't like Nicor wouldn't see in a few moments.

"Boyfriend?" Mandy asked shocked. "Since when?"

Nicor grinned at her and held out his hand for her to shake. "Pleasure to meet you. Jordan's told me wonderful things about you."

Mandy snorted, but shook Nicor's hand anyway. "I highly doubt that."

Jordan coughed awkwardly. He loved Mandy. The

woman had put up with his shit for five years and still managed to make him a hell of a lot of money along the way. But he might not have always been flattering about her when he was telling Nicor stories.

"What's the big rush in getting me down here?" Jordan asked, wanting to change the subject.

"What's the big rush?" she repeated back at him in a slightly sarcastic tone. "Oh, I don't know. We only open your next exhibit in three days, and I *still* need your final approval on the layout. No big deal."

Nicor coughed beside him and Jordan had the grace to blush. "Sorry. I kinda forgot."

"You kinda forgot?" Mandy asked, her voice raising several octaves.

"Come on. Let's go inside and get this over with before you have a heart attack right here on the footpath."

"And who's fault would that be?" she asked as she allowed Jordan to steer here towards the gallery door.

The windows were all covered from top to bottom with black paper. Big white letters proclaimed across the centre of the windows that a new Jordan Makan Exhibit was opening this Friday.

Jordan and Mandy stepped inside, when Nicor tried to follow them Mandy turned around and held her hand up in the universal sign of stop.

"Where do you think you're going?" she asked.

"Inside, with Jordan."

"I don't think so buddy. No one gets to see until opening night," she assured him adamantly.

"I'm not just anyone. You can trust me."

Mandy scoffed.

"Let him in, Mandy."

Mandy stared in disbelief.

"I trust Nicor with my life. He's not going to betray me."

"Never," Nicor promised.

Mandy sighed and stepped back. Not that she had any choice in the matter.

They closed and locked the door behind Nicor. Jordan kissed his mate tenderly on the cheek before he stepped back.

"Why don't you wander around while Mandy and I go take care of the details? I'll try not to be too long," Jordan said.

Nicor's gaze had wandered off to the side, his eyes widened as he stared at Jordan's work. "You did all this?"

Jordan shrugged. "It's taken a while."

"Go," Nicor told him. "Do what you need to. Don't worry about me. I'll be fine. Take all the time you need."

"Thank you."

Nicor walked over to the portrait of his mother and stared at it with open wonder on his face. Jordan wanted so very much to go over there and be with Nicor, but Mandy had a point. They had work to do if they were going to open on time. They'd already delayed the opening by several months due to his council project and all the shit that had gone down when he'd met Nicor. He was looking forward to the exhibit finally being done, however, Jordan had completely lost track of the days recently.

He and Mandy headed to the office to go over the paperwork side of things. Then she had her assistant, a preppy looking young man with glasses and a bowtie follow them around with an iPad making notes as they walked the studio, studying where every piece was placed, what Jordan wanted moved and why. They checked and double-checked every name plate to make sure they were correct, along with the description plates.

Jordan was fairly particular about how his art was showcased, it wasn't something he could describe or explain to someone else. Mandy did the best she could with what she was given. But there was a feeling Jordan got. A flow to his work that only he could feel and see. And that was what he'd always fallen back on when setting up for shows like this one.

Mandy didn't question him. She and her team made notes and made it happen.

Jordan even went so far as to pull pieces off the walls and placed them on the floor, leaning against the wall in their new spots so he could verify what he needed to.

He saw Nicor several times out of the corner of his eyes as they worked. His mate stayed quiet and left them alone. If it wasn't for the occasional glimpse as he moved about the gallery no one would even know he was there.

Jordan's stomach growled loudly letting him know he'd been here longer than he'd planned. He glanced at his watch and swore when he realised it was nearing seven and they'd been there for nearly four hours. God,

Nicor must think he was an ass for dumping him for so long.

"I'm so sorry," Jordan apologised as he found Nicor staring at a painting of himself in hound form.

Nicor glanced at him quizzically. "What for? The painting? It's stunning. As are all the other pieces in here."

"No, for leaving you for so long."

Nicor looked at his watch then and his eyes widened in surprise. "Holy crap."

Jordan laughed. "Okay, I don't feel so bad now."

"You shouldn't feel bad. Your work is incredible, I think I've told you that before. I could look at it for hours without getting bored. I love what you did with the surfboards."

"Thank you." Jordan felt himself blushing slightly under the praise from his mate. "You ready to get out of here? I can feel Netflix calling our names."

"Sounds like a plan."

Jordan linked his fingers with Nicor's and together they left the gallery. Mandy would change what needed to be done and have the place ready to go by Friday. The drive back to Nicor's place was quiet, the radio playing softly in the background.

"What do you feel like for dinner?" Nicor asked as they parked under the building and climbed out of the car.

"You feel like pizza? Though I don't think I'm up for making any. Mind ordering in?"

"Sounds good to me. Anything in particular?"

"Nah, not fussy. As long as there is no pineapple

and no black olives." Jordan pulled a face to show his true dislike of those two things. His mate had a weird sense of adventure with food sometimes. Today he needed normal.

Nicor laughed. "I totally agree. Black olives are the devil's food. And who ever thought of putting pineapple on pizza deserves an eternity in hell for that blasphemy. Make yourself at home," Nicor told him as they entered the apartment. "I'll place the order for dinner then come and join you. You remember where everything is?"

"Thanks, yeah, I'm good." Jordan took a seat on the large plush sofa and picked up the remote to the TV. He might have grinned when he noticed each of the hounds had their own Netflix profile.

Jordan clicked into Nicor's to see what kind of movies and shows his mate had been watching.

He glanced away from the TV a few minutes later when he heard the clicking of nails on the tile floor and was surprised to find himself looking at a large hellhound.

"Well hello, you," Jordan said in surprised delight.

He patted the couch next to him in enthusiasm and the large hound practically leapt onto it from where he'd been standing. Jordan laughed as the hound licked his face several times. Jordan patted the short silky hair and scratched behind his ears.

Nik let out a low whine of enjoyment.

"You like that don't you?" he asked as he kept scratching. Nik flopped down on the couch beside him, his large head, heavy in Jordan's lap. He didn't mind.

He'd missed this guy. "I take it you don't care what we watch then?"

Jordan flipped through the movies until he found something interesting and pressed play. He put his legs up on the coffee table and got comfortable, patting and lightly scratching his hound the entire time.

They were interrupted by the sound of the internal phone ringing.

Nik whined but got up and headed toward the sound.

Jordan lost sight of him, and moments later he heard Nicor's deep timber of a voice answer the call.

"Pizza's here!" he called out not long after.

When Jordan saw him again the large hellhound was only wearing his jeans riding low on his hips.

There was a snatch of conversation and then Nicor appeared again carrying a couple of pizza boxes, a garlic bread and a large bottle of coke.

"Yum," Jordan said, he couldn't take his eyes off his nearly naked mate. The man pulled off the "jeans and nothing else" look really well. The light smattering of hair on his stomach lead to a tantalising trail down below the waistband of his jeans.

"I know, smells delicious." Nicor placed the boxes down on the table before disappearing again.

Nicor walked back into the room carrying a couple of empty glasses. Jordan looked at his mate. Really looked at him, and decided he liked what he saw. He thought he might be starting to fall for this man. The fact that he'd shifted and let Jordan spend time with his hound had really opened up Jordan's eyes and heart to the lengths that this man was willing to go for him.

There would be time enough to think about his emotions later, though. Now, it was time for pizza.

They settled back on the couch with their pizza and soft drinks. Jordan happily ate slice after slice of garlic bread—that shit was delicious—and pressed play again on the movie. Halfway through the movie he had to stop chowing down. No way could he keep up with his mate anyway. Where did Nicor put all that food?

Groaning, Jordan collapsed back into the corner of the couch and patted his now full belly. "So full."

The pizza had been too good to stop at just two slices. He burped, quite loudly and blushed at the unexpectedly loud noise.

Nicor laughed beside him, then burped himself.

"Oh my god, that's so wrong, but still funny," Jordan said while trying to hold back a laugh.

Nicor winked at him then burped again.

Jordan threw a cushion at him, which Nicor caught, tucked behind his bod and settled back into the opposite side of the couch. "Thanks for that."

"Hey, thief, give that back, it's my cushion," he complained as he held out his hand for his property back.

Nicor snorted. "Shouldn't have thrown it at me if you wanted to keep it. It's mine now."

"I don't think so." Jordan lunged for the cushion.

Nicor wasn't giving up without a fight though and soon the pair of them were completely ignoring the movie and laughing so hard as they play fought over the ownership of a cushion.

"Omph." Jordan groaned as they rolled, and realised there was no more couch for them to lean on, the pair of them crashing to the hard floor below them. He shivered as the cold floor seeped through his clothes.

His breath hitched as Nicor lay atop him, their faces mere inches apart.

Their laughter died suddenly as they lay there and stared at one another.

Before either of them could say a word, the sudden tension in the room was broken by the shrill ring of a phone. Nicor closed his eyes and Jordan knew what that meant, his mate was being pulled away again.

Nicor climbed off him and Jordan missed the warmth of his mate's body against his own. He grabbed the helping hand his mate held out to him and climbed up.

He snatched the cushion off the couch and placed it behind his back as he sat back down again.

Nik glared at him and pointed. "This isn't over, not by a long shot." Then he answered the call. "Hello?"

Jordan watched as Nicor's shoulders tensed and his entire body went on alert. He was being called away again. Jordan knew it. He felt a sudden pang at the thought of his mate once again being pulled away from him. He hated how much this must be tearing Nicor up, worrying about his pack, and about how Jordan was going to react to his need to go.

Nicor's expression didn't change as he nodded and listened to whoever was on the other end of the call. It was time he gave some serious consideration to moving to Melbourne.

Nicor hung up the call, before he could say anything Jordan beat him to it. "You have to go?"

"I'm sorry," Nicor whispered, pain clearly etched on his features for Jordan to see.

"Hey," Jordan said and stood. "There's nothing for you to be sorry about. We knew going into this that you would get called away if your pack needs you."

"But I'm going to miss your opening," Nicor said sadly.

"That's not important. There will be others. What's important is making sure your pack is safe, and for that, they need you. When do you have to go?"

Nicor glanced at his watch. "Adze has me booked on the first flight out in the morning."

"So, we still have the rest of the night?" Jordan smiled.

"Yeah," Nicor grinned wickedly, then dodged around Jordan, grabbed the cushion and flipped over the back of the couch. He held it out, taunting Jordan.

He growled.

"Hey! Give that back." Jordan climbed onto the couch and reached out, but Nicor stepped back, then took off laughing.

Jordan followed his mate, chuckling just as hard. If this was how they were going to spend their last night together for who knows how long, he wasn't about to complain. He'd worry about how much he was going to miss Nicor tomorrow.

EPILOGUE

ne Year Anniversary in Sydney...

Nicor pulled at the black tie around his neck. He'd never liked wearing these things and avoided it at all costs. It felt like he was choking. But now that he was dating a famous artist, he had to get used to them. For some reason a lot of gallery openings were black-tie affairs and there was no way he was going to miss his mate's hard work being put on display for the sake of a damn tie. He'd already missed Jordan's first gallery showing when he'd had to leave Sydney suddenly all those many months ago.

Now, though, they were back and he had another chance.

The glass of champagne he held had long since gone warm so Nicor placed it on the tray of the first waiter he saw. Jordan had thankfully warned him to eat something beforehand. Nicor had listened to his mate and had a quick burger before he arrived. If he hadn't, Nicor would've been starving by now. The trays of food always seemed to empty before they arrived to him. Not that there was much on them to begin with. The servings were tiny and could be swallowed whole.

It had been nearly two hours since Nicor last laid eyes on his mate, Jordan having been swept away by first Mandy and then god knows who else. The gallery was packed, which was great for Jordan, not so good for Nicor. He'd never liked crowds much, especially in confined spaces.

Nicor made his way through the people, who were all gathered around Jordan's art. He did notice several sold stickers on the pieces as he headed to the front door. Nicor wasn't leaving, he just needed some fresh air.

He nodded to the security guy they had on the front door tonight and stepped out of the crowded gallery and onto the footpath out front. The cool breeze on his face was wonderful after the warmth from inside.

His phone vibrated in his pants pocket. Nicor had turned it to silent, not wanting to be *that person* who had their phone ring loudly in the middle of an event.

Nicor's heart sank when he saw Adze's name on his caller ID. Knowing what his boss was about to say, Nicor sighed and answered the call.

"Hey boss," he said lightly.

"Nicor. How's things?" Adze asked.

He knew Adze wasn't asking for the sake of it, but actually wanted to know how he was getting on. All his packmates followed Jordan's shows now, wanting insider news about themes and such. Callum had even talked Jordan into a commissioned piece for Pyro, though they hadn't shared what it was with everyone.

"Good. Really good, I think. Jordan's gallery exhibit opened tonight. You've seen his work. You know how good he is," Nicor gushed a little. His mate was a very talented man.

"Glad to hear things are going well." Adze sighed.

"Please don't tell me you're calling me in. We just got here two days ago, Adze," Nicor complained.

"Nah, just wanted to give you a heads up. Between you going with Jordan on his exhibition trips and Oriax's trouble with his mate, we don't have enough team members to deal with the situation so I've called in the others to take this one."

"You think they're ready?" Nicor asked speculatively. They'd been training for months with Aamon's Beta team, having them shadow and help out on their calls. Adze had apparently been working on getting approval for a second Aussie team for a while, which Nicor loved the idea of that coming through finally. There was far too much activity and land for just the one team to handle anymore.

"There's only one way to find out," Adze said confidently.

"True that. So what are they hunting?"

"A possible Lamia in Cairns."

"What the fuck is a Lamia?" Nicor asked. He

couldn't ever remember hearing that name before.

"Child eating demon." Adze sighed. "They're very rare. Women can turn into them after the death of their own children."

"Fuck, seriously? That's messed up!"

"Yeah. Nothing like throwing them in the deep end of the swimming pool, but it couldn't be helped."

"Thanks, man, I really appreciate you not calling me back in so soon."

"Don't mention it, you'll both be back in a few days anyway right?" Adze asked.

"Yeah, we'll be home in a couple of days."

Nicor smiled wide. He'd been so ecstatic when Jordan had agreed to pack up and move to Melbourne so they could spend more time together. They still hadn't officially mated, but Nicor was in no rush. He had the rest of his life to spend with Jordan.

Adze had purchased one of the apartments right below their own and decked it out so that Jordan could use it as an art studio and room. Lately though, Jordan had been spending more and more nights falling asleep cuddled up to Nicor, and sharing soft gentle kisses, then in his own place. He was loving that his mate felt comfortable enough around him to do that.

They were currently staying at the hound's apartment in Sydney since Jordan had sold his house.

"No worries, we'll see you when you get home, unless anything else pops up before then."

Nicor disconnected the call then ran his hand through his hair, grateful Adze hadn't called him back. He glanced at his watch and realised it was nearing midnight. It was about time he found his mate and rescued him from whatever hell he'd been dragged into. Jordan wasn't a fan of crowds either. He'd much prefer to lock himself away in his studio than deal with people —unless it was Callum and Archie. Jordan got along famously with those two.

Nicor nodded to the security guard on his way back in, then made his way through the crowd, looking for the one and only person he wanted to see.

Jordan's expression lit up when he saw Nicor heading towards him. His heart skipped a beat at the effect he obviously had on his mate. Time had been slowly bringing them together and making them closer.

To Nicor's utter surprise Jordan stepped right up to him, wrapped his arm around Nicor's neck and pulled him down for a tender kiss.

"Missed you," Jordan whispered when he pulled back, smiling up at Nicor.

Nicor's heart melted, he leaned down and kissed his mate again. "Missed you too," he whispered back. "Can we talk?"

Tension coiled under his mate's shoulders. The man definitely needed a break.

Jordan's expression didn't change, but Nicor could see the hint of something mischievous in his eyes. He had to stop himself from laughing at how badly Jordan wanted to escape his current situation.

"If you'll all excuse me," Jordan said to the group he had been chatting with before Nicor found him. "My partner needs a moment of my time."

Jordan took Nicor's hand and led them off the

gallery floor. They escaped down a passage to Mandy's office.

"Quick, in here, before someone stops us," Jordan said.

Nicor followed Jordan in and was surprised when Jordan pushed him up against the closed door and stepped right into his personal space.

"Did I tell you how good you look in that suit?" Jordan asked as he kissed Nicor's neck, lightly scraping his teeth against the pulse point.

Nicor groaned, his cock waking up and wanting to play. Nicor wrapped his arms around Jordan, pulling him close. He trailed his hands down his mate's back until he cupped Jordan's perfectly shaped ass. He squeezed and lifted.

Jordan didn't hesitate. His arms went around Nicor's neck and his legs wrapped around his waist. Nicor flipped them, pressing Jordan against the door. His mate's eyes were half lidded, Nicor leaned in and kissed his man, lips, teeth and tongue battled for supremacy. His mate tightened his hold on Nicor.

Nicor broke the kiss at the unexpected feeling of Jordan's hard cock pressing up against his stomach. He didn't let go, but leaned his head against the door, next to Jordan's. His breathing came out hard and fast as he tried to get his body under control.

"Fuck, fuck, fuck," he swore. "Just give me a minute, *please*."

Jordan's fingers wound into the back of his hair and he tugged lightly, trying to get Nicor to look at him.

"It's okay. I wanted this," Jordan whispered.

"That's not the issue," Nicor said then swore again.

"Oh." Jordan sounded unsure and Nicor didn't want that.

"I should let you down," Nicor said as he loosened his grip and tried to step back to give Jordan room to stand.

Jordan had other ideas though and continued to cling to him.

Nicor chuckled. "Gonna be like that, is it?"

"Yep. Now what's the problem?" Jordan wasn't one to beat around the bush.

"Adze called."

"Oh," Jordan's expression dropped and he loosened his grip on Nicor. "You're not being called away already are you? I was supposed to have you all to myself for a week."

Not wanting his mate to fall, Nicor set him down and didn't let go until he was sure Jordan was steady on his feet.

Nicor gently lifted Jordan's face so they were once again looking at each other. "Not at the moment. He called to let me know of a situation happening in Cairns and the Beta team is dealing with it. But if something else comes up in the meantime, he'll have to call me back."

Jordan was quite for a moment after that as he thought. "Fair enough. It was nice of Adze to call and give you a heads up."

"I love you." Nicor blurted out of the blue. This incredible man in front of him had packed up his life and moved to Melbourne to be with him. He never got angry when Nicor had to disappear at a moment's notice to go hunt down some creature who was wreaking havoc on the population. Nicor's emotions all kinda bubbled over in that moment and words happened.

Jordan laughed, a happy sound Nicor never tired of.

"You know what?" his mate asked, a twinkle in his eye.

"What?" Nicor asked.

"I love you, too."

Nicor crushed his mouth to Jordan's and kissed his mate like his life depended on it. Tender and sweet had gone out the door with those four little words.

When they finally broke apart they were both breathing heavily.

"Let's get out of here," Jordan said as he took Nicor's hand and started leading him towards the door.

"We can't leave, Jordan. This is the opening night of your new exhibition." Nicor pulled his mate to a stop.

"Of course we can leave. As you said, it's my exhibition, which means I can leave whenever I damn well want to, and that's right now." Jordan tugged once more on Nicor's hand.

Who was he to argue with the man of the hour?

They found Mandy on the edge of the crowd and told her they were leaving. She didn't look happy, but Jordan didn't seem to care. Nicor wasn't going to add his two cents worth as this was Jordan's business, not his.

Nicor didn't feel the cold night breeze as they

stepped outside, his body felt like it was on fire. They were soon in his car and heading back to the apartment.

The second the apartment door was closed behind them Jordan jumped him. Buttons went flying when Jordan ripped open Nicor's shirt. He wasn't going to complain though. His mate *wanted* him, was pushing to have him. No way would he stop. Nicor staggered down the hall, a very determined mate clinging to him, driving him wild with teeth, lips and hands the entire way.

"Off," Jordan rasped and Nicor shrugged out of his jacket, letting it fall wherever it did.

He reluctantly had to break their kiss as his tie was loosened and pulled over his head. He fiddled with the shirt sleeves as he stumbled along, finally shrugging out of that as well. His shoes disappeared in the passage.

By the time he made it to the bedroom, all that Nicor had left were his underwear and socks.

Jordan had managed to lose his jacket and tie—that was it.

"Your turn now." Nicor growled as he dumped Jordan in the middle of his bed.

He'd fantasised about this moment ever since meeting his mate. He didn't think it would actually happen tonight, though. Nicor watched Jordan scramble out of his clothes, Jordan's eyes glued to his own. He didn't even look down when Nicor pushed his briefs down and removed his socks.

Nicor grinned as he knelt on the bed then crawled up it until his was hovering over his naked and trembling mate.

"You sure about this?" he asked, wanting to make sure Jordan was fully on board. He'd never do anything to hurt his mate. If Jordan said no, then he'd go run a cold shower and they could curl up on the couch again and watch Netflix until Nicor had to leave.

Jordan reached up and cupped Nicor's face. "I've never been surer of anything in my life."

He pulled Nicor down and they kissed again. Their fully naked bodies touching for the first time. Nicor could feel Jordan's excitement at what was happening as much as Jordan could probably feel his own.

Nicor trailed a line of kisses down his mate's dark reddish-brown neck. He pulled back slightly so he could take in the full picture of his mate laying under him. Nicor leaned down and ran his tongue over one dark brown nipple. It pebbled as he withdrew and cool air hit it. Nicor licked the other, this time biting the small nip at the end.

Jordan groaned above him, his hands tangling in Nicor's hair, gently guiding him down his mate's body. Nicor chuckled then kissed and licked at his own pleasure, completely ignoring what Jordan wanted. He'd take his time and enjoy the journey now that it was finally happening.

Nicor was surprised to find his mate completely hairless, and he found he liked the feeling of the smooth skin against his lips. When Nicor finally reached his prize he admired the sight before him.

The engorged shaft sat flush against Jordan's stomach, the tip dark pink in colour already gleamed with drops of precum. His balls sat high and tight letting Nicor know how much his mate enjoyed what they were doing.

He leaned down and ran his tongue from Jordan's balls all the way to the tip of his shaft. Jordan groaned, and when Nicor looked up, his mate had bitten his bottom lip, his fists clenched in the bedsheets beside him.

This time, when Nicor licked the same path, he sucked Jordan's head into his mouth then lowered himself halfway down his shaft. He could deepthroat with the best of them, but why give away all his secrets right at the start? He continued to look at Jordan, whose eyes shut tight. His mate looked like a man who was concentrating more on holding something back than enjoying the pleasure he was receiving.

Not wanting this experience to be soured by anything Nicor pulled back.

"What's wrong?" he asked as he ran his hands over his mate's body, unable to stop touching him completely.

"Nothing," Jordan replied, almost too quickly. He still hadn't opened his eyes though.

"Liar." Nicor leaned down and lightly nipped at the tip of Jordan's cock. Not biting too hard. He didn't want to injure his mate after all.

Jordan groaned, his hips lifting off the bed as he tried to follow Nicor's mouth.

"What's wrong?" Nicor asked again.

Jordan sighed. "Nothing's wrong...." He took a deep breath before he continued, "I'm just... it's been a while, and I'm finding it hard not to *Feed*," he finished quietly. "I need *more*."

Nicor understood then. He crawled back up Jordan's body and kissed his mate. Jordan willingly surrendered and opened his mouth. Their tongues tangled together, and his mate's body relaxed beneath his own.

When he pulled back, Nicor stared into the half-lidded eyes of his mate. "You're mine and I'm yours. Take what you need from me."

"Are you sure?" Jordan asked hesitantly.

"Positive. I have no issue with you feeding during our time together. It's who you are, and I'm not about to deny a part of you."

Jordan kissed him then, his arms going around Nicor's back, holding him close.

"I love you," Jordan whispered against his lips before he kissed Nicor again.

Nicor couldn't have been happier in that moment. He was here, with his mate, who loved him.

He rolled onto his back, taking Jordan with him, so his mate straddled Nicor's lap. He reached out to the edge of the bed and fumbled blindly in the bedside table drawer for the bottle of lube that lived there. When his fingers grasped the bottle he removed it triumphantly and threw it on the bed beside them.

Jordan pulled back from the kiss as he sat up. His ass rested perfectly on Nicor's hard erection. Jordan grinned down at him, then wiggled back and forth. Nicor groaned and gripped Jordan's hips, stilling the teasing man.

"You like that?" Jordan asked him with a smile.

"A little too much. You're a very tempting man, Jordan."

"Why thank you." Jordan winked. He ran a finger over Nicor's chest, his nail catching then flicking at his pebbled nipples.

"I think you're enjoying having me under you," Nicor said.

"Not sure what could have possibly given you that idea." Jordan spied the bottle of lube on the bed next to them and grinned. "Oh, I really like the way your mind works."

He picked up the bottled and poured a small amount onto his fingers of his left hand. He placed his right hand in the middle of Nicor's chest then leaned forward and reached behind himself.

The expressions Jordan made changed as his mate stretched himself. Concentration filled his face at first, then it moved to relaxation, ending with Jordan staring at Nicor with want and desire. Normally, Nicor enjoyed stretching his partners, but it had been a long time for Jordan and the last thing he wanted to do was to hurt his mate. He was happy to lay back and enjoy the sight and sound of his mate pleasuring himself until he was ready.

Nicor reached down between their bodies and cupped Jordan's balls, tugging lightly before he released them and stroked his mate's shaft a couple of times. His man was still rock hard.

"You look so fucking incredible above me like that."

Nicor growled. He wanted to devour this man. Make Jordan his in every way possible.

"You don't look so bad yourself," his mate said, then grinned.

Jordan pushed up on his knees and shifted forward a little. He picked up the bottle of lube again and this time poured a generous amount into the palm of his hand. He reached back and took Nicor's shaft into his hand, liberally coating it with the slick gel.

Nicor growled at how good that felt.

Jordan lined himself up, holding the base of Nicor's shaft at the angle he wanted. His fingertips dug into Jordan's hips, as his mate gently and so slowly Nicor wondered if he'd be able to last, sank down on his cock.

"Fuck, fuck, fuck." Nicor swore as the tight heat of his mate's body engulfed him. His cock felt like it was in a vice.

Nicor looked at Jordan, wanting to make sure his mate wasn't in any pain. The expression on Jordan's face was pure pleasure.

Little tendrils of his mate's powers reached out. They hooked onto god only knew what and then lit up like a beacon. Nicor felt like his whole body had been lit up by electricity. Above him Jordan relaxed. His eyes glazed over as Nicor bottomed out. They sat there, together, for several moments.

"You okay?" Nicor asked.

"Never better," his mate replied. He sounded a little drugged, his grin wide. He leaned forward and placed both hands against Nicor's chest, raising slightly off his cock.

"You okay if I move?" he asked, wanting to make sure he didn't hurt Jordan with anything he did.

"Yes, please," Jordan begged.

Slowly Nicor lifted his hips then lowered them again, holding his mate still. The tingling in his body intensified and above him Jordan groaned, his head lolling back as he gave himself over to the pleasure. Nicor set his feet on the bed to give him the leverage he wanted, then thrust, slowly at first, then increasing in speed and force. Jordan cried out as their bodies joined over and over again. His hard cock rubbed between their bodies, leaving a thick trail of precum behind.

Nicor's entire body felt like it was aflame from the inside out. He had never felt anything like it before and couldn't wait to feel it again. His orgasm built quickly, those tendrils of fire felt like they were in his very soul.

"I'm close," he growled out, not wanting to finish before Jordan. The sound of their bodies joining and their heaving breathing were the only noises in the room.

Suddenly Jordan sliced a line across his right peck with a sharp nail, Nicor groaned as the pain mingled so perfectly with the pleasure. Before he realised what Jordan was doing the man leaned down and latched onto the lightly bleeding cut, sucking Nicor's blood into his body, mating them in incubus' customs.

Nicor cried out as he felt the bond start to form between them. Not wanting to be left out, Nicor pulled Jordan off his chest and up, pushing his head to the side and bit down, piercing the skin at the juncture of his mate's neck. As the first drops of his mate's blood hit his tongue Nicor thrust once, twice, three more times, then buried himself inside his mate as his orgasm slammed through him.

Jordan moaned, his body tense in Nicor's hold. He released Jordan in time for his mate's back to arch and his own orgasm to splash across Nicor's chest. The hot semen felt like it seared his skin.

Jordan collapsed on top of him. Like his body couldn't hold him aloft a second longer. His head rested on Nicor's chest, in the crook of his own neck. He could feel Jordan's hot breath against his skin as his mate panted.

"That was..." Nicor didn't know quite how to finish that sentence.

"Yeah. It certainly was..."

"I look forward to doing it again." Nicor chuckled.

"You and me both... Although I don't think I'll need to feed again for a while."

"Oh no?" Nicor asked.

"No, I may have gorged myself a little. It was probably the most satisfying meal of my life."

Nicor preened a little at that. His cock, which had started to soften, twitched at Jordan's words.

Jordan groaned above him.

"Thank you for waiting for me," Jordan said softly beside him.

"You were worth the wait."

Jordan cried out in surprise as Nicor rolled them over. He stared into his mate's sleepy, satisfied gaze then gently leaned down to kiss the man he would have happily waited an eternity for.

TRIGGER WARNINGS

Hellhounds hunt the bad monsters that go bump in the night, keeping the human world safe from supernatural evil. High stakes and deep passions follow Adze's Australian pack as they try to deal with sudden mate discoveries while trying to do their difficult and hazardous jobs.

This book has situations containing: violence, torture, kidnapping, a sex slave ring and underage trafficking.

THANK YOU READERS!

Thank you for purchasing ***Jordan's Accidental Adoption***. We hope you enjoyed this new world Toni has created. She loves being able to have more sexy men around to fight for their love, and who can blame her? Look out for the next book in the Smokey Mountain Bear series coming soon!

Want to let us know what you think? Please consider leaving a review where you purchased this ebook or on Goodreads. Reviews and word-of-mouth recommendations are *vital* to independent publishers.

Want more gay paranormal or fantasy? Freddy has a couple urban fantasies out, *Snow on Spirit Bridge* and *Waiting on the Rain.* You may also want to give Evelyn Benvie's *Something to Celebrate* a spin for a sweet holiday romance!

We love hearing from our readers. You can email us at mischiefcornerbooks@gmail.com. To read excerpts from all our titles, visit our website: http://www.mischiefcornerbooks.com.

Sincerely,
Mischief Corner Books

YOU MAY ALSO ENJOY 1 ...

www.mischiefcornerbooks.com

YOU MAY ALSO ENJOY 2 ...

YOU MAY ALSO ENJOY 3 ...

www.mischiefcornerbooks.com

YOU MAY ALSO ENJOY 4 ...

www.mischiefcornerbooks.com

YOU MAY ALSO ENJOY 5...

ABOUT TONI GRIFFIN

Toni Griffin lives in Darwin, the smallest of Australia's capital cities. Born and raised in the state she's a Territorian through and through. Growing up Toni hated English with a passion (as her editors can probably attest to) and found her strength lies with numbers.

Now, though, she loves escaping to the worlds she creates and hopes to continue to do so for many years to come. She's a single mother of one and works full time. When she's not writing you can just about guarantee that she will be reading one of the many MM authors she loves.

Feel free to drop her a line at info@tonigriffin.net anytime.

Webpage:
http://www.tonigriffin.net

ALSO BY TONI GRIFFIN

Available from **Mischief Corner Books**

My Christmas Present

Once a Cowboy

As Fire Rains Down (Coming Soon)

SMOKEY MOUNTAIN BEARS

A Bear in the Woods

Wreath of Fire

A Bear's Bear

HOUNDS OF THE HUNT

Archie's Accidental Kidnapping

Pyro's Accidental Shooting

Holiday Hijinks

Jordan's Accidental Adoption

THE BORILLIAN TWIST

Finding Connor

THE HOLLAND BROTHERS

Unexpected Mate

Determined Mate

Protective Mate

Forbidden Mate

*A Very Holland Christmas**

*A Very Holland Valentine**

A Wolf in Cop's Clothing

*Available together as *A Very Holland Collection*

THE ATHERTON PACK

Liam

Ben

Corey

Kieran

Corey's Christmas Bundle

ABOUT MISCHIEF CORNER BOOKS

Mischief Corner Books is an organization of superheroes… no, it's a platinum-album techno-fusion group… no, hold on a sec here…

Ah yes. Mischief Corner is a small press publisher offering queer romance and fiction for readers, intent on making some mayhem with our books. Diversity and positive representation for all members of the queer community is important to us, and MCB works to make those voices heard because those who travel the off the beaten path are a gift and their stories make the world a more interesting place.

In addition to making mayhem, we live to break molds. MCB. Giving voice to LGBTQ fiction.

Website:
http://www.mischiefcornerbooks.com

CPSIA information can be obtained
at www.ICGtesting.com
Printed in the USA
LVHW022359091220
673729LV00013B/1123